THE MAN FROM LANCER AVENUE

THE MAN FROM LANCER AVENUE

Trudy J. Morgan

REVIEW AND HERALD® PUBLISHING ASSOCIATION
HAGERSTOWN, MD 21740

This book was
Edited by Richard W. Coffen
Designed by Helcio Deslandes
Cover Illustration: Greg Fitzhugh
Type set: 10/11 Sabon

PRINTED IN U.S.A.

96 95 94 93 92 91   10 9 8 7 6 5 4 3 2 1

R&H Cataloging Service
Morgan, Trudy
    Man from Lancer Avenue, The.

    I. Title.
        813.5

ISBN 0-8280-0643-1

Dedication

For Jennifer

who would have been, and is,

a disciple

and who taught me a lot

about being one . . .

Also by Trudy Morgan

All My Love, Kate
Roommates

Contents

Chapter One

The grimy Coca-Cola clock on the wall of Pete's Garage showed 5:30. Pete wiped his hands on a reddish utility rag, threw it aside, and snatched his jacket off a peg on the wall. Shrugging into it, he said good night to Tony, the high school kid who pumped gas in the evenings.

" 'Night, boss," Tony said, not looking up from his comic book. A Grand Prix drove onto the lot and pulled up in front of the pumps. The driver waited expectantly and so did Pete. Pete's Garage was one of the few full-service gas stations in town, but the news hadn't seemed to have filtered down to Tony yet. The kid, still not taking his eyes off the Mutant Ninja Turtles, was fiddling with the radio, adjusting it from Pete's favorite oldies station to WHBM, the local heavy-metal blaster.

Pete jingled his keys, very slightly.

Tony's head jerked back, flicking his hair out of his eyes and enabling him to see. Suddenly his entire body shot into action. He bolted out the door and approached the car before Pete had a chance to yell at him. One of the few things the kid respected was his boss's temper.

Pete left, mildly annoyed at Tony for having gotten past him. Andy was just closing up the garage, when a green Honda Civic turned onto the lot, coughed, sputtered, and died in front of the garage doors. Pete shrugged and shook his head at the driver, but Andy was closer and flashed a sympathetic smile to the harried-looking young woman who slipped out of the car.

Pete shook his head. "For heaven's sake, Andy," he muttered under his breath, "can't you just tell a customer we're closed?"

9

Since he would never bawl out his brother—or any other employee—in front of a customer, he chose to let off a string of curses at Tony, who was loping back to the office.

"Look, I filled up the car, OK?"

"After the poor jerk sat there long enough to write up an arms limitation treaty, for crying out loud! Whaddya think this is, a five-star restaurant? We don't keep customers waiting for their order. We *serve* them, OK?"

"OK, Mr. Johnson."

"Smart kid. Now maybe I can get out of here and leave things in your hands—if only my stupid kid brother would figure out that *closed* means closed."

"Aw, he's a soft touch. You know that."

Pete ambled over to where Andy was leaning over the Honda's open engine compartment. Even as the obviously harried woman talked, Andy looked relaxed. His calm smile and his sympathetic blue eyes usually put people at ease, but this customer was too wound up to notice. She had a kid straddling her hip and another one clinging to her leg, both whiny. It was easy to see where they got it from.

"It can't be the gas filter, can it? That's what was wrong with it the last time. I knew they wouldn't fix it properly at the dealership . . . they never do. My friend told me I should bring it here, but it's just luck I came here this time, you were the closest place . . ."

"No, ma'am, gas filter wouldn't make 'er stall that way. Too bad it's not; I could fix it for you right now."

Pete ground his teeth while Andy explained—patiently, simply, and in as few words as possible—that he would have to buy the part from the Honda dealer, which couldn't be done sooner than tomorrow, at the earliest.

"But I'm desperate!" the woman whimpered. "This is the only car we got; I can't take the bus home with two kids, can I?"

"Listen, lady," said Pete. "You're lucky we even looked at your car, 'cause we're closed. See the sign? Now my brother here likes to be the Boy Scout and do his good deed for the day, but he could be the Archangel Gabriel for all I care and it still wouldn't get the car fixed one minute sooner, because the part's not available till tomorrow!"

"I'm really sorry," Andy said.

One of the kids started to cry.

"I got no way home . . ."

"How far do you have to go?" Andy asked.

"Division Street and Birch."

An awkward pause. "Oh, what the . . . It's not too far out of our way, we'll drive you. Hurry up, we're late already." Pete was, as always, surprised to hear his own voice making the offer.

Driving back from the dingy row houses on Division Street, Pete and Andy got snarled in the 6:00 traffic jam. Pete swore softly and regularly, cursing the sun in his eyes, the other drivers, and the woman with the whiny kids. He ran his hand through his brown hair—a little thinner in the front than it used to be—and fiddled with the rearview mirror. Andy hummed along with the radio. A smile twitched the corners of his mouth.

"What's so funny?"

"You are."

"Me?"

"First you rip a strip off that poor woman, then you go halfway across town to drive her home."

"Her and her screaming brats, who probably kicked a hole in the upholstery back there." Pete made no attempt to defend his contradictory behavior. The paradoxes of his own personality were the only things in life he admitted he couldn't explain.

He thought of that again when they walked into the house and he dropped his jacket onto the floor. "What kind of man," Audrey was fond of saying, "at 36 years old still wears his high school jacket?" She hung it up—as she would again later tonight and had every night for 15 years—with a shake of her head.

Pete wouldn't have parted with that jacket for diamonds. It had the Marselles Central High crest on the front, the team name, "Raiders," emblazoned across the back, and the words "Captain" and "Rocky" on the sleeves. He'd come a long way since Marselles Central High, but he was still proud of that jacket. It—along with the jump shot he was teaching Randy in the backyard on Sunday afternoons—was the only trace left of Rocky, "The Rock," Johnson, captain of the Raiders, basketball star and uncrowned king of Marselles Central High. Sure, you moved on and up, but it never hurt to remember. And Audrey—a screaming, short-skirted freshman girl in the bleachers . . .

Audrey, he supposed, was currently an annoyed housewife in the kitchen. He rushed in to calm her and assure her he didn't mind eating a cold supper. But his plate was already in the microwave, and Audrey was laughing along with Andy at the story of their errand of mercy. Pete, embarrassed at being the object of their amusement, brushed his wife a quick kiss on the cheek. She caught him around the waist and kissed him firmly on the lips.

Jenny was at the table, dawdling over a piece of cake. Pete sat down next to her. "Hi, Angel, what's up?" The screen door burst open as Randy and Kevin tumbled over each other and into the kitchen.

"Daddy! Uncle Andy! Look!"

"I got a blue ribbon in the track meet! That's first place!"

"I got a red one! For the high jump!"

The tangle of children swallowed up Pete. Audrey slid his dinner out of the microwave and placed it before him. Andy slipped his own plate into the oven. Pete dug his fork into a pile of mashed potatoes.

Pete Johnson. One lucky guy. And he knew it.

Chapter Two

Marie pulled up her chair to the cluttered dresser and switched on the lights surrounding the makeup mirror. Dusk was clouding the sky. Time to go to work. She began to smooth foundation over her still-silky skin, careful to use upward strokes. As always, almost unconsciously, she appraised her face with a mixture of concern and approval. This kind of life aged girls fast: looking her age could cause a drastic decline in her standard of living. She must zealously guard against every wrinkle.

Not a bad face, she thought, brushing powder on it. A soft cry came from behind the closed door. Shirley was having another of those nightmares that haunted her. To be like Shirley—now that was something to be avoided at all costs. She was 23, five years younger than Marie, but she looked easily 10 years older. It was the drugs mostly, of course, no question about that. That was what really tore a girl apart, tore away her youth and beauty to expose the hungry wretched skeleton beneath. But it was a no-win situation, for how could you survive the pain and emptiness without the drugs to give a little pleasure, an hour's escape? Marie drank—more than she should if she hoped to keep her looks—and smoked marijuana, but she had stayed off the hard stuff so far. Her escape route, her survival mechanism, was a harder, sterner one. It involved cutting off memory, speculation, and most of all feeling, as soon as they began. Ripping them out by the roots.

She wriggled into her skirt, buttoned her blouse, pulled on her jacket. Black Spandex, red lace—the look was hard to mistake, but at least she wore it with a touch of class. She hoped. A final touch of the brush to her cloud of black hair, and she was out the door,

13

high heels teetering on the dingy narrow staircase.

At least it's better than the house on Berman Street, Marie thought with a shudder. And she and Shirley were on their own now . . . no one to answer to. She was luckier than most.

The shortest way to Ellesmere Avenue, the nightclub strip where girls like Marie headed as twilight seeped through town, was past the hospital. Shirley always avoided it, taking the longer route. She couldn't bear the stares of the well-heeled neighborhood people around Mercy General, the perfectly coiffured doctors' wives who sat on committees begging City Council to "clean up Ellesmere Avenue." Marie, on the other hand, took a perverse pleasure in walking past the hospital parking lot as the elegant matrons left the Auxiliary meetings. There was Mrs. Denver now, getting into her BMW and shooting Marie a look of contempt mingled with frustration—because, of course, you couldn't arrest a girl for walking down the street. She could not, no matter how much she wished to, literally get Marie "off the streets." Did Mrs. Denver suspect that Marie was at least as well acquainted with the good Dr. Denver as was his wife? Whether she knew or not, the knowledge gave Marie a silent power over the uppity physician's wife, a power that enabled her to hold up her head and look straight into Mrs. Denver's steely eyes—and of half the other matrons on the Mercy General Auxiliary.

It can't go on forever, Marie reminded herself as she turned the corner and saw the lights of Ellesmere Avenue blinking in the distance. She was staying away from hard drugs and too much booze and keeping herself healthy for a reason. Someday she'd leave behind Ellesmere Avenue and this whole shoddy town. In a plush hotel in New York City, she'd be sought after by rich and important men. Maybe one of them would set her up in a fancy apartment, buy her cars and clothes and diamonds, and just maybe someday *love* her. . . .

As soon as the forbidden word flitted through her mind, the blinds automatically snapped down behind her eyes and across a corner of her mind. Safe, stone-cold, hopeless as night, Marie strutted onto Ellesmere Avenue, lit a cigarette, and waited.

Chapter Three

Perfect shot," Pete said as the dart hit its target. James Fisher, shooter of the perfect shot, allowed his usually grim mouth a smile.

"Now, if only you were as good at playing darts as you are at shooting pool, I'd have some competition!"

"Yeah, and if you were as good at running a business as you are at playing darts, *I'd* have some competition." Pete set down his glass and picked up a dart thoughtfully.

"Gets ya right where it hurts, doesn't he?" Phil said thoughtfully. James, Pete, Phil, and Nat were as close as billiard balls before a break.

"Oh yeah, Pete's always ready to cut me down," James agreed, trying to sound good-natured. "But it's no good criticizing me, ol' buddy, unless you're going to tell me what's wrong. What's the secret of success I'm missing out on?"

Pete let the dart fly before he turned to face James. "Aw, don't gimme that, Jim. You know what's wrong with your business and so does everyone else in this joint."

"Oh yeah?" James clenched his fists and set his jaw and leaned forward, ready to take a swing. Nat slapped him on the shoulder and said, "Take it easy," then had to dodge a swipe.

"Gotta give it to ya straight, Jim," Pete continued. "When a customer disagrees with you over a bill, you don't punch him out. When a car acts up, you don't crack off the antenna. You pull a few stunts like that, word gets around. You lose business."

Lightning-quick, Nat put his hand on Jim's shoulder to hold him back. "And it's a shame," Pete went on quickly, "because

15

you're a better mechanic than I'll ever be. Probably the best in town. You deserve the business, bud."

The lines in James's face relaxed a fraction. He satisfied himself with a fist-crunching blow to the bar. Pete's annoyance with him was replaced by a flash of pity. James had graduated from Marselles Central in the same class as Pete, but his heavy, lined face looked years older. Of course things hadn't been easy for him. His marriage hadn't worked out, he had a widowed mother to support and a family business to run ("Into the ground," Pete added uncharitably). And his only help was a younger brother who was something less of a right-hand man to him than Andy was to Pete. True, Jim's bad temper made things worse for him. But it was all a vicious circle, wasn't it? Pete tried to throw a bit of business his way, special jobs he knew James did better, but how could he recommend that his customers take their cars to a man who might crack their windshields if he got annoyed?

John, as usual, was ignoring his brother and all his surroundings. Pete wondered why he was even here tonight. Normally he avoided James's friends, and easygoing coupla-beers-and-a-game-of-pool hangouts like Ranger's Bar. Of course, he was only a young guy—10 years younger than Andy, whom Pete thought of as "the kid." With his jeans tight over his slim legs, his pierced ear, and his stylishly long hair over the collar of his army surplus jacket, John looked like an alien in the smoky, friendly, blue-collar Ranger's.

Six o'clock most evenings, John would already be headed to one of the trendy downtown pubs, or else off at the library. He read constantly, silently smoldering in his fury at not being able to go to university. Not only did the family not have the money to send him, but his help was needed to keep his father's garage going. John wore resentment as proudly as he wore the army jacket. Idly, Pete wondered again what he was doing here.

The guys had calmed Jim down a bit, and now Nat glanced at his watch. "Time to head back home," he said. "You need a ride, Pete?" Nat and Pete were the only two family men in the gang. James didn't have a wife anymore, and Phil wasn't overly fond of his.

"Not tonight. Audrey's got the kids out shopping for school clothes."

"Come to think of it, I think Sue's going over to her sister's tonight. Maybe I should give her a buzz, tell her I won't be home till later."

16

"Aw, sure," Phil urged. "If all you're going home to is a TV dinner, might as well stay here and have a burger with us."

"Hey, I can cook, OK?" Nat protested. "But I don't guess I've got to cook for Sara and Mike, do I?"

"They're teenagers, they can take care of themselves," Pete assured him. He liked the idea of hanging around Ranger's with the guys for a few more hours. Going home to a house empty of Audrey and kids didn't do much for him.

Nat left to call his wife. "Where's Andy tonight?" James asked.

Pete shrugged. "Had to go uptown to drop off a car for some ritzy customer. I figured he took the bus back; don't know where he went after that." He picked up his glass and gulped another swig of beer. "Am I my brother's keeper?"

"I sure wish I wasn't," James said, with a sidelong glance at John.

John's sullen face was suddenly animated. "Oh, right. You're the brother's keeper? You think I'm in this hick hole because this is where I like hanging out? I like the country music or something? I'm burning my brain cells out here because Mom told me she wants my precious big brother home early tonight—not drunk and not beat up! So you can just shut up about . . ."

James was on his feet in a flash, hurling curses at his brother. With the speed of those practiced in their art, Pete and Phil moved to hold the brothers off each other, and Nat, back from the phone, attempted to change the conversation. Easing an irate John back onto his stool, Pete reflected that with all the energy the Fisher boys spent fighting each other, it was amazing they still had the strength left to fight outsiders too.

Despite not being his brother's keeper, Pete was relieved to see Andy stroll through the door a few minutes later. His easygoing kid brother, the guy everyone liked. No fights got started when Andy was around.

Tonight, though, an uncharacteristic tension stiffened Andy's step, an urgency marked his glance.

"Pete! You've got to come with me. I've met this amazing guy . . ."

The fellows laughed. "Shouldn't that be 'amazing *girl*'?" Pete cracked.

"Or is there something you're not telling us?" Nat teased, laying his hand on Andy's arm in an overly friendly gesture.

Andy shook Nat's touch off impatiently. Andy, impatient? The

17

two words didn't fit together in Pete's mind.

"Down on Lancer Avenue," Andy continued. "This guy's a street preacher, and, man, he's amazing. I met him this afternoon. Couldn't believe the stuff he was saying—and doing. You've gotta meet him!"

It crossed Pete's mind to ask what Andy was doing on slummy Lancer Avenue when he was supposed to be delivering a car to Westchester Park. But there were more pressing matters to discuss just now. "Have you lost your mind?" he demanded.

"No. But I might have found it."

"Wait a second," Phil said. "I know the guy you're talking about. Drives a blue van and works with ghetto kids, right? I met him last week at a house where I was doing a job. Remember, Nat? I told you you had to meet this guy. Chris Carpenter, right?"

"I think that's his name," Andy agreed.

"An amazing guy from Lancer Avenue?" Nat commented quizzically.

"Wait a second—why are you getting all worked up over some social worker type?" James asked.

Pete settled back for another sip of his beer. "He said a *preacher*, Jim. My kid brother's got a sudden attack of religion."

James waved his hand in dismissal. "If you're into that kind of thing, send a few bucks to a TV evangelist and ease your conscience, but leave me out of it."

Maybe it was just the opportunity to disagree with James, but John suddenly looked interested, even eager. One of the few times Pete could remember such a look on his face. "I've heard of this guy too," John said, rising. "He sounds like a real radical. I want to meet him."

Pete looked at the others. Phil, normally so cynical, had his jacket on already. Nat was looking at Phil. Used to trusting his friend and business partner, he was obviously curious about Phil's new enthusiasm. Pete glanced at James. "Should we go along for the ride?"

Chapter Four

The blue Buick station wagon — "Addison and West, Plumbing and Heating" painted on its doors — pulled up in front of the run-down Lancer Avenue Community Center. Its four doors opened: Phil and Nat emerged from the front, Pete and Andy slid out from the back. Behind them James and John's battered Impala clattered to a halt.

Pete had seen the place before — as he drove through the neighborhood with all his doors locked. It was always dark and empty, broken windows boarded up, paint peeling off the sign. The brave community-improvement schemes of a more liberal age had faded under lack of funding and lack of commitment. As he stepped out onto the sidewalk, Pete could hear John's strident voice lecturing James on that very subject, cursing a government that chose to ignore places like Lancer Avenue.

Tonight, though, lights were blazing out of the few intact windows. A buzz of voices rose to greet them as they pushed the doors open.

In a large open room that looked like an underdeveloped high school gym, about 40 or 50 people were milling about. There were the usual groups — women standing around talking to women, men talking to men, children playing tag in and out between the adults' legs. But most of the people seemed clustered around some central attraction — what, Pete couldn't say. The place had a faint odor.

Two women came toward them — both roughly middle-aged. One was large and Black, the other small and Spanish-looking, Pete thought.

"Hi, I'm Erica," the Black woman said. "You want to come in?

You missed the meeting, but we'll be around for a few hours."

The other woman didn't seem as openly friendly. She frowned slightly. "You're not from around here, are you?"

Pete looked at his buddies uncertainly. Andy, who had dragged them all here, looked at Pete as if expecting him to say something.

"No, we're not," Pete admitted. "But we heard about this guy—Carpenter, Christopher Carpenter, is it?—and, uh, we wanted to meet him."

"I was down here today," Andy volunteered, finding his voice at last. "Chris asked me to drop by this evening."

Erica laughed. "They don't need no excuse to be here, Martha. People been coming from all over town to see Chris."

Martha's tight face seemed to relax at the mention of the man's name. "He's been here all week, and the place has been packed every night."

"I thought this place wasn't open anymore," John commented.

"No, it just kind of died out a few years back," Erica said. "But when Mr. Carpenter came around here a few weeks ago, well, we needed someplace bigger than my kitchen to hold the people who wanted to meet him, and I called up Martha here—"

"I used to work at the Center when it was open," Martha said. "Erica and Mr. Carpenter talked me into getting it going again. We still don't have any government money—it's all volunteer right now—but Mr. Carpenter says we should just take it one day at a time."

John seemed interested in discussing Center politics with the two women, and the other men drifted away but stayed on the edges of the group.

"Funny thing," Pete said, trying to find words for what they were all feeling. "I'm just an ordinary guy, a mechanic, and there's people who can make me feel real lower-class, but here—here I feel like I'm rich, and I got no right to be."

The others, looking around at the people in the room, nodded silently. The crowd in the middle seemed to be breaking up; some leaving, others just dispersing. A lone man walked away, headed toward a group of children—then noticed the five men standing uncertainly and turned to them.

"Andy! You made it!" he called, his voice glad. He held out a hand to shake Andy's. "These your friends?" He was an average-looking guy, moderately tall, well-built but slim, dressed in jeans and a blue T-shirt. His brown hair was unremarkable, as was his face—except for the broad welcoming grin and unusually lively eyes. *It must be his voice*, Pete thought—but was unable to complete the sentence.

Andy was making introductions. "I think you've met Phil—" he began.

"Sure!" Chris replied. "Fixing the sink in Hernandez' apartment, right?"

"And looking for the contact lens," Phil added. He and Chris shared a laugh.

"Their teenage daughter wanted to know if her lens was anywhere in the pipes," Chris explained. "She'd lost it, oh, maybe six or seven months ago. Seriously, though, Phil, I was really impressed with the way you treated those people. They're so used to getting ripped off, and respect isn't something they see much of."

Phil looked at the ground and shrugged. "Satisfied customer's a repeat customer."

Christopher Carpenter turned to Nat. "Nathan Addison—the most honest man in Marselles," he said, putting a hand on Nat's shoulder.

Nat looked at Phil, startled. "What have you been telling him?"

"Nothing," Phil insisted. "I didn't say nothing."

"Aw, I know you, Nat," Christopher assured him. "Didn't I see you sitting in your car out in the Ranger's parking lot tonight, going over the day, making sure you'd given everyone a fair deal? You're a decent man, Nat Addison."

Nat's eyes widened until he looked almost comical—a short, plump man with a thatch of graying hair, staring with his mouth half-open at this stranger. The look on his face reminded Pete of a man who'd just been told he'd won the lottery—a shock too big to absorb all at once. But Chris was already turning to Peter.

"Rocky Johnson. I've been waiting a long time to meet you." His handclasp was firm; no nonsense here. Pete glanced automatically at his sleeve for the telltale name tag—on the jacket he wasn't wearing.

"How'd you know to call me Rocky?" he blurted out.

Mr. Carpenter smiled. "That's your name, isn't it? You still think of yourself that way, and I do too. The Rock—someone you can build on and lean on. Some people call me that too. You're a born leader of men, Peter Johnson."

For once, somebody got a word in ahead of Pete. "Who *are* you?" James exclaimed.

21

"I know who you are," Nat said. Quietly. Nat, still awestruck. "You're sent from God, aren't you? You're the leader, the one who's going to save the world." The huge impossible words would have sounded ridiculous in this everyday setting—except . . . Christopher Carpenter was there.

He smiled, almost as if something were funny. "You believe that, just because I knew your names?" he said in a gentle, faraway tone. "What will you think when you see the sky split open and angels pouring down on Marselles County?"

Lively wasn't the right word for his eyes. *Piercing,* Pete thought.

A shy-looking girl on crutches came up behind Chris and stood there, too hesitant to reach out and touch his sleeve. "Sir?" Andy said, and nodded toward the girl. But Chris was already turning around.

She beckoned him over, away from the men, and he bent to talk to her for a few moments. Pete looked at the other guys. No one seemed to have much to say. When the girl walked away, Pete noticed the happy, confident tilt of her head before he realized that her crutches were gone.

"He can do that?" Nat breathed.

"He can do anything," Andy said simply.

"It could be a trick . . ." suggested James.

"Shut up. This is no trick," Pete said roughly, not knowing how he knew.

They stayed and watched him in action for another hour, talking to people, listening to them, healing them. Andy moved right into the crowd, helping out where he could, directing people to Christopher. The others got involved more tentatively. Pete found himself in the Center's cramped kitchen, making a sandwich for a drunk and wondering, "What am I doing here?"

By 9:00 the crowd had thinned a bit. Chris came into the kitchen and sat down with some of the volunteers who were taking a break. Martha was pouring juice into paper cups.

"Folks are taking their kids home now," Erica said. "Should be ready to shut down by 10:00 or so."

"And we should get Mr. Carpenter home by midnight," her husband, Bob, said, "after he's done talking to every bum on the streets." They laughed the comfortable laughter of people who know each other's habits.

"Well, I gotta go," Pete said, standing. "Audrey and the kids'll be home by now, and . . ."

22

"We'll give you a ride," James offered. "Mom expects us home early, eh John?"

"At least she'll have no worries about either of us coming home with a black eye tonight," John said. "Ah, Mr. Carpenter, I'll be down tomorrow night, like I said, OK?"

Carpenter smiled at him. "Thanks, John. I'll be counting on you." He said goodbye to the others. Then, just as Pete reached the doorway, he said, "Rocky!"

Pete turned. Those eyes again.

"I'm counting on you, too."

☆ ☆ ☆

Back at the house, quickly and silently Andy went down to his basement. "He's got a lot on his mind," Pete explained to Audrey. He sat down across the kitchen table from her. "Me too. Sorry I'm late."

"The kids wanted to show you their new stuff, but tomorrow will be time enough."

"I'll go up to say goodnight to them in a few minutes." He sat looking at her, at her hands moving in the little pool of light the lamp cast on the table. Her dark blonde hair, pulled away from her face by a gold clip, shone a little in the light. Her fingers moved deftly between pen, paper, and calculator. She was paying the household bills. "So, what happened tonight?" she asked pleasantly.

"Audrey, I—we—met the most amazing guy." He tried to explain about Christopher Carpenter. "It would have been spooky," he finished, "him knowing our names and all that, but—it wasn't, see? It was just like—like he'd met us before."

"The way God knows us, I guess," Audrey said gently.

"He said I was—a leader of men. Someone to build on, like a rock. And I . . . Audrey, I'm just an average guy, right?"

She put down her pen, cupped her chin in her hands, and smiled. "No, honey. You're a bigmouth with a quick temper and a kind heart—both of which you usually keep hidden—and you have a lot of frustration bottled up inside because you've never found a challenge that will let you be the man you're meant to be."

"And now . . . I think I've found it," Pete said.

Audrey looked back down at her checkbook. "I'd like to meet this Mr. Carpenter."

Chapter Five

Matthew switched off the TV with the remote control. "I've gotta study," he insisted for the fourth time that evening. "No loss to me," murmured Jude, who was glancing idly through a law textbook. Then he glanced up, a grin curling the sides of his mouth. "You, study? Your sources fail you?"

" 'Fraid so," Matt said casually, trying to mask the paralyzing fear that always gripped him when he couldn't get hold of the answers to an exam beforehand.

Jude shook his head, still grinning. "Those who live by the cheat sheet shall die by the cheat sheet."

"Thanks a lot, pal." Matthew stretched full-length on the floor and tried a few sit-ups. "You can afford to be flip. You haven't got an exam tomorrow."

"Matter of fact, I have." Jude picked up two snapshots from the desk. "Do you think Susan or Gail is a better bet for this dinner party? Who's going to impress more profs?"

"You're a first year law student with an exam tomorrow, and all you can think of is dates?"

"I prefer to think of them as test drives, my romantic little friend. Or interviews with candidates for the highly coveted position of my charming wife."

"Your charming first wife, you mean."

Jude waved both book and photos aside casually. "Torts and tarts—equally irrelevant. But both necessary to get to the top." He paused in thought. "Not Gail. She's too cutesy—too much of a cheerleader. A high school date. Even to go out with her in undergrad was pushing it. Definitely not a law-school date. She's — perky."

Matt had abandoned sit-ups in favor of running in place. "I wish I could take things as casually as you."

"Not to worry. You'll learn that, as you've learned everything else." Jude pulled the book toward him again, this time seriously. The very action discouraged Matthew. Jude looked so confident.

Whereas I, Matthew had to admit to himself, *am worn out from an evening of watching TV, and I haven't opened the book yet.* For a moment his degree seemed light-years, rather than three years, away. *Tailored suits and paisley ties do not an MBA make,* he reminded himself. *I've got the image and precious little else.*

At least there was a cure for tiredness. Matthew picked his way through the clutter of the living room. Though the place had the ramshackle look of most bachelor apartments, under the clutter it was better furnished than most other grad students' places. Both guys had the money and the taste to make it look right. The apartment, too, fit the image.

In the bathroom, in front of the mirror, Matthew swallowed two pills and studied his reflection in the mirror. Flawless haircut, clear skin, good face, athletic body looking sharp in crisp Adidas shorts and mesh tank top. With the blond hair and blue eyes, he looked like a negative of his roommate. Both were tall, well built, well dressed—only Jude had dark hair and eyes. Bright Young Men on the way up. Both had already attracted attention in the first years of their various schools.

"The difference is," Matthew told his reflection, "that Jude is the real thing. A winner. And you're just a well-covered-up loser, coasting on uppers and crib sheets."

His muscles tensed, jumping with nervous energy. He drummed his fingers against the counter without even realizing it. Much too lively, now, to settle down to studying. He grabbed a towel off the rack and slung it over his shoulders.

"I'm going down to the weight room to work out," Matthew called to Jude. "Wanna come?"

"No, I think I'll do a bit of real cramming," Jude responded, without looking up.

Sweating, straining, pulling at the weight machine, Matthew couldn't stop comparing himself with his roommate. Jude would take advantage of anyone, use anyone, step on anyone's face to get to "The Top." In short, he would ruthlessly do any of the barbaric things within the range of professional ethics. He'd taught Matthew all those tricks. But he would never do anything as stupid and classless as buying—or selling—exam answers. Nothing that could get him kicked out, or even questioned.

The killer was, he didn't have to. *No, buddy,* Matthew thought as he switched to the rowing machine, *there are a few things I can't learn. How can I face a night of studying till dawn—which is what I'll need to scrape through without a crib sheet—knowing I'll still be no smarter when the sun comes up?*

As if on cue, Charlie Smith strolled into the otherwise empty weight room. Short, pudgy, red-faced, Charlie didn't look like an angel. But for Matt, he was.

"Good news, kid," Charlie said.

"You got it?"

"Bonnie held out a little longer than usual. Sorry it's late." Charlie held a manila envelope just out of Matt's reach as he quoted his standard price.

Matthew pulled his wallet from his pocket and handed over the cash. Silently he thanked God for Masterton's secretary Bonnie, who stole exams for guys like Charlie, and for guys like Charlie, who sold them to desperate students like Matt.

"Gotta run," mumbled Charlie. "Got a few other anxious customers in this building."

With the precious envelope under his arm, Matthew bypassed the elevator and sprinted up eight flights of stairs. No studying! Only a good night's sleep was needed, so he'd be alert enough not to get caught—even a veteran cheater like Matthew Levy, MBA, had to be cautious. If only he didn't have all those now-useless chemicals surging through his bloodstream. But that was easily solved.

The apartment was dark. No light shone from under Jude's bedroom door. His "real cramming" had lasted less than an hour. Great!

Back in the bathroom, Matthew refilled his plastic glass and reached into the medicine cabinet. He took another look at himself—handsome, sweaty, triumphant, one hand on the plastic tumbler and the other on the bottle of sleeping pills. And in that moment, Matthew Levy knew he was looking at a creature for whom he felt nothing but utter contempt.

Chapter Six

Not yet seen, Pete Johnson leaned against the hood of a rusted-out pickup, watching. The Fishers' yard was, as always, filled with vehicles in various stages of repair. Right now James and John were both under the hood of a 1979 Toyota Corolla that should have been given up for dead long ago. James was clearly in charge, John his assistant. Pete wondered how long that would last without a blowup. Maybe several hours. Both of them seemed to have a bit more patience than usual these days.

Andy was just cleaning up from working on a Jeep. Both he and Pete had been stopping by more often than usual to help out when they'd finished their own work for the day. The Fishers, who were always going through hard times financially, seemed lately to be going through harder times than usual.

Somewhere inside, old Mrs. Fisher was puttering around the kitchen. *Cantankerous old . . .* Pete cut off the thought. He should be feeling sorry for her. Thinking of Mrs. Fisher reminded him that Audrey's mother was staying with them again. No wonder he was on a short fuse when it came to old ladies.

Pete strolled over to an Olds Delta 88 in the middle of the yard. A pair of legs protruded from beneath it. "How's that one going?" he called.

The man underneath, greasy and sweaty, wriggled out and smiled up at Pete. "I think it's a bit too much for me." He sat up, wiping an arm across his forehead. "I'll have to give James a look at it—unless you want to." When Chris was helping out with a car, he always deferred to the others, but he was picking up the skills so quickly Pete knew there wasn't really much he needed help with. It was just his way, to give credit to anyone with more expertise.

Christopher Carpenter had surprised them. Well, that was an understatement. He had surprised them in a lot of ways, including his willingness and ability to help fix cars. Pete had figured this guy for a university-liberal type, never having done a tap of work in his life. Not so. Apparently Christopher's background was in construction, and he'd run a small contracting business with his father until just a few years ago. He understood not only the work, but also the headaches of running a small business. It made him an easy man to respect.

James walked over to the Delta 88 and sat down on the ground. "I'm not going to bother with it anymore today," he said. "Getting dark now anyway."

Pete could hear James fighting to keep the edge of discouragement out of his voice. He was surprised to see John shoot a look of—could it be concern?—at his brother.

"Still nothing coming in?" Chris asked gently.

James shook his head. "I'm hoping if we can get paid for the last two jobs by Wednesday . . . but there's nothing after that. And Rutger still owes me for the truck. . . . I didn't even open the mail today. I'm scared to get any more bills."

"Maybe you *should* open the mail," Chris remarked quietly.

"Does your mom know how bad it is?" Andy asked.

It was John who answered. "We haven't told her. We've had bad months before, and scraped through. We didn't want to worry her."

"We never had this many bad months before," James said dully.

Pete felt uncomfortable. His own business was doing OK, and his friends were on the brink of bankruptcy. James wouldn't normally accept charity, but lately he'd been desperate enough to take a little help—except the kind of help Pete could give him wasn't nearly enough. Both Pete and Andy had been putting in as many hours as they could spare to help out—and so had Chris Carpenter, maybe to repay the hours the Fishers had spent with him down on Lancer Avenue. But it wasn't enough.

"If you could go after Rutger—" Pete began.

"It'd only scratch the surface," James said. "I can't afford to get the money out of him anyway, but—even then. A couple thousand dollars. We need a good 10 thousand to put us back on our feet. And there's nowhere to get it." He shrugged, then frowned.

"Things have never been as bad before—but yet I don't feel as worried as I should."

"I do," John said. "What's going to happen to Mom if we don't have the business?"

James stood up and turned toward the house. "S'pose I should go face that mail."

The four men left in the yard were quiet. "Jim has got a point," John admitted after a few minutes. "It won't be the end of the world if we go under. Look at some of those people down at the Community Center. They're a lot worse off than us, but some of them seem to be . . . happy, I guess." He suddenly turned to Chris. "Even you. You don't really have any security. You're just living one day to the next—how do you do it?"

Chris leaned back, stretched out his legs, looked at the sky. "There's more to security than having a paycheck coming in. It's a waste of time to build your security on material things. It can all be taken away—as you're finding out." He stared thoughtfully at the swallows on the utility line outside Mrs. Fisher's house. "Do the birds worry about stuff like that? No, they just figure someone's going to take care of them—and Someone does. Trusting God to take care of you—that's the only real security."

"It's not easy," Pete replied.

"No, it's not easy, but it's real. Look for God and His kingdom first, and everything else will fall into place. I can promise you that," Christopher added in the odd voice that made Pete somehow feel calm. Only John still looked a little troubled.

"*John!*" James roared in the voice usually reserved for fits of extreme rage. He was running across the yard, waving an envelope, and on his face was not anger but some kind of joyous awe. He thrust the envelope into his brother's hands.

John scanned the paper quickly. "It's the bank statement, but—" He looked at James and then back at the paper. "Where did this huge deposit come from?"

"I don't know," James said. "I thought it had to be a mistake, but there's a letter explaining that an unidentified person made a deposit—"

"Of $15,000 to our account on October 25," finished John, who was reading the letter. "This is for real! Somebody gave us 15 grand! Man!"

They all crowded around John excitedly, except for Mr. Carpenter. He stood off to one side, hands in pockets, staring at the road. Pete walked over to him and stood there, uncertainly.

"You're behind all this, aren't you?"

Chris smiled, a half smile. "God is behind every good thing."

"And you're God, right? Or you're sent from God, or you're the Son of God. Look, I don't even think I should be hanging around you. I'm just an ordinary guy. This stuff is way over my head."

Carpenter turned and looked at him with eyes that made Peter grow cold all over. He felt as if he were standing at the edge of a chasm. On this side, he was Pete Johnson, mechanic, family man, ordinary guy. On the other side—what? Life completely different. Christopher Carpenter. Involuntarily, Pete stepped back a pace or two.

Chris turned to face the others. John was looking toward him, awe in his eyes. Suddenly he dropped to one knee. "I don't know how you did this, but I know you had something to do with it. Uh—thank you." His eyes shone. John was so young, so idealistic—then Pete, who was middle aged and cynical, noticed that he too was on his knees. As were they all. On their knees in front of Chris, who just a minute ago had been underneath an Olds Delta 88.

Chris, too, dropped to the ground and sat down across from them. "Listen, guys," he said. "Things are changing. God's kingdom isn't something far off in the future. It's starting here and now, and you're part of it. I need you to help me tell people. Instead of filling people's gas tanks, you could be filling up empty lives. Instead of fixing broken engines, you could be showing people how to let God fix their broken hearts." He was quiet a moment, meeting each of their gazes in turn. "What I'm asking you to do is to leave all this behind . . . and follow me."

Chapter Seven

Audrey tossed Pete a dish towel. He was slowly becoming a liberated husband, but not as slowly as he'd have liked. He picked up a cereal bowl and wiped it thoughtfully.

"You've been awfully quiet lately," Audrey observed. "Something on your mind?"

When Audrey got to the point of asking, she not only knew something was wrong, she usually knew what it was as well. This time, however, she was off base. "You're still upset Mom's here, aren't you?"

"No I'm not upset your mother's here! Well, all right, she's not my favorite houseguest, but I'm not going to kick a sick woman out onto the sidewalk."

"I'm afraid if she doesn't get better, she won't be able to go home at all. We can't keep her here forever, and I hate the thoughts of putting her in a home. . . ." Her voice trailed off.

Pete reached for a glass, dried it, held it up to the light. Spotless.

"You still haven't told me what's wrong. Is it anything to do with work? Are things OK down at the garage?"

Pete was, again, uncharacteristically silent. A lot was happening down at the garage. He was making plans to turn the place over to Stan Carey. Pete would continue to be the owner, for now, but Stan would run it. And he felt guilty, because he had never even considered such a major career move without consulting Audrey. Ever since his bid for senior class president, 18 years before, Audrey had been involved in his every decision. But now—how could he tell her he wanted to walk away from it all? What did Mr. Carpenter's invitation mean?

31

James and John were closing up shop. With their unexpected windfall, they had been able to pay off their debts and leave their mother a little security. They were with Chris Carpenter all the time now: working at the Center, gathering groups to listen to his street-corner sermons, going with him to visit some of the scummiest neighborhoods of Marselles. Andy spent little time at the garage now. He, too, was usually with Chris. Nat and Phil were seriously considering selling out their plumbing and heating business.

Pete knew himself to be impulsive. His immediate response to the invitation had been "Yes! Of course I'll follow you!" He'd even spoken first, while the others remained in shocked silence. Only as he made his way home did the question of Audrey and the kids drill into his vision-soaked brain.

Audrey didn't mind the time he spent with Mr. Carpenter. She liked Christopher; even spent some time down at the Center herself. In her quiet way, she seemed almost more impressed than Peter himself. But what would she say if he told her he wanted to leave the business? Or worse—what if Chris wanted to visit towns other than Marselles? Would he be expected to leave Audrey, Jenny, Randy, Kevin? And for how long?

Audrey sighed and shut off the tap. "Forget it. I can see I'm not getting anything out of you this morning." Footsteps thundered on the stairs, and she raised her voice so it would carry, "Are all of you ready for church?"

"I can't find my shoes!" Kevin yelled.

"He's got on my sweater, and I want to wear it!" Randy chimed in.

Churchgoing was a regular weekly ritual at the Johnsons'. Audrey made sure of that. Pete had always taken it for granted. He'd never been overly religious, but as soon as Randy was born Audrey had insisted on weekly church attendance, and he'd complied. Lately, church had confused Pete. *With all the time I'm spending with Chris Carpenter,* he thought, *I should be getting more religious. Instead, I'm getting impatient with church.*

He tried to say some of this to Audrey on the way to church, as if sharing his thoughts now might make up for his earlier silence. "All the stuff Chris does and talks about . . . well, it seems a lot more real than what they say in church," he tried to explain.

"I find it that way too," said Audrey. She combed Jenny's

blonde hair as she spoke. Andy, wedged in the backseat with the boys, leaned forward.

"It's not just what Chris says or does," Andy put in. "It's who he says he is."

"Yeah, that too," Pete agreed. "When you're hanging around all the time with a guy who believes he's the Son of God, church just seems kind of—I don't know, kind of out of it."

"Mr. Carpenter always goes to church, though," Audrey pointed out. "By the way, you want to invite him home to lunch today?"

"Sure. He's got no place of his own to go, and he's never been to our place for a meal. It won't be too hard on your mother, will it?"

"I don't think having Mr. Carpenter around is hard on anybody," Audrey said. "I'm glad Mrs. Fisher was able to come in this morning, though. I hate to leave Mom alone."

"Chris is preaching today," Andy added quietly.

"He's *what?*" Pete narrowly missed hitting a bus.

"He's the guest speaker."

"That'll be nice," Audrey said placidly. "Kevin, leave your sister's hair alone."

"Nice is the one thing it won't be," Pete said grimly. "A disaster is what it'll be."

"Oh, you're such a pessimist."

Pete felt no need to revise his prediction when Christopher Carpenter stood up behind the pulpit later that morning. Nobody else in the large congregation looked worried, though. They all knew him well by now—a few of them had even volunteered time down on Lancer Avenue. They described Chris Carpenter as "interesting" or "challenging" or "intriguing" and settled back comfortably in their seats and hoped to hear an inspiring sermon about the need for social action.

Pete knew better.

He glanced across the church to where Nat Addison sat with his family. Phil West sat just behind them. Somewhere in the back, James Fisher sat alone. John was up in the balcony with some of the younger people, his long hair, earring, and army jacket defiant in the sea of suits and ties. Except for Nat, Pete couldn't remember seeing any of his buddies in church until a few weeks ago. Right now, they all had something in common: they all looked as uneasy as Pete felt. They knew Chris.

The text he chose for Scripture reading was innocent enough—

seemed to fit in with what most of his hearers were expecting. "The Spirit of the Lord is on me, because he has anointed me to preach good news to the poor. He has sent me to proclaim freedom for the prisoners and recovery of sight for the blind, to release the oppressed, to proclaim the year of the Lord's favor."* Christopher read it over again when he got up to speak, then fixed the congregation with those eyes that made Pete stop caring whether people were shocked or not.

"Friends," Chris began in his clear, ringing voice, "we all know that this text tells us what God wants us to do in the world. But we also know it's much more than that: it's a prophecy about what God's Chosen One will do when he comes to save the world. You've all looked forward to His coming; all your lives you've heard sermons about how this world will change when God sends His special messenger to lead you out of blindness and captivity and poverty. Well, I'm here to tell you that you don't need to wait any longer. That time is here! God's Chosen One is here! Today, in this church, this scripture is being fulfilled."

A low murmur ran around the edges of the congregation as Chris went on talking and the impact of his words sank in. People leaned forward to catch what he said.

"The kingdom of Heaven—the kingdom of God—that perfect world of peace and goodwill that you've all been waiting for—it's not something far-off in the future. It's not a fantasy or a fairy tale. It's here now. You have to make a choice, and if you choose to believe, this kingdom will begin right in your heart. It will begin . . . here in this church. It will begin here in Marselles, with all of you who choose to believe in the one sent by God."

Murmurs grew louder now. A few people got up to leave. A man across from Pete got to his feet and called out, "Just what are you trying to—" but was firmly yanked down by his wife.

Mr. Carpenter met the man's eyes. "What I'm trying to do is this—wake up the good people of Marselles and tell them a new day is coming. What I'm trying to say is that you can be a part of this new day—all of you—if you'll be willing to leave the safe lives you know, and believe me, and follow me." He stretched out his hands and looked out into the congregation for a moment, then turned quickly and sat down.

The elder who had to announce the closing hymn scrambled uncertainly to his feet after a moment and waited in vain for the talking to cease. Finally he gave up and plunged in, signaling to the organist to begin.

Pete held the edge of Audrey's hymnbook and sang lustily.

> We are living, we are dwelling
> In a grand and awful time. . . .

He wondered if Chris had picked the hymn.

☆ ☆ ☆

Back home Audrey was concerned about getting dinner on the table as quickly as possible. The only way they'd managed to get Christopher away from the mob scene in the parking lot was to tell everyone where he'd be in the afternoon. Obviously Audrey was afraid people—the angry, the eager, the curious—would be ringing the doorbell before her roast was even out of the oven.

Chris seemed pleased and a little amused by the response to his sermon. "I wish I'd gotten this much of a positive response when I preached that sermon in my hometown," he said with a smile on the way home from church.

When at last they were ready to sit down, though, Christopher Carpenter was nowhere to be seen. "I'll go find him!" volunteered Jenny, kicking back her chair and racing away from the table.

"No, me!" shouted Randy, tearing off after her.

"He couldn't have left, could he?" asked Audrey. She was arranging a plate of food to take upstairs to her mother.

Randy reappeared in the doorway, suddenly quiet. "Mr. Carpenter was upstairs with Grandma," he announced solemnly. Down the hall behind him came Audrey's mother and Chris, with Jenny in between clinging to both their hands.

"Mom, what are you doing out of . . ." Audrey's sharp voice faded away. Pete looked at his mother-in-law and had the strange feeling of being caught in a time warp. This white-haired woman with the steady step and clear eyes was Ethel Delaney as he remembered her looking the day he married her daughter (though without the look of sorrowing disapproval she'd worn that day). She bore little resemblance to the frail, sickly woman of recent years.

"It's all right, dear," Ethel said in a firm voice. "I'm fine now. Mr. Carpenter has healed me. Is there anything I can do to give you a hand?"

☆ ☆ ☆

As they'd expected, the house was busy all afternoon and evening. Church people and neighbors dropped by to meet Chris Carpenter and talk to him. Some tried to challenge him on what he'd said that morning, but Pete didn't hear any loud arguments developing. Nat and Phil and their families, and the Fishers, were there all afternoon. Audrey's mother and some of the other women worked in the kitchen, preparing snacks and drinks for the hordes of visitors. Andy had organized some of the people with cars to pick up those who wanted to come over but couldn't find a way. The phone rang till Pete thought he might go crazy. Fortunately, he didn't.

It was late that evening when the crowd finally thinned. James and John and their mother were the last to leave, except for Christopher himself, who sat in the lamplit kitchen with Jenny on his knee and Kevin beside him. They watched attentively as Chris showed them how to do tricks with their new yo-yo. The kids adored him—hung on to every word he said, even when he told those Bible stories that Randy declared "bor-ing" if Audrey tried to read them at bedtime.

Randy was out in the living room watching TV with his grandmother. After almost the whole day on her feet, Ethel still seemed to be all right—amazing, considering how weak she'd been just that morning. Audrey was clearing up the kitchen, so Pete gave her a hand. "You kids should be in bed now," she told Kevin and Jenny. They started to protest, but quieted down when Christopher said, "C'mon, I'll take you upstairs."

"Will you tell us a story?" urged Jenny, sliding off his lap.

"If you're good . . . there's a very strong chance I might," he promised.

Pete hadn't had a moment to talk to Audrey all day. Now he tried, tentatively. "Quite the day, wasn't it?"

"It sure was."

"You didn't mind all those people here?"

"Well, how could I mind? They came to see Chris Carpenter. After what he did for Mom, I wouldn't want to keep anyone from seeing him." She paused, wringing out a cloth to wipe up the table. "Pete?"

"Mmm-hmmm."

36

"Do you believe in Chris? I mean, do you believe he is who he says he is?"

Pete was quiet, too, leaning at the sink to look out the kitchen window. "It's really weird, but . . . yeah, I guess I do. I mean, the stuff he does, like healing people . . . but it's not even that. It's just the way he is—you've got to believe him." Another pause. "What about you?"

Audrey nodded. "Well, it's either that or else he's crazy, and he sure isn't crazy. But believing he's the Son of God means I have to totally rearrange everything I've ever thought. He asked you guys to come with him, didn't he?"

"Well . . . he wants us to help him out. Full-time, I guess."

"I had a long talk with him today," she went on. "He explained why he needs you, and how he asked you to give up everything to follow him. He asked me to . . . give up some things too, I guess."

"And?"

"Well, if I believe in him, I can't hold anything back, can I? I've enjoyed the security of your having the garage, but security's not everything. You could give it to someone else to run, or even . . . sell it, I suppose."

Hesitantly, Pete admitted his plan to turn over the garage to Stan. "I'm sorry I didn't talk to you first."

"It's OK. . . . I wish you'd trusted me enough to ask me about it, but I understand. And Mr. Carpenter says he'll be going on the road for a while, maybe taking you and Andy and the other guys with him. I need you around here, of course . . . but I can manage for a while. Anyway, some of the girls and I were talking, and we think the work he's been doing in Marselles shouldn't just be let to slide when he goes. Martha and Erica could use some more help down at the Center, and, well, there are lots of people who still need to know about Christopher Carpenter here in Marselles. Sue Addison wants to help too. So I'd be doing my work here, while you were away."

Pete was very nearly speechless. "You've really thought this through, haven't you?"

"Well, of course I have. It's the most important thing that'll ever happen in our lives." She bent down to tie up the garbage bag. "I think Mom should stay here with us, at least for now, so I can keep an eye on her and she can help with the kids. And maybe in the summer, when the kids are out of school, we can drive to wherever you are and spend some time together."

"I'd like that," Pete said simply. He reached out to touch her cheek as she straightened up, and covered his action by brushing back a stray wisp of her hair. Then he took the garbage bag from her. "I'll carry this downstairs."

"One more thing," Audrey said as he headed for the basement door. "I asked Mr. Carpenter to stay here tonight. He can sleep on the couch. He's got no place of his own to go, you know."

"Fine by me."

---

*Luke 4:18, 19, NIV.

Chapter Eight

I understand why he had to leave, but it sure is different around here without him," Erica said. She laid her head on her hand and allowed a note of discouragement to slip into her voice. Down at the Community Center, Erica Washington was known as a pillar of strength and a source of good cheer. Here in Martha Castillo's kitchen she just looked like a tired, middle-aged Black woman, dressed in a faded print dress and scuffed loafers.

Her companion was a marked contrast. Martha, short, thin, and wiry, was younger than Erica, still a few years short of 40. Her dull brown, whip-straight hair tied with an elastic hung listlessly down to the middle of her back. Martha didn't allow herself the luxury of sitting at the table with her head in her hands. She had been raised on a store of reliable proverbs, all a good deal easier to believe in than God. "Idle hands are the devil's workshop" was one of her favorites. Her own hands were bony, callused, and rough-skinned, with nails clipped (not bitten) sensibly short. No showy nail polish or gaudy rings had ever brightened those hands. They were hands that justified themselves by being constantly at work, and right now they were polishing the bottom of a copper pot in the cramped but spotless kitchen.

The note of discouragement would not have sounded alien in Martha's voice, though perhaps a listener would have been more inclined to call it resignation. Martha Castillo had long ago steeled herself to expect nothing from life—nothing but simple duties and small pleasures. Until the appearance of this Christopher Carpenter person on Lancer Avenue, life had obligingly met her expectations. Now that he had gone, the disquieting element of hope could be put to rest too. She was disappointed, of course, but disappointment was the easiest emotion to deal with.

Of course she said none of this to Erica—she couldn't even have expressed it, in so many words, to herself. What she said was, "Well, I suppose things will settle down a bit now."

"That's what I'm afraid of. Things settling down on Lancer Avenue is just what we don't need."

"Of course, now that we've got people together, maybe we can work on City Hall to improve some things. There's that petition to get funding for the Center . . ."

Erica rubbed at a patch of the table's shiny surface. "Yeah, there's stuff like that, we got to keep that up, but . . . I don't know, when Chris was here it was more than just that. More than politics—there was a new spirit. People were different. I don't know if we can keep that up, with him gone."

Martha edged away from the subject. It bordered closely on religion, and religion made her uneasy, except when it involved collecting clothes for the needy or putting on baked goods sales to raise funds for a new church roof. "Mr. Carpenter certainly made a change in a lot of people," she conceded.

"Well, your brother, for instance," Erica pointed out.

Martha nodded shortly. The easiest way to annoy her was to mention Lazario. His broad smile, his whistle, his easy stride, all made her hackles rise when she thought of all the trouble he'd caused. "We'll just see how long that lasts, now," she told Erica.

"Oh, give him a chance. He's such a nice boy, and now that he has that good steady job, I'm sure he'll do all right."

"Yes, if it was the first time he had a good steady job." Martha pulled a sock out of her bag and sat down to darn. "When he was a teenager, mom always said he'd be OK as soon as he finished high school—only he never did. Then it was when he got married, he'd settle down a bit. Married! How long did that last?"

"How long did it last?"

"Not quite two years, till Sally got sick of him being so shiftless. She got a much better deal her second time around, you can be sure." Martha stabbed the sock firmly. Paradoxically, she hated her former sister-in-law for leaving. *How dare she do that to my brother?* Martha had asked herself at the time, knowing full well the reasons why.

Lazario had been the family's hope. He fitted in neatly between his two sisters, so different and so difficult. While their widowed mother fretted over her pretty younger daughter, whom boys wouldn't leave

40

alone, and her plain older daughter, whom boys wouldn't notice, all three of the Castillo women had pinned their dreams on the tall, handsome charmer with the ready smile. He would grow up, go to college, get a good job, and move them all off Lancer Avenue.

Lazario inherited his unfortunate name from a great-uncle who died without leaving him any money—perhaps there had been nothing to leave. At home he was always Lazario, but as a teenager he was called "Larry" by the guys he hung out with.

Too late Mrs. Castillo noticed those boys and worried. They were Marselles' version of a street gang, and Lazario was not just a member but a leader. "Poor Mom," Martha said aloud. "All three of us ended up being a worry to her in the end."

"Now, you couldn't have been much of a worry," Erica said. "You were such a big help to her."

"Yes, well, she worried I'd never get married. But I think in the end she was just as glad I didn't. Who else would there have been to care for her, after Maria nearly broke her heart and then she got so sick? And after Sally left, Lazario came back home and Mom would never have died peacefully if she hadn't known there was someone to look after her boy. As it was she didn't have a worry in the world when she died, except not knowing what happened to poor Maria. And I would have gladly spared her that trouble, if I could have."

"No, you couldn't do anything about that, could you now," Erica agreed. Her eyes strayed involuntarily to Maria's picture on the shelf, and Martha's gaze followed hers. Martha had often wanted to put the picture away, but Lazario wouldn't hear of it. He had adored Maria—they were so much alike, and Martha was the odd one in the family, being so serious and hardworking. The picture showed Maria at 13, four years before she left home. Dark eyes peeked out from under a stylish tangle of dark curls. Her mouth was crooked up at one end into that teasing grin that drove Lancer Avenue boys wild.

Lazario successfully kept his street-smart buddies at bay by making it clear that anyone who touched his little sister would have to answer to Larry Castillo personally. His warnings didn't diminish Maria's popularity, but they did save her some trouble, at least until she reached high school. Martha, too, wanted to protect Maria, but wasn't sure how. The few times she tried to talk to the girl about men and boys, she felt Maria was amused by her awkwardness. Martha was in her twenties by then, but she realized that her teenage sister knew things she herself didn't know. The knowledge Maria lacked couldn't be supplied by Martha or kept from her by Lazario. Maria would find out on her own.

"Well, there's nothing I can do about it now, either," Martha told Erica decisively. "No sense crying over spilled milk, is there now? I suppose we'll go on having the meetings down at the Center and all, same as we did when he was here?"

"Yes, I imagine so," said Erica, getting up to leave. "He'll be back to visit soon, he said, and you know he told us to carry on."

After Erica had gone, Martha began to scrub the kitchen sink vigorously, as if she hoped that her brisk strokes could erase the memories that had been called up. All the while Christopher was in Marselles, he had tried to talk to her alone. Lazario spent long hours sitting out on the front step with him, but Martha avoided being alone with him as much as possible. Now it seemed that in his absence he was forcing her to do what she'd not done in his presence—to go over the past, shaking out old memories she had long since folded and put away.

It had taken years of effort for Martha to look at that kitchen door without seeing Maria huddled there, crying and trembling; without hearing her own voice ordering Maria to get out of the house and never to show her face again. Lazario would have stopped her, but he was newly married then and had moved out. And their mother was helpless, reduced to tears and disbelief. Seeing Mom like that was what drove Martha to rage . . . knowing that Maria, like Lazario, could cause the old woman so much heartache just by being charming and sweet and thoughtless. Better to end all the hurt, to drive Maria out into the rainy night. Where had she gone? What had she done? Over the years Martha had trained herself not to ask these questions, but tonight they echoed in every stroke of her scouring pad. Most of all she wondered if Maria had ever had the baby. If she had, it would be a gangly boy or girl of 11 now. Martha liked children, actually, and when she thought of Maria's child and the baby whom Sally had taken with her when she left Lazario, she blinked against tears. Had her brother and sister robbed her of everything that might have given her life meaning?

For once, Martha's hands were still at the kitchen sink. She stood there, her thin freckled arms braced and her head bent, until she heard Lazario's key in the lock. But as her hands moved firmly back to their work, it was not her brother she longed to talk to, but Christopher Carpenter.

Chapter Nine

Matthew elbowed through the lunchtime crowd, balancing a cafeteria tray while trying to keep hold of his attaché case. From a relatively secluded corner table, Jude waved to him. "Have a seat, Matt. You look like you've been through a major war—or a final."

"Whichever comes first." Matt twisted the top off his Perrier bottle. "O'Toole's class—it was a killer, not the kind of thing where a cheat sheet was much help."

"Don't tell me you had to resort to studying," Jude replied in mock horror.

"Mmm. Unfortunately that wasn't much good either. How many more have you got?"

"Just one . . . then it's off to sunny California."

Matt shook his head enviously. Jude, with his usual ability to settle himself in an ideal situation, had snared a summer job at a law firm in Southern California. "Of course I'm taking the job because the connections are excellent—just mention the senior partner's name and doors magically swing open," Jude explained. "But that doesn't mean I'm going to ignore the sun and surf, naturally."

"Or the women."

"Ah, the lovely ladies of L.A.—no, of course I wouldn't dream of hurting their feelings by ignoring them. I couldn't be so hardhearted."

Matt wasn't too thrilled about his own summer plans, which involved staying on campus and working for a local company. Surely, with a little effort, he could have found something as impressive as California. Lately he felt he was running harder and harder to keep up with Jude, but he was falling behind anyway. He ran a hand through his blond hair and looked down at his plate of lasagna as if he wasn't sure what he was supposed to do with it.

"You look tired, Levy," Jude said. "When was the last time you got any sleep?"

"Oh . . . two nights ago, maybe. I don't know," Matt said dully.

"Better watch it. The chemical high only lasts so long, you know. What if you'd crashed in the middle of O'Toole's exam?"

"Wouldn't have made much difference," muttered Matt. He wished Jude could learn to keep that note of sarcasm out of his voice.

Jude was enthusiastically attacking his dessert. "Well, eat something. It'll keep your strength up. Hey," he added, looking closely at his roommate's eyes, "we're talking more than a little sleep deprivation here, aren't we?"

"Go ahead, say it."

"You're hung over."

"Thank you. I needed that."

Jude rolled his eyes. "Matt, I thought I'd taught you something. I thought you were catching on. Did you get plastered alone again?"

"No, not this time." Matt was glad to be able to answer honestly on that score. Drinking alone in the apartment was a habit he'd picked up fairly recently, and it scared him. He could have pretended to himself that it wasn't happening—he was an expert at that—but Jude never failed to comment if he found an empty bottle or a tumbler on the coffee table. "No, I went to a party over in Riley last night . . . some guys who'd finished exams . . ."

"That's hardly much better."

Matt reflected that there were times when Jude sounded exactly like a disapproving parent. This was one of them. He was counting off Matt's faults on his fingers. "First, one does not celebrate the end of exams until one's exams are actually over. Second, one does not waste one's time partying with overgrown frat boys. Social occasions should be opportunities for advancement and should not involve making a fool of yourself with a bunch of Animal House dropouts. Third—"

"I get the point, Jude." Matt decided to try the lasagna. It was cold. He looked at the limp yellowish broccoli. *No*, he thought.

"Third, unless one is anxious to end up in the University

Medical Center, one is careful about mixing alcohol with the other drugs that, knowing you, are certain to be floating around in your system."

"Yes, all right." The Perrier definitely was exactly what Matt's stomach did not need.

"I'm warning you, Levy, you've got to be careful. You could very profitably have spent that time studying for the exam you found such a killer. And you've got to be careful about the booze. The other stuff you're on, well, that's one thing, if you really need it to perform. But there's no practical purpose to getting hammered out of your mind two or three times a week."

Matt looked wearily up at his mentor/tormentor. "It does help me forget that I'm a failure, for a while," he said quietly.

"Don't give me that melodramatic drivel!" Jude banged his fist on the table, an act Matt and his headache deeply resented. "The point is, Levy, you don't have to be a failure. You've been steadily learning to be a success—but lately, you look like you're about to throw it all away. If you don't watch where you're going, you'll find yourself eating the dust of your wiser cohorts."

"Like you?"

"Like me," Jude agreed. He picked up his tray and left.

Matt ate the rest of his meal in blessed silence, wondering how he would get through the day. Two things helped. One was that his attaché case held what he believed to be the only free-floating copy of Dr. Masterton's final exam, scheduled for tomorrow morning. He'd gotten it himself this time, no middleman involved, and was mildly proud of the accomplishment. For the curve's sake he hoped he could keep his windfall a secret, but just in case someone else found out and wanted it, Matt had made a few extra copies. If he couldn't be the only one with an unfair advantage, he could at least make some spare change. A win-win proposition.

The other thing that held out some hope was the unopened bottle of vodka back in the kitchen. OK, OK, he'd planned to stay stone cold sober until the exam and celebrate afterward, but the grueling harangue Jude had just subjected him to demanded that he have just one drink—to relax. Then he'd study—even with an advance copy of the exam, he'd need some preparation.

As he left the cafeteria, Matt ducked into the men's room to straighten his tie, comb his hair, and splash water on his face. Although it took an effort, he walked out straight-shouldered and confident onto the campus, with his attaché case swinging. The sun's glare seemed unusually harsh and he had to squint, but the smiles and "hi's" he got from girls on the sidewalk reminded him that, on the outside, he was still the Bright Young Man.

Don't-screw-it-up-Matt, don't-screw-it-up, he chanted in his head, and began walking in time to his chant.

Rounding the corner past the library, Matt noticed an uncommonly large crowd gathered in the square. The square was the place where official and unofficial speakers climbed up on their soapboxes to sound off about nuclear disarmament or academic freedom or whatever the issue of the day was. Once in a while a concert was held there.

Today it seemed to be a speaker. Matt craned his neck to see a not-particularly-striking guy in jeans and T-shirt at the center of the crowd. He overheard the words "kingdom of Heaven." Ah, another religious freak. The square attracted plenty of those, but usually no one stopped to listen.

This guy sounded different—less hysterical, for one thing. Mildly curious, Matt moved closer, hoping Jude wasn't around to catch this display of unprofessional behavior. *Why worry?* he thought. *Jude's success formula is killing me, and on my own I'm a surefire failure. I need all the help I can get—street preachers, shrinks, the whole bit.*

"I know a lot of you out there have burdens—things weighing you down, worries and pressures you think you can't escape," the man was saying. "But you *can* escape them! God wants you to be free from those burdens. Come to me, and I'll show you how to let Him take all your cares. If you're exhausted, if you're about to give up, come to me. I can give you rest."

A murmur ran through the crowd. Matt ran his fingers through his hair. This was almost spooky.

"Of course life will always have problems," the man went on, "but if you'll take the burden I have for you, you'll find it a light load compared to the one you've been carrying—that load you made for yourself or allowed other people to place on your shoulders. Forget about meeting their standards of success. Come with me, learn what I have to teach you—and I can promise you you'll find the rest, the inner peace, that your Father in heaven wants all of you to have."

Matt shook his head. He'd heard lots of religious talk before, and most of it seemed to be advice about what to do and what not to do. This guy was the only one he'd ever heard who seemed to suggest that he himself had some kind of solution to offer — as if he had a direct line to God. Obviously he must be crazy. Too bad.

"Do you know who this guy is?" Matt asked a fellow next to him.

The boy — long-haired, an arts undergrad type, Matt figured — nodded enthusiastically. "I work with him," he said. "Isn't he something?"

"I can't get over how he talks," Matt admitted. "Like he has all the answers."

"He does," the boy said. "My life has changed totally since I met him. By the way, I'm John Fisher."

"Matthew Levy. This guy here —"

"Christopher Carpenter."

"Carpenter, he talks like he's really got something great to offer, but he doesn't tell you what it is, know what I mean?"

John grinned. "He does that on purpose. He wants to get you curious, so you'll go talk to him. What he really has to offer is himself. See, we believe he's God's Chosen One, sent from God."

To hear this last sentence spoken by such an apparently rational being shook Matt's composure a little. "He's what?"

"I know what you're thinking, man, but I'm not on anything. A little high on God, maybe, but that's natural. I know it sounds crazy, but don't knock it till you've talked to him."

Someone tapped Matt on the shoulder, and he turned. The smiling face of his classmate, Nancy Evans, greeted him. "Didn't expect to find you here, Matt."

"Just passing through," Matt said easily.

"Me too. I hear through the grapevine you've got the Masterton final?"

Confirm or deny? Unable to think quickly, Matt said, "Uh, yeah."

"Got any extras?"

"I might, for a price."

"How much?"

He named the first price he thought of.

The girl looked shocked. "Charlie Smith only charges half that," she protested.

"Get real. This is a final."

Matt listened to himself haggle with the girl till they reached a price they both agreed on. Nancy opened her purse and pulled out several crisp bills. Matt glanced around briefly, then opened his case and took out the envelope. Pulling out one copy of the exam, he handed it to Nancy and took the money.

When she had gone, Matt stood there for a moment, looking around. Chris Carpenter had stopped speaking. The crowd was thinning. *Where was I going?* Matt wondered.

Again, he felt a touch on his shoulder. "Matt?"

The man standing there was only a little shorter than Matt himself. He smiled.

"You're—Mr. Carpenter?"

"That's me. John told me about you, but I wanted to see you anyway."

"Me? How did you—why did you want to see me?"

"Because I think you need what I was talking about today."

"Rest?"

"Don't you?" He surveyed Matt quickly, his warm eyes taking in the manila envelope, the money, the silk pocket square, the bloodshot eyes. Matt had the odd feeling that this man disapproved of his lifestyle just as much as Jude did, but his look and tone were entirely different from Jude's. Come to think of it, Christopher Carpenter would probably disapprove of Jude too. But disapproval wasn't what came through—sympathy was. And, maybe, hope.

"Leave all your burdens behind, Matt. Come with me. It won't be easy, but I can at least promise you peace of mind."

"I—I can't. I'm—I'm an MBA student. I've got an exam tomorrow. I can't just run away and join some—some cult, can I?"

"Can you go on the way you are?"

"No," Matt replied promptly. Chris Carpenter held his gaze.

A gust of wind swept across the square. Matt loosened his grip on the precious manila envelope and the bills. The money and Masterton's exam fluttered out of his hand and across campus. Matthew laid down his attaché case. "I'm coming with you."

Chapter Ten

Late afternoon sun slanted across the hills, filtered through trees just turning red and gold, and spilled across a dozen men sprawled on the ground. A very battered blue van was parked in a nearby lot.

Pete reached for his jacket, which he had been using for a pillow, and put it on. The air was getting nippy. They had just driven away from a small town where things had gone really well for a week or so, until some of the local religious leaders got a little upset by things Chris Carpenter had said. The crowds liked Christopher. They followed him around for days, listening to his sermons, bringing sick people to be healed—but then there had been some threats, and Chris had said it was time to move on. It was a familiar pattern by now, and one that seemed to be growing more frequent.

"Soon be winter again," Pete observed to no one in particular.

Jim Fisher, sitting nearby, nodded agreement. "I'm not looking forward to that," he said. "I don't mind summer so much, sleeping on the ground, but I'm not sure I want to go through another winter like last winter."

"No, I don't like having to depend on other people to put a roof over our heads," agreed Phil.

" 'Specially now, when things seem to be getting more tense all the time," Pete pointed out.

"Why is that, I wonder?" asked Phil. "I mean, Chris Carpenter is getting more and more popular, but there's just more and more trouble everywhere we go."

John, also lying on the grass, had been quiet so far. Now he

49

leaned up on his elbows and started to explain things in the tone of voice that particularly grated on Pete's nerves. "It's perfectly obvious, man. The more people take to Chris, the more miracles he does, the more worried the establishment gets. He's chipping away at their power. He's already the biggest force in the country, religiously, and he could be a big force politically if he wanted to. They're afraid he . . ."

Pete, who usually felt that whatever intelligent thing John said was exactly what he'd just been thinking, tuned out the voices. That was one technique they'd all learned in order to survive living in cramped conditions with 12 other people.

Two summers and one long winter had passed since they had driven out of Marselles. The Boss's original group of six men had grown to 12, and they were a motley crew. The Marselles guys were bad enough. Pete had known his brother, the Fishers, Nat and Phil, for years, but he'd never envisioned roaming the country in a van with them for more than a year. The newcomers had made it even worse.

The college boys were probably the worst. Big, strapping, successful-looking guys with college degrees—it annoyed Pete that mere kids could be so polished. Matt had turned out not to be so bad. He was pathetically happy to be anywhere near Chris and gladly took on the grubbiest jobs. A bit like Andy, that way. But unlike Andy, Matt suffered from an absolutely towering inferiority complex that sometimes made the others want to shake him. That was really his only major fault. His buddy Jude was another matter altogether. Smooth-talking and super-organized, he'd tagged along with them a few months after Matt showed up. He handled the money, the P.R., the details of the organization. Jude had frequent run-ins with Chris, since both of them obviously had a game plan for where this traveling road show was heading. Jude's plan certainly seemed destined for success—the guy was a born leader, even if he was annoying as all get out. Chris, on the other hand, seemed to be taking a very roundabout route to success, often doing things that destroyed everything he'd worked so hard to build. But Chris was Chris, and not even Jude could challenge him. He was why they were here.

Probably the member of the group who'd caused the most discomfort was Simon, the skinhead. Head shaven, stomping around in black jeans, a black shirt bearing the logo of some punk band called "Bauhaus" or something, and vicious-looking Doc

Martens, Simon had been eyed warily by all of them at first. Thad, the only Black member of the group, almost left when Simon showed up. Skinheads were notorious racists, everybody knew that, and while Simon didn't appear openly bigoted, he also didn't make a point of saying he wasn't a White supremacist. Christopher had talked to both men separately, and they'd both stayed, though hostility had simmered unspoken. Where hostility had been spoken was between Simon and John. Pete was never too clear on the differences between all these radical young people. As far as he was concerned, John and Simon both dressed funny and got angry at "society" a lot. But apparently their philosophies were directly opposed to each other, on top of which they liked different music. Some of their fights had gotten pretty physical before Chris broke them up.

Fights, actually, were pretty common. James and John still had the distinctive Fisher temper. Not only did they argue with each other and the other guys in the group, but also Chris often had to restrain them from attacking people who weren't receptive to him and his message. Sometimes they seemed to be improving, but they could have pretty nasty relapses.

I guess that's true for all of us, Pete thought uneasily. All the guys were complainers, most of them got on each other's nerves, nobody knew the meaning of the word "tact." *OK, OK, so I'm a little outspoken, too, sometimes,* he admitted to himself. *But it's not just me.* The only one who wasn't prone to get in a fight was James—not James Fisher, of course, but James Goodridge, an older man, a quiet farmer whose only outstanding quality was his extreme shyness. Even easygoing Andy got riled occasionally.

If Pete had to pick his own pet peeve, the least favorite of his traveling companions, it would have to be Tomas. Tomas was a tall, muscular Mexican from down in Texas somewhere, and Pete, on first seeing him, had assumed he was a migrant farm worker. So much for racial stereotypes. Tomas turned out to be a high-school science teacher with an unusually keen mind. Carpenter's group was composed of a generous mix of educated and uneducated men, but Tomas was the only one who considered himself an intellectual and had the degree to prove it.

At first Pete and Tomas got along famously, because they shared a love for argument. They'd while away hours on the road as they'd debate politics, religion, sports—anything. What Pete lacked in book learning and long words, he made up for in passionate conviction. Which was why Tomas eventually began to irk him. The man took no firm position on anything. He could poke a hole in any argument, even his own. He could switch sides in a debate without batting an eyelash. He questioned everything, even stuff Chris Carpenter said. It was inquiry itself he loved; he had no desire to find answers. Tomas wasn't sure he even believed in God. Tomas didn't even support one particular ball team, though he could argue for hours about anyone's chances of winning the pennant. To Pete, who chose his convictions quickly and defended them fiercely, such a wishy-washy attitude toward life's basic matters was unfathomable.

In fact, they had had a run-in earlier today, just after they'd stopped driving and Chris had taken off on one of his solitary walks. Pete had goaded Tomas into a fight—something to do with religion, which was uppermost in all their minds these days. And Tomas had again come out with his big one-liner about how he wasn't sure if there was even a God.

"What is this!" Pete exploded. "How can you talk like that? You gotta believe in *something*! How can you not believe in God, you dumb wetback?" He threw in the ethnic slur because it made him mad just to look at Tomas, standing there with his arms folded, black hair tied back in a ponytail, muscles rippling under his tank top, his face an unperturbed mask. He always stayed so calm, so cool—calling him a wetback eased Pete's frustration a bit, even though he'd often been told—calmly—that there was absolutely no question about Tomas' citizenship.

"I never said I didn't believe in God," Tomas shrugged. "Just that I'm not sure. Don't you agree that there's a lot of evidence to suggest that there may not be any Higher Power?" He seemed, as always in his arguments with Pete, slightly amused.

"I don't get this!" Pete shouted, gesturing into the air. "If you don't believe in God, what business have you got going around with Chris Carpenter? What are you doing here at all? Go back to cutting up frogs in your lab, don't waste your time with us!"

For the first time, Tomas' face lost its mocking detachment. He was silent a long time, and when he spoke, his eyes glowed with an emotion Pete could recognize. "When I met Chris Carpenter," Tomas said slowly, "for the first time in my life I found something I couldn't argue with. I have never wanted to believe in anything . . . but I was compelled to believe in him. No, I'm not sure he's the Son of God, the way you seem to be so sure. I don't know if I will ever be that sure of anything. . . . I don't know what I believe *about* him, but Chris himself—his character, the power he has over people, the power he has over me—whatever it means, I *must* believe in him." Then Tomas turned and walked away.

Pete was nearly struck speechless, but he saved himself in time. "Well, I'm glad to hear you say *that* much, anyhow!" he yelled at Tomas' back.

Reflecting on the argument now, he realized—grudgingly—that Tomas had hit on something vital. Despite their differences, despite the difficulties of life on the road, all 12 of them, as well as the many hangers-on who often joined them, were irresistibly drawn to Chris Carpenter. Most of the time, he was enough to keep them on this crazy trail, even when the approach of another winter left them all a little discouraged.

Pete snapped out of his reverie to notice Phil getting up and walking away. He looked at the Fishers. "Where's Phil off to?" he asked.

Jim shrugged. "Probably gone to look for Nat."

"Yeah, Nat's been pretty down lately," John agreed.

"Well, no wonder! Look at the way his wife's been treating him—getting a legal separation and all that garbage! Sure, Sue was really supportive when he started out with Chris, but look what she's doing to him now. I don't know how he stands it!"

"Don't be too hard on her, Pete," Jim cautioned. "Not every woman's like your Audrey, you know. I figure I couldn't do this if I was married—even with Mom, I think she's only putting up with it 'cause she knows The Boss has got a pretty big future and we're going to be part of it."

"Audrey *is* pretty amazing," Pete admitted. "There she is, working full-time—well, she's got her mom there to help with the kids but even so, having her mother there is as much of a burden as a help. And then she drives out to see us every chance she gets, brings the kids along when they're out of school, does so much with Chris's work back in Marselles—yeah, she's quite the girl."

"You're lucky," John said simply. "Poor Nat—he and Sue used to be so close, too. And he's not the only one who's having some family problems."

"Is it really all worth it?" Pete wondered aloud. "I mean, we take off and leave our jobs, leave our families with no real security and traipse all over the countryside, and what do we accomplish? Chris gets his name on the evening news and draws a few crowds, then some preacher or politician gets mad and we're on the road again. Don't you ever just want to pack it in? I mean, is it really going anywhere?"

"I think it is," James said. "Look at all the attention we're getting, nationwide. Jude says Chris could even run for Congress and win, probably, next year."

"Jude's full of it," said Pete.

"I don't care if we *are* accomplishing anything," John said. "Look, we're with Chris, right? I don't know about you guys, but he's the whole world to me. I'd follow him anywhere, even if I knew he was bound to fail."

"Well, sure—" Pete said.

"You're a kid, you can afford to talk like that," Jim began, pointing at his brother.

"By the way, either of you seen Chris lately?" Pete interrupted. The diversion worked.

"No, but he's been gone for hours," John said. "I was just going to go look for him."

"I think I'll join you," said Pete, getting up. Jim fell in beside them.

One great thing about Chris Carpenter was that you could never bother him. He had a lot to put up with, what with his powerful enemies and his contentious friends, and he often slipped away for some solitude. But if one or more of the guys strolled up while he was sitting alone, praying as he usually was, he never seemed annoyed.

And indeed, his smile was wide and welcoming when they saw him a few minutes later, walking toward them on a twisting path.

"Hi! I was just coming back looking for you guys. Wanted to take you with me," he greeted them. The four of them angled off together on another path that wound uphill.

"Where are you heading?" Pete asked.

Chris smiled. "Off to meet someone," he said but didn't elaborate. His mysterious silences and his sometimes equally mysterious speeches took some getting used to. But all the guys felt completely relaxed with him. They not only admired him, they enjoyed being with him. He made life interesting. Not that any of them, even Jude, ever thought of him as an equal. He was younger than some of them, less educated than some, but he was unquestionably their leader. In serious moments they called him, "Sir," and even when they laughed and joked together he was usually "Chief" or "The Boss."

Yet Pete knew for certain that The Boss was the best friend he'd ever had. Chris Carpenter knew him better—and loved him more—than Nat or Andy or, yes, even Audrey. Climbing the hill beside him, Pete was ashamed to think that a few minutes ago he'd considered leaving Chris.

"I came here to talk to the Father," Chris said when they reached the top of the hill. "I want you to join me." They knelt awkwardly in the grass, and Chris knelt a little farther off. Pete bowed his head to pray—an activity he'd done more of recently than in his whole past life—but Christopher raised his face to the sky.

Pete's mind wouldn't stay on prayer. He was thinking how great it was to be up here alone with The Boss, just the three of them and none of the others. He wasn't surprised it was he, James, and John. Though Chris spent a lot of time alone with each of the men, he seemed to single these three out more often. Pete and Jim liked to rub this in a little with some of the other guys, especially with Matt and Andy, who were so nauseatingly good so much of the time. Never hurt to remind them who Chris's closest friends were. John had caught them at this game one day and laughed himself silly.

"You guys are something else," he told Jim and Pete. "You really think Chris spends the most time with us 'cause we're the best? Get real, man! Who does he most often have to haul out of a fight? Who gives him the most headaches? Man, Christopher Carpenter takes time out for us cause we're the ones who *need* him the most!"

The memory of John's words made Pete squirm. *You're praying*, he reminded himself, when James whispered, "Look!"

Pete opened his eyes and wondered how he could have failed to notice how intense the light had grown. Looking toward the source, he saw Chris Carpenter standing with a stranger on either side. But were they strangers? The figures were familiar, pictures in old Bibles, maybe. One was ancient and white-bearded, with flowing robes and a staff in hand. The other was slightly younger, clad in rough garments, with a visionary look in his glittering eyes.

"They—they look like—Moses and Elijah," John whispered.

"It is—that's who they are!" murmured James.

The figures did not speak, but seemed to agree. Their faces beamed at the shocked men, who then turned toward Chris.

"This is amazing!" Pete blurted out. "This is—it's a holy place! We should do something here—build a monument. To remember it!" His tongue, excited, was running ahead of his brain. "*Three* monuments—for Moses, and Elijah, and Christopher Carpenter! Nothing like this has ever—" He broke off, noticing the odd stillness of the hilltop and of his companions. His words tumbled into silence, as if he'd gone on singing a song after the music had stopped. He looked at Jim and John, sure that they'd be staring at him with that "Shut-up-Pete" look.

But they were staring at Chris.

Christopher Carpenter—was this the same man who had changed a flat on the van that morning? Pete couldn't see the worn jeans and familiar T-shirt. Chris seemed to be clothed in light— light that glowed and shone from his body. His face had a new dignity, and his incredible eyes glowed with a power not earthly. It was as if every momentary glimpse they'd caught of his godlike majesty was fulfilled beyond their wildest dreams. Beside him, Moses and Elijah in their beards and biblical robes looked positively ordinary.

Then the Voice came. It came from the sky and the ground; it burst from inside Pete's head and pressed on him from the air around. It was deep and commanding as only one Voice in all the universe could be, yet filled with a wild passion, a passion both of joy and sadness, of tenderness and steel.

"This is My Son, whom I love dearly. Listen to him!"

That was all the Voice said, but Peter Johnson knew he would never cease hearing it. His eyes were closed now, but the light still burned against them. He pressed his hand to his heart and felt it pounding. He touched his face and found it damp with streaming tears. Had he said something stupid, five minutes ago? Had he thought of leaving The Boss, an hour ago? He remembered nothing, only this moment.

He was huddled on the ground, but a moment later he felt a tap on his shoulder and he heard Chris's voice saying, "Get up. Don't be afraid." Opening his eyes, he was surprised to see Jim and John on either side of him.

The light had faded. The echoes of the Voice had stilled; once again the wind blew and the birds chirped. Moses and Elijah had vanished without a trace. Chris stood alone in front of them. "Let's go down and find the others," he said.

He wore faded jeans and a blue T-shirt. His voice and his walk were familiar. His face seemed to glow, holding a hint of unearthly glory. But perhaps that had always been there? And he was still their best friend, traveling companion, Chief. But perhaps, even in that moment of glory, he had never been anyone else.

Chapter Eleven

Clyde Bankhurst's world had once been very wide. Now it had narrowed considerably, and shortly it would be very narrow indeed. True, it had started out narrow. A small midwestern town, a house that was large enough but seemed crowded with parents and children and extra relatives. Even at the age of 10, Clyde felt crowded there. He'd sit on the back porch on summer evenings, reading a book or teaching himself to play the guitar. From the yard, sounds of his brothers and sisters and cousins and neighbors playing drifted up—screams and shouts of laughter. From beyond the screen door, sounds of his mother and aunts wafted out—chatter and tinkling plates. In the background was the steady hum of his father, uncle, and grandfather watching the ball game. Ten-year-old Clyde, a tiny island in this sea of sociable noise, wished fervently for the day when he could get out.

High school failed to improve things. Clyde was smart, shy, mostly alone. He wasn't an athlete. He felt uncomfortable at parties. The only place he shone was in drama club.

"Drama? What are you going to do with drama? Useless foolishness!" his father thundered when Clyde announced his intention to major in drama at college. "Actors don't make any money! You'll wind up working as a waiter!"

In fact, Clyde did work as a waiter, not to mention grocery-store clerk, gas station attendant, janitor, and pizza delivery boy. But he never thought of these jobs as anything more than stops along the way. He was acting all the time, but it was a long time before he was able to make a living at it.

It was a thrill, at the university, to discover that other people in

58

the world thought like he did, were interested in the same things, valued his talents. Clyde became popular. Girls who'd always admired his deep brown eyes and blond hair now considered it a mark of distinction to be seen with him. And Clyde, dateless throughout high school, took full advantage of his newfound popularity. His roommate laughed about it—there was a new girl every week, all of them pretty, all of them intelligent. Actually, Clyde developed a reputation for treating women badly—using them and discarding them. When a female friend told him what the girls said about him, Clyde couldn't have cared less.

"All my life I've been nice, sweet, shy Clyde. Now things are finally starting to open up for me. I'm finally starting to enjoy life—and I'm going to enjoy it. And if that means having every girl I can get my hands on, tell them they'll just have to take their chances."

Later, he remembered that conversation and was both ashamed and amazed. They didn't sound like his words, nor did they express his feelings. The playboy phase had been heady excitement at first, but it quickly lost its allure, though the game went on. Clyde got less and less satisfaction and absolutely no joy out of his brief conquests. Some of the girls were actually nice people, and he wanted to get to know them better. He had several close friends who were girls, girls he talked to comfortably and didn't sleep with. But when it came to developing a deeper relationship with any one girl, Clyde felt as if some part of him were frozen. He just couldn't make it happen—and when it seemed to be happening on its own, he quickly ran in the opposite direction. Yet it didn't make sense; he felt so lonely.

Two years after college graduation, Clyde met Danny. At this point Clyde was still living in Pendleton, the university town, and working as a tour guide at the museum. He was a member of the Spare Change Players and had won the part of Happy in *Death of a Salesman*. Danny was playing Biff in the same production—very well. Clyde admired Danny not only for his skill as an actor, but for his day job, which was teaching drama at a local high school. The two young men quickly became friends.

About two months after Clyde met Danny, he made two startling discoveries. The first was that Danny was homosexual. The second was that Clyde was, too.

Of course it didn't hit him straight out of the blue like that. He had struggled with the feelings for years, pretending they didn't exist. He grimaced, looking back, at the thought of all those sweet, sincere girls he had hurt, trying to prove to himself that he was a "real man." Now, with Danny to confide in and advise him, the pretense was over. Danny helped him admit who he was and talk openly about it. Clyde had never felt so free, so relieved, in his life.

Clyde lived with Danny for a while, but they were really friends more than lovers. When Danny moved to New York to try to make it in the theater there, he left Clyde his apartment, his teaching job, and a wide circle of friends who liked and accepted Clyde as he was.

The next years—roughly from his twenty-fifth to his thirty-fifth birthday—were the best of Clyde's life. He moved around a bit from place to place; he even followed Danny's footsteps and worked in New York for a while. Unlike so many other aspiring young actors, he actually met with a small measure of success there. In the end, though, he decided to go back to performing in regional theater, where good roles were easier to get and the pace of life wasn't so hectic. No, he'd never been tempted to try movies or TV. The stage itself was what Clyde loved—the stage and the exhilarating world backstage.

His social life couldn't have been better, either. He had many friends in the theater world, both gay and straight. Clyde was well-known and well-liked, and his acting was much admired. When he did go up occasionally to New York to do a play, he stepped easily into a glittering circle in which his place was secure. Back home, in Pendleton, he was a local celebrity, much in demand for TV commercials and public appearances. He had finally settled back in Pendleton, and taught drama part-time at the university. Between that and his near full-time acting, he managed a lifestyle that was both busy and financially secure.

As for relationships . . . well, in those first exciting years after Danny, when he felt so liberated, naturally he had played around a bit. He'd experimented. Later, of course, there was the AIDS scare. It took too many of his good friends—including Danny. Clyde and Danny hadn't lived in the same city for years, but they'd kept in touch, and the death of his old friend hit Clyde hard. Frightened him, too. He was more mature by then anyway. He stopped playing around, settled down to more steady, long-term relationships.

His family was a problem, though. During and after college, Clyde had drifted away from them, though his mother still tried to keep in touch. Over the years, his gay friends had urged him to "come out" to his family. But the family was now such an unimportant part of Clyde's life that telling them didn't seem necessary.

Then his mother contracted cancer, and Clyde was once again drawn into the family circle. During the long months of her illness, Clyde dutifully called, wrote, and visited home. He was touched by how impressed his brothers and sisters were by his success and how proud his mother was of him. Even his father admitted to a grudging admiration. Even while he endured their constant ribbing about "When are you getting married, Clyde?" he knew this could not be the time to tell them. His mother should be allowed to die believing that Clyde was all she'd ever hoped he'd be.

But when he went back for his mother's funeral, Clyde felt he owed it to them to tell them the truth. The results were predictable. His brothers were disgusted and wanted nothing to do with him. His sisters shied away from him, obviously scared he had come to spread AIDS or molest his little nephews. And when he told his father, the old man almost went up in flames. Clyde felt 17 again, standing in the living room listening to his dad's irate lecture and being told never to set foot across the threshold again.

He never did.

Clyde's family had been an important part of his adult life for not quite 10 months. In the three years since his mother's death, he hadn't heard a word from any of them.

Should I write and tell them? he wondered. *Will they find out somehow?*

His thirty-fifth birthday stood out in his mind. He had just returned from a successful nationwide tour with a play that was getting rave reviews. To celebrate both the play and his birthday, Clyde and his partner, Jeff, had planned a party at their apartment in the evening. That afternoon, between taping a talk-show interview and shopping for party supplies, Clyde sandwiched in a trip to the doctor's office to get the results of some blood tests taken at his last routine checkup, a few days before. Then he went home, cooked a superb dinner for Jeff and a few friends, and played the gracious host as people dropped in and out all evening. When the last guest had gone, at about 2 a.m., Clyde sat down with Jeff in the kitchen and told him that he had AIDS.

Jeff moved out. Clyde couldn't blame him, really. He was much younger than Clyde, still in college. He was still full of life, and he didn't want to linger in the presence of death. Clyde could understand that. They'd been together less than a year, and Clyde had been touring a lot of that time. There were no ties holding Jeff there.

Jeff packed his suitcases and left that same night. He was angry and wanted to start an argument, but Clyde couldn't spare the energy he felt he was hoarding for the ordeal ahead. He sat silently, listening to Jeff yell and swear. After Jeff left, Clyde drifted around the apartment, picking up empty glasses, paper plates, and napkins. In the kitchen, he stacked the champagne glasses in the dishwasher, turned it on, and stood looking out the kitchen window, watching dawn streak the sky.

For a while, Clyde went on much as usual—teaching, acting, living. But soon he made his first trip to the hospital, then his second and third—and after each one he came back a little weaker. More and more of his friends found out. Almost all his straight friends disappeared, and even many of his gay friends drew away, as if Clyde were bad luck. He grew close to a small circle of men with AIDS, and they shared the endless search for the best doctors, the most effective treatments, the most promising drugs, the best ways to cope. But even those men all had lovers or family or close friends to help them when, one by one, they became too weak to care for themselves between hospital stays. Clyde, of course, had no one.

And so he was here. The hospice was called Serenity House. It wasn't in the nicest neighborhood in Pendleton. Everybody thought an AIDS hospice was a great idea—as long as it wasn't on their street. Clyde had been staying there for four months. Right now 27 men were living there. They ranged in age from 19 to 62. One was a heroin addict who had slept on the streets most of his life; another was a corporate lawyer who had owned a deluxe condominium near the university. They did, however, have some things in common. All of them had AIDS. None of them were well enough to care for themselves. None of them had anywhere else to go.

There hadn't always been 27. New ones came and old ones left, though few left alive. People came here to die. During Clyde's stay, Serenity House had had as many as 40 residents, and as few as 12.

Clyde was playing cards in the lounge with Jerry. Jerry was 42 and had been a car salesman. He had also been married, but his wife, more disgusted at learning about his double life than by the disease itself, had left when she found out he had AIDS. He wasn't allowed to see his children. He was in slightly better health than

Clyde, who was recovering from a bad bout of pneumonia and expecting another anytime.

"I've got a few of those lesions on my legs, I'm sure of it," Jerry said. "I know I'm gettin' it. The drugs are supposed to be doin' something for it, but they're no good."

"You better say something to the doctor," Clyde responded, gazing out the window. He glanced down at the cards in his hand and then looked back out the window again.

A knot of people seemed to be gathered at the top of the street. Clyde couldn't see what the attraction was, but he could guess.

"Jerry, remember the guy who was on the news last night? Christopher Carpenter?"

"No . . . oh, the preacher? That crazy one?"

"He didn't look crazy to me, Jerry."

"Well, no, lots of them don't *look* crazy. But think about what they said about him—that he thinks he's God, says he can heal the sick, stuff like that. You know he's gotta be crazy."

"That's what I was thinking about—what they say about him curing people."

Jerry dropped his cards on the table. "You don't believe that, do you? Faith healing and stuff? That's a load, Clyde, that's complete and total crock."

"So what if it is?" Clyde challenged. "What have we got to lose? We're dying anyway—may as well live a little. Take some chances! Loosen up, big guy!" He felt oddly lighthearted.

"I don't know what you've got to be so happy about," grumbled Jerry. " 'Course, you're not the one with the big purple sores on your legs."

"No, I'm the one who gets pneumonia," Clyde said quietly. "Doctor said he doesn't know how I survived that last attack. If I get another one—"

"Well, that's it for you, then," Jerry said discouragingly. "You and me both." He scooped up his cards and began sorting through them carefully.

Clyde got to his feet, a bit shakily, and leaned out the window. The crowd was still at the top of the street. A boy of about 9 or 10 came running down the street, past Serenity House.

"Hey!" Clyde called.

The kid looked up, startled, and backed away toward the curb.

"Don't worry," Clyde wanted to tell him. "I'm two stories up. I'll try not to breathe down on you." But instead Clyde called,

"What's going on up at the corner?"

"It's Christopher Carpenter," the kid yelled back.

"Wait—can you do me a favor? Can you run up there and ask him if he'll come by here?"

"*Here?*" The kid shrugged, then turned and ran back up the street.

"What are you, crazy?" Jerry sputtered as Clyde sat back down. "We don't want no religious crackpots around here."

"If it's a religious crackpot who can heal sick people, then yes, I do want him here," Clyde said. He still wasn't sure what he believed about Mr. Carpenter, but it sure wouldn't hurt to try. He could act as if he believed—a leap of faith, so to speak.

"Well, I don't want anything to do with it," Jerry said decisively. "If he comes in here, I'll be up in my room and I don't want to be disturbed."

"Oh, come off it, Jerry. I mean, what can possibly—"

A racking cough broke off Clyde's speech, and before he had a chance to resume, he heard voices in the street below.

"Don't go in there, sir. You don't want—"

Chris Carpenter and the crowd surrounding him had moved down the street, and people were trying to dissuade him from going into Serenity House. He ignored their comments. He glanced up at the building and his eyes met Clyde's. "Hi—did you ask me to come by here?"

"Yes, sir," Clyde answered. "I—we—need your help."

Chris walked toward the door. "Stay outside," he said unnecessarily to the bystanders, who were edging away from the entrance.

"What? Is he coming in? Then I'm outa here!" Jerry announced, standing up.

"Jerry—no. Stay. It's not going to hurt you."

"It would hurt my pride to give that rip-off artist the satisfaction of trying to heal me! I don't support people like that . . . and I'm surprised you do."

"I'm a little surprised myself," Clyde said to Jerry's retreating back.

Seconds after Jerry had left, Mr. Carpenter was there, standing in the doorway, knocking gently.

"Come in."

Chris smiled and walked across the room to where Jerry had been sitting. "Mind if I sit down?"

"No, go right ahead," Clyde said, strangely shy. He wasn't sure what kind of person he had expected Christopher Carpenter to be, but nothing could have prepared him for the quiet calm and absolute certainty that seemed to shine out of the man's eyes.

"What's the matter with you, Clyde?"

"Uh—how did you know my name?"

Christopher smiled. "A little secret I have. I know everyone's name." He was silent, obviously waiting for Clyde to answer the question.

"Well—to put it bluntly, I have AIDS. I'm sure you guessed that anyway, since this place is an AIDS hospice. So—I've just gotten over pneumonia, I think I may be getting it again, every bout's a little worse than the last—and, well, to be frank, I'm dying."

Mr. Carpenter's next question was totally unexpected. "Is that all?"

"What more would you like?" Clyde wanted to snap. Instead he said slowly, "No . . . that's not all that's wrong . . . but the other things are things you couldn't . . . cure."

"You'd be surprised."

Clyde was surprised. Surprised to hear himself telling this stranger things he'd never even admitted to himself. He had looked back on the years before his illness as happy ones—and they had been—but pain lurked beneath the pleasure. To Chris Carpenter, Clyde confessed the loneliness of life without permanent relationships, the frustration of life without any higher purpose than his own pleasure, the hurt of life without his family's love and acceptance.

This guy's religious, Clyde reminded himself. *There's no way he'll approve of my lifestyle.* And when he talked about his life, Christopher's eyes didn't mirror approval or approbation. But they didn't show censure, either. Only concern and what seemed to be understanding. *How can this guy understand my problems?* Clyde wondered. *He's never lived like I've lived.*

When Clyde was finished, Chris reached out and laid a hand on Clyde's hand. The touch felt unfamiliar—AIDS patients didn't get touched a lot. In the hospital doctors and nurses wore surgical gloves when they touched them. The volunteers and staff at the hospice were better about touching the patients, but still it somehow felt clinical, unnatural. And even back in the "real" world, no straight man would be likely to touch a gay man in such a way—could be misinterpreted, you know.

This, the first friendly touch Clyde had known in months, seemed full of love and strength. "Do you want to be healed?"

"Yes, I do."

"And do you believe I can heal you?"

"Yes."

"Then . . . you are healed. You can go see your doctor—he'll confirm it. I have to go now, to see the others. But I'll drop in again before I leave."

"Mr. Carpenter, there's a guy upstairs—friend of mine. He says he doesn't want to see you, but he really needs your help. Can you try—"

"I'll do everything I can," he said.

Clyde's heart pounded as Chris Carpenter's footsteps receded down the hall. He *felt* good. He *felt* different—but *was* he any different? He stood up. Since his last illness, he'd had to use the wheelchair for any distance more than a few steps. Now he walked away from it firmly. His muscles tightened with energy he'd almost forgotten—the power of being able to walk, even run, as far as he wanted. He took a few deep, clear breaths and felt no urge to cough.

Clyde went to the window and stood there, just listening to his body. Yes, he would go to the doctor. He would have blood tests, but they would be only a formality. He knew.

He was still standing there some time later when Chris slipped back into the room. "How are you, Clyde?" he asked, sounding half-amused.

Clyde turned quickly. "Oh, thank you. I don't quite . . . know what to say. Um . . . did you see the others?"

He looked sad for a moment. "All but Jerry. He wouldn't even let me in."

"Maybe when he sees that the rest of us are—well, better . . ."

"Yes, you could try talking to him. It won't be too late—I'll be around for a while. And now, Clyde, what are you going to do?"

Go back, Clyde thought. His fantasies about a sudden cure for AIDS had always ended with his going back to his apartment, his job, his acting. Not to his old lover, but to a new one, no doubt. But he'd always expected to be cured by a drug or a treatment—not by a person. "What do you want me to do?" he asked.

Chris responded promptly, as if Clyde's question were perfectly normal. "Leave behind your sinful life, and live a new life in God's kingdom."

The strange words hit Clyde between the eyes. "I'm not sure what you mean, Mr. Carpenter. I don't really know what sin is or how to leave it. And I don't know what God's kingdom is or how to live in it."

"I can teach you all those things, if you'll come with me," Chris said. "You could travel with my friends and me for a while before you go home."

Home. Clyde figured Chris had used the loaded word casually, as anyone might. But, being Christopher Carpenter, he might not have.

"I have a call I have to make," Clyde said quietly.

"I know."

"It can wait. I'll come now."

"No. Go see the doctor, and talk to your friend Jerry. Tell the other men they're welcome to come too—if they want. I don't think they will," he added, looking sad again. "Then, tonight, after you've done those things and made your phone call, you can find me at the Central High gym. We're staying there."

"I'll be there. And—thank you."

"Praise God," Chris said, as though it were an instruction rather than a cliché. He waved, and headed for the stairs.

Clyde's legs were firm as he walked to the phone; his fingers were unusually steady as he dialed the number. Only his voice trembled when, in response to the long-distance greeting on the other end, he said, "Hello? Dad?"

Chapter Twelve

Marie's shoulders ached as she walked, and the chilly wind numbed her fingers. She considered setting the grocery bags down for a moment, but knew that would only slow her. She'd just have to pick them up again, anyway.

When Marie was little and walking back from the grocery store, Mom would always give her the bag with the bread in it to carry, because that was light. She'd swing it as she walked, swing the bag in a wide arc ahead and behind her as she skipped down the sidewalk. Martha, walking primly on the other side of Mom, would scold, "Don't do that, Maria, you'll break the bag." Mom used to say it, but after a while she didn't need to. She had Martha, her apprentice. "Mom-in-training," Marie called her. Martha always carried a heavy bag of canned goods. Sometimes she was allowed to carry eggs.

They fought a lot. Or rather Marie fought, screaming and crying at her sister with wild passion. Martha would fold her lips tightly and look away. She seldom said anything in response. If she did, it was brief and to the point.

Marie shifted her grip on the bag's plastic handles, which were cutting into her palms. She tried to bring her thoughts back to the present. It was a habit with her to avoid all thoughts of childhood and family. Marselles didn't exist on her map anymore. Living the life she did, it was easy to distance herself from the past. But simple homely activities, such as grocery shopping, sometimes brought back the past in a rush. Now she couldn't stop thinking of Martha, Mom, and Lazario.

The family of four was evenly divided: Mom and Martha,

hardworking and sensible, made up the dominant half; on the other side were Marie herself and Larry—she was the only one in the family to call her brother by the nickname he preferred. And he was the only one who understood her, who sympathized when she got into trouble at school or disobeyed Mom or Martha. Larry, too, liked a good time. He told her they must both take after their dad, though neither of them remembered him well.

Only Martha never got in any trouble. "Maria, why can't you be more like your sister?" her mother pleaded. Marie knew the other side of Martha though: she never got in trouble with the teachers or brought home bad report cards, but she wasn't popular at school either. She had few friends; no boyfriends. She wasn't pretty and didn't have any fun. When Marie was 12, Martha was 19 and should have been getting phone calls from guys. But when the phone rang, it was always for Marie.

Marie slowly climbed the steps to her apartment. The door was ajar and she could hear Shirley humming along with the radio. She shouldered the door open and staggered to the kitchen table, where with relief she dropped the bags.

Shirley, fixing Kraft Dinner for supper, was in a chatty mood. "What's the matter with you tonight, Marie? You're awful quiet."

"I'm always quiet."

"Yeah, but not *this* quiet. What's up?"

"Ah, nothing. Well, I don't know, I was just thinking about my family."

"Oh yeah? What about them?"

"Oh, nothing." Marie kicked off her shoes and put her feet up. "It's stuffy in here, even though it's so cold outside."

Shirley tugged the window open. The yellowish curtains waved in the sudden breeze. She stuck an empty tin can under the window to prop it open. "Mostly I just forget I ever had a family," she said over her shoulder. "After all, they forgot I existed, why shouldn't I do the same?"

"Yeah," Marie agreed. "I mostly forget my family too. My sister threw me out of the house when I got pregnant."

"No kidding?" Shirley said. "Isn't it strange we've lived together so long and we don't really know anything about each other's past?"

"Not really," Marie said, lighting a cigarette. If the past didn't exist, how was Shirley going to know about it?

Only . . . it did exist. Her offhand comment to Shirley called up a flood of horrible memories. If she had to remember, couldn't she remember something pleasant? She searched her mind for happy memories and came up with Larry sitting on the steps of their house. He was so handsome, her big brother, with his brown curly hair and his brown eyes crinkled up in laughter. They were teasing and joking, but he was worried about her.

"Marie, a girl with your looks is bound to get in trouble if you're not careful," he warned. Mom and Martha told her the same thing, but on their lips it sounded like an accusation. "Is it my fault I'm pretty?" she'd shoot back, glancing sideways at Martha, hoping the words would wound. But to Larry, she said only, "Well, you don't have to scare away every guy who tries to talk to me."

"Sure I do. Those guys I hang around with, they're always asking me about you. But none of them's good enough for you; I know that. I'll take care of you till you're old enough to take care of yourself." His warm grin made her feel safe and protected. And while it was true that she dated plenty of boys behind Larry's back, it was also true that she'd often been grateful for his fierce protectiveness when things got out of hand.

Back then she'd have been, what, 14? She met Simon at a party when she was 15, brave enough by then to risk Larry's displeasure and date openly. Anyway, Larry's reputation, a thing to be feared on Lancer Avenue, meant nothing to Simon Noble. Simon wasn't from their neighborhood: he went to St. Vincent's, uptown, and lived in Westchester Park. Larry Castillo didn't exist in Simon Noble's world. But Marie Castillo did. Very much so.

Yes, Simon was a good memory, for a while. Marie had been really proud that Simon wasn't ashamed to openly acknowledge her as his girlfriend. He took her to Westchester Park parties where she was never properly dressed but always made a hit anyway. Yes, she was flattered and excited—and completely in love. After all the hasty, embarrassed encounters with boys in the alley or in the back of the theater, she knew she'd found something utterly different with Simon, who treated her like a princess. Her mother's and Martha's prim lectures had always been easy to ignore. But even Larry's dire warnings about men, and her own instincts for self-preservation, fell completely under the force of her love for Simon, and his for her. She would have followed him to the ends of the earth—and it was only a happy coincidence that following him would be certain to lead her off Lancer Avenue. Was it any surprise that for the first time she was willing, even eager, to give herself with no restraints?

Marie took a last long drag on her cigarette and stubbed it out fiercely in the ashtray. But memory, once lit, was not so easily extinguished. Shirley scraped the macaroni out onto plates and sat down across from her. Below the dark roots of her bottle-blonde hair, Shirley's eyes looked as deadly tired as Marie felt. "I never knew you were pregnant, though," Shirley probed. "What happened?"

The question called forth all the images Marie was trying to keep back. Reluctantly she said, "It's no big story. I told my mom and sister, because I figured, well, my brother got his girlfriend pregnant and it was no big deal, they just got married and that was it. But when I told them I was pregnant? The place blew up! My mom locked herself in the bedroom and my sister told me to leave and never come back." Words, so stark and simple, disguised the voices and tears and pain that time couldn't erase. "So I left. I went to see my boyfriend. We'd been going out a long time so I figured probably he'd marry me."

"Ha! Bet you got a surprise."

"Oh yeah. He dropped me like a hot potato. His family was real rich, and I guess he didn't want to hit them with a big scandal, you know? He did give me some money. I was mad of course. I didn't want to take his money, but I was pretty desperate too. So I used the money to get out of town." The pain was tearing at her chest now. Maybe Shirley would be content, would stop asking questions.

"So you came here?"

"Uh huh."

"And what happened—you know—to . . . to the baby?"

"Shirl, why am I telling you this? I don't even talk about this. Look, I got here and I met a guy and he helped me find someone to do an abortion."

"But this was, what, 10 years ago? That must have been illegal here then, wasn't it?"

"Yes it was, and it wasn't very nice." Blood and pain and blood again. She closed her eyes and drew a new cigarette to her lips. "So this guy took me in till I got better, and since he loaned me the money for the abortion, when I got well again I had to pay him back, and there was only one way I could make money so I went out on the street for him."

"Oh, that's awful." Marie could see Shirley just itching to tell her own life story. No. Not tonight. Enough of her own memories; she couldn't carry someone else's too. She stood up. "Well, Shirl, I've got to go to work—thanks for supper. You going out tonight?"

"Yeah, later. See ya."

Ellesmere Avenue was slow tonight. Marie knew why. That religious dude was in town, preaching in the park and getting everybody worked up. Some people didn't like him, but an awful lot went out to hear him. And a guy didn't just go from hearing this Carpenter fellow preach straight down to Ellesmere Avenue to pick up a girl. Not only was this religious kick bad for business tonight, Marie knew it would lead to another round of crackdowns and arrests in the next few weeks. The good citizens would be eager to clean up the town—at least temporarily.

No cars slowed down, no one strolled up to her. The street was almost empty. It was a cold night. Marie pulled her jacket around her and shivered. How much longer? When she spotted a lone man walking down the street toward her, she decided it was time to take a risk. Normally she waited for customers to approach her; to approach them was soliciting, and that was asking for trouble with the cops. But tonight she needed the money, and she felt lucky.

Not lucky enough. When the man made eye contact with her but didn't walk over, she called out to him softly. He listened to her offer, came a little closer . . . and pulled out his badge.

Marie said nothing in the police cruiser on the way to the station. She had never been picked up before, and she was feeling scared. Normally the penalties were light enough, but now, with this sudden tide of morality sweeping the town, they might choose to make an example of her. And no matter what they did, she'd have to spend the night in the lockup. She shivered.

A crowd thronged the square outside the building that held the town hall, courthouse, and police station. The floodlights were switched on.

"Is that guy still out here?" one cop asked the other.

"You kidding? Does he ever go home? He's been out here preaching all day, and there's been a crowd like this the whole time. We had to have guys out there round the clock, crowd control, you know?"

"I don't think the mayor's too happy with this," the first cop said.

"Happy? He's dyin' for an excuse to run this Carpenter fellow out of town. But what can he say? The guy's so popular. Anyone says a word against him and they come off looking like they're anti-God or somethin'."

They both held Marie's arms as they led her out of the car and up the steps, their hands brushing her body. She hated cops—hated the fact that in their eyes the same greedy lust she was used to seeing in her clients was coupled with righteous indignation. *Pigs*, she thought.

As they jostled through the edges of the crowd, Marie overheard snatches of talk. About Chris Carpenter, no doubt.

"You can say what you like, but look, he healed my kid. What am I—?"

"It all sounds great now, but this isn't good for the town. People will—"

"I've never heard anyone talk like him! Is it true that he—?"

"What he says is all very well and good, but does he really expect—?"

One shrill voice rose above the rest. "*That's* the kind of thing he ought to be concerned about!"

Marie's escorts stopped, and Marie looked around with a sinking feeling. She saw the smooth blonde head of Mrs. Denver, the surgeon's wife, saw Mrs. Denver's beautifully manicured fingers pointing at her. The shrill voice had attracted some hearers. "It's all well and good for Mr. Carpenter to talk about the kingdom of Heaven and tell *us* to clean up our act, but if he's really concerned about morality, he ought to have something to say about *this* kind of thing."

This kind of thing, also known as Marie, felt her heart racing beneath her scratchy lace blouse. Voices joined in with Mrs. Denver's, "Let's see what he *does* have to say."

"This should be fun," one of Marie's cops said to the other, over her head. Mrs. Denver was ascending the steps. Her red-nailed fingers tore Marie's arm out of one policeman's grip. Head held high, she charged back down the stairs, dragging Marie and the other policeman behind her. The cop caught her crusading spirit, and he and Mrs. Denver elbowed through the crowd so forcefully that Marie stumbled, half-running, trying to keep up. Mrs. Denver's nails dug into her arm.

This whole scene would be funny, Marie thought, if I weren't so scared. She did not want to meet this man. With ordinary men she always counted on their desire to temper their disapproval. But she'd seen ministers and religious fanatics before. They were far worse than cops. The lust was there, all right, but they felt so guilty for it that they covered it up with passionate hatred. They weren't kind to women. She understood why in olden days these men—these holy men—used to whip and even stone prostitutes. The fire was still in their eyes.

Then the crowd parted, and she caught a quick glimpse of a man in front of her before Mrs. Denver and the cop—aided by a few people behind them—thrust her roughly forward. She fell onto her hands and knees—holes in her nylons, gritty stones drawing blood—and stayed there, fighting back sobs. Above, she could hear them challenging him, asking what should be done with her. Oddly, she thought that he seemed almost as much the target here as she. But that wouldn't make them allies. He'd use her to score points, one way or another.

She became aware that he was no longer towering over her. She looked up to see him crouched in front of her, looking steadily at her. She glanced up at the ring of solid citizens around them, illuminated by the floodlights' glare. Marie's eyes were driven away from their cold stares, but she could not meet his eyes, either.

"Maria."

It was just a whisper—her name. Her old name, her childhood name. It drew her eyes up to his. At first she couldn't understand what was missing in his gaze. Then she knew. Though his face seemed to promise kindness and concern, there was no hint of lust there. He was seeing her not as a beautiful woman but as a human being. Other men's eyes had undressed her body; this one bypassed it to undress her soul. She cringed, but could not turn away. Since she was—what?—11, no man had looked at her without desire—no man except Larry, of course. She was drawn to this man whose gaze was so warm, so like her brother's. Yet this stranger's face had a strength that Larry's had lacked. Her brother had wanted to save her: this man really could.

He looked away, up at the spectators. His voice was clear, with a sharp note in it. "Perhaps," he said slowly, "whoever is perfectly innocent here ought to step forward and condemn her."

Utter silence. Marie kept her eyes on Christopher Carpenter, but he still looked at the eyes of the crowd, as if challenging someone to step forward. The moment grew very long—Marie was reminded of a schoolteacher asking a question no one in the class could answer.

Then Chris looked down at the ground. With his finger, he began to trace patterns in the gravel and sand beside him. Curious, the onlookers strained to see. Marie could tell that he was not simply doodling, but writing. She could not pick out the words, but apparently someone in the crowd could. An exclamation broke the silence, and someone hurried away. A murmur ran round. Christopher Carpenter kept writing—it looked as though he was writing words, names, dates. Marie didn't take her eyes off him, but she dimly heard more feet shuffling away.

She was amazed at how he made her feel. Not attractive, as men had once made her feel, nor angry, as most men now did, nor defiant, as authority figures did. Only safe, and loved . . . and known.

Mr. Carpenter had just finished writing what might have been a man's name, though Marie couldn't make it out. She heard a strangled gasp behind her—wasn't that Mrs. Denver? From the other side she heard the cop whisper, "I'm not stickin' around to find out what he knows about me." Footsteps. More murmurs. Then quiet again.

Chris stopped writing and faced her again. He balanced on the balls of his feet, his large hands resting on his knees. He was smiling, half-amused, half-sad.

"Where are the people who are accusing you?" he asked. The smile on his lips and in his eyes had seeped into his voice. He looked around the square, and her gaze followed his. The ring of spectators was gone. She looked back at him and shook her head.

"You mean there's no one here to condemn you?"

"No one."

His smile broadened, and he stood up, then reached out his hands to pull her to her feet. When she stood in front of him, he kept hold of her hands. His face grew serious again.

"Then I don't condemn you either. You can go, Maria—but leave this life of sin behind."

Marie could say nothing. A chill wind blew across the square, but she hardly felt it. Still looking into his eyes, she dropped again to her knees before him. It was the only thing to do.

Chapter Thirteen

Pete shifted uncomfortably. He lay on his back, arms folded under his head. Beside him Audrey breathed deeply and steadily. *What a place for the wife and kids to have to come visit me! Not that they seem to mind. It's only for the long weekend, anyway—kids have to be back in school on Tuesday.*

His eyes, adjusted to the irregular light cast by a flickering neon sign in the street outside, could see shadowed shapes all around— men, women, and children huddled on the floor. It wasn't so warm. Must have been about 40 people there, all told. The usual crowd of 12, and some who were traveling with them—Audrey and the kids, a few of the other guys' families, Erica and Bob Washington from Marselles, people like that. And people they had just met today, who had stayed so late talking and listening to Chris Carpenter that they just never bothered to return home.

Another town. One town after another. Pete didn't like this one; it was too big. Marselles, where he'd lived all his life, had maybe 20,000-30,000 people, but it wasn't a city. The city was a great place to visit, take the kids to the science museum and let Audrey go shopping, but it wasn't a place he'd ever wanted to spend long periods of time. And it was a dangerous place to be when they were with The Chief, too. Crowds still followed him everywhere, but so did the disapproval of a lot of the top brass.

Take that little scene in front of City Hall tonight, for example. The girl was here somewhere now, sleeping on the floor too. Or was she also lying awake? Pete frowned. He had been embarrassed by the whole thing—then quickly ashamed of his embarrassment, because that was like being embarrassed of Christopher Carpenter.

And he was proud of Chris, proud of the way he handled things. But it didn't seem as though Christopher could see what was so obvious to Pete—that scenes like this weren't doing him one bit of good. The minister who had offered them the use of his church basement for tonight had almost withdrawn the offer when he saw how easygoing Chris was with the girl, not to mention how he'd offended the people standing around. They'd wanted some little speech about morality and community standards, and instead he does his forgiving-sins line, which always made people uncomfortable. Was it worth risking his reputation to save the self-respect of one cheap little Spanish hooker?

If The Boss himself couldn't see it, others certainly could. Jude, for sure. Jude was an obnoxious jerk, of course, but Pete couldn't help agreeing with the guy sometimes. Jude was so happy when crowds gathered around Chris, when flashbulbs popped and microphones were thrust in front of him. Jude adored publicity. But Chris turned down so many of the great opportunities Jude lined up. Requests to go on a nationwide talk show. An offer from a major publisher—would Chris like to write a book about his ideas and experiences? A possible movie deal even. When Chris Carpenter passed up chances like those, or annoyed important people, or wasted his time with people who were no better than scum . . .

"I feel like tearing my hair out!" Jude had confided to Pete that evening, in a rare moment of camaraderie. "How's he ever going to get anywhere? He's the hottest property in the country, but he has no idea how to market himself. The guy needs management, definitely."

Jude's choice of words made Pete a little uncomfortable. "I'm not sure he really sees it that way. I mean . . . maybe that's not what he's trying to do."

"So?" Jude shrugged. "Whatever he's trying to do, he still needs to market it. And I'm starting to worry. Remember how it used to be . . . last year, and even before that?"

"Oh yeah. Boy, everybody loved Chris Carpenter then, didn't they?" Pete felt almost nostalgic. "But the stuff he was doing then—the big miracles, feeding the crowds, and stuff like that, you know? He was giving them just what they wanted." Pete knew he wasn't expressing this as well as he wanted, but Jude seemed to understand, perhaps because he wasn't listening to anyone but himself.

"Exactly! And why does he have to go around alienating people now? Have you read some of the editorials in the papers about him these past few weeks!"

Pete laughed. "Sure! The Boss had to talk James and John out of going over and bombing the newspaper offices. They were pretty steamed up."

"Great—that would have really done wonders for our publicity! At least Chris had the sense to talk them out of *that*." Jude rolled his eyes in despair. "The thing is, he's got so many good instincts—but then he's just so stubborn when he gets it into his head to do something. He just won't listen to anyone. I try to tell him to hold back on his Son-of-God, sent-from-heaven line for now—concentrate on the moral teaching, the stuff people want to hear. Work through the system, and later, when he's got some kind of power base and he's not so vulnerable, then he can say whatever he likes."

Pete eyed the younger man suspiciously. "Can I ask you a question I've always wondered about, college boy?"

Jude's expression was pained. "I'd be happy to tell you anything you don't already know."

"Do you believe in The Boss? I mean, do you believe he is who he says he is?"

Again, a shrug. "Maybe. As much as I believe anything." There was an uncomfortable pause; Jude looked away. Then he brought his eyes back to meet Pete's. "Look, the point is, people are looking for a leader. The country—well, hey, the whole world—needs someone to look up to, someone who's got the answers. Chris Carpenter thinks he's got the answers, and his sure aren't worse than anyone else's. So maybe things will swing around our way, people will decide he's what they need. And when that happens, I want to be part of it." He put his hands in his pockets and rocked back on his heels, half-smiling.

"I love your attitude," Pete said, turning away.

"Hey, what am I even talking to *you* for, caveman?" Jude countered. He stalked off in the other direction, sullenly kicking a pebble in his path.

Remembering, Pete sighed. He, personally, would tear apart anyone who tried to hurt The Boss. And he resented Jude for trying to—well, to make Christopher Carpenter something he wasn't. But all the same, he couldn't help wishing Chris would be a bit more careful.

More minutes flickered by. He remained awake. Even in these

recent months on the road, Pete was a sound sleeper. But tonight sleep just wouldn't come. Across the room, someone cried out in sleep. Then more silence.

Pete sat up, trying not to disturb Audrey. Kevin, Randy, and Jenny slept clustered around their parents, Jenny on her mother's side, the boys next to Pete. Slowly, Pete got to his feet and stepped across their sleeping bodies. He picked his way carefully across the room, between a tangle of legs. The whole dingy church basement was silent, except for breathing and snoring sounds. Pete couldn't believe everyone else was sleeping so soundly.

He stopped to look at faces—Phil, Nat, Jim—his old buddies. Some new faces, too. The unmarried women and men slept at opposite ends of the room, the women nearest the exit. There, with her hair tangled and an arm thrown across her face, was the girl they had brought to Chris in the square today. A frizzy-haired blonde slept nearby—looked like another of the same kind. Great. Traveling companions like these would do wonders for The Boss's reputation!

That silver-haired woman sleeping by the door, now—she wouldn't hurt their image any. Except that her husband, some big shot government guy, probably wasn't thrilled about her being here. What was her name? Joanna—Hirsch, wasn't it? Whatever. Chris had found her on the cancer ward at the hospital a few days ago. Since he had healed her, she had simply refused to leave him. A lot of people were like that. That guy Clyde from down Pendleton way who'd been with them the last little while—there were rumors it was AIDS The Boss had cured him of, but no one dared talk about it openly or treat him any differently as long as Chris was around. Whatever it was, it sure had made him devoted to Chris Carpenter.

Pete pushed open the door marked "Exit" and crept softly upstairs. It was colder up here. He stood in the cramped foyer, shivering, until he noticed a sliver of light under the sanctuary door.

He pulled open the door that led into the sanctuary. One dim light burned there, up near the pulpit. A man sat on the front pew, leaning forward, looking up at the stained glass window above the choir loft. Pete could hear Chris's voice, though he couldn't pick out the words. So, not everyone else was asleep.

Pete gripped the doorjamb tightly. He wanted desperately to talk to Chris alone, but he didn't go in. This was too private a moment to interrupt. Though Chris never minded. Perhaps it was just that Pete wasn't sure what to say.

Nighttime—being awake, alone in the middle of the night like this—stripped bare those thoughts and feelings that a man wouldn't admit to in daytime. Pete Johnson was scared. He looked down the dim aisle to the man who sat at the front. Chris's voice rose a little, and though Pete still couldn't pick out all the words, he could clearly hear the anguish, the pleading, in his tone. Disconnected phrases drifted back, phrases that told more than he needed to know. "How can I . . . ?" "Why don't they . . . ?" "I try so hard . . ." Did Christopher Carpenter, too, fight with despair? How could he not?

Chris's voice broke off, his head dropped. He sat there in silence, holding his head in his hands, looking down at the floor. Pete shivered. After what seemed a very long time, he heard him begin to speak again, his voice calm and steady this time. His face was once again raised to the towering stained-glass window. Involuntarily Pete moved forward, straining to hear. Again, he caught only phrases. "Thank You, Father . . ." ". . . know You're with me . . ." ". . . Your strength . . ."

Pete stepped back, out of the sanctuary and into darkness again. He didn't understand all that he'd seen, but he was glad he'd waited to hear some kind of conclusion. The picture of Christopher Carpenter in pain and discouragement was more than his heart could carry.

Oh, how easy it was to be sure when he was face-to-face with Chris! Just a few weeks ago, one of The Boss's sermons had upset a lot of people. When Chris had looked sadly at the 12 of them and asked, "What about you? Are you going to leave me too?" wasn't it Pete who had spoken up almost before the words had left Chris's mouth? "Who else would we go to? You're the only one who can show us how to live forever!" How easily the words had come then. Probably it was only the sleepless night that made him doubt.

The next day, Chris Carpenter showed no signs of the past night's wakefulness. They went to the biggest shopping mall in the area, and Chris started to speak in the courtyard outside the main entrance. Before long the crowds had grown huge. Shoppers who crowded the mall to enjoy holiday bargains stood shoulder-to-shoulder in the frost-tinged air, listening to the ringing voice that had no trouble carrying to the back of the crowd. As always, the children squeezed closest to Chris. Pete smiled to see his Jenny pressing as near to him as she could. "Mr. Carpenter," she had confided to her dad, "is my favorite person—next to you and Mom and Uncle Andy and Grandma." Another little girl about Jenny's age stood near him also, looking up into his face with unabashed wonder. Some of the adults wore that expression, too, though most of them were more guarded.

"This world is a dark place," Chris was saying. "Much of the time we seem to be surrounded by darkness, groping to find our way. But it doesn't have to be dark in this world. It doesn't have to be dark in your hearts. I've come to bring light into this world. I've come to bring light to your heart. I *am* this world's Light, and if you follow me you'll never have to live in darkness again!"

A hush followed His words. It always took a moment for the boldness of the promise to sink in. People just weren't used to hearing sane, rational men claim to be sent from Heaven. Pete shook his head and started moving back to the fringes of the crowd. The Boss sure wasn't pulling any punches lately. No more mysterious stories or cryptic hints about the kingdom of God. He was laying it on the line, and that had a tendency to upset people.

A voice close to Chris broke the silence. "So we're supposed to believe you're sent from God, just because you say so yourself?" Other voices joined in. "Haven't got much backup for that claim, have you?" one challenged.

Pete didn't hear the specific words of reply. He could pretty much predict what The Boss would say, anyway—scenes like this were getting pretty common. Though this city crowd was even rougher than those in some of the towns.

On the edge of the crowd he saw most of his friends. Andy and John were working the crowd as usual, talking to people, urging them to listen. Jude, too, was patrolling the square in his own way. He checked to make sure any TV cameramen who might be there got clear shots, and he smilingly introduced himself to anyone wearing a press badge. No doubt some of the others were inside the mall, inviting shoppers to come out and listen to Christopher Carpenter.

Pete opened one of the doors and slipped inside. Behind glass, the whole scene in the courtyard had an air of unreality to it. He turned and walked aimlessly down the mall.

The huge bank of TV screens in an electronics store caught his eye. One or two were showing a soap opera, but almost all displayed the same program, a talk show. Pete was about to turn away when he realized that the panel was discussing Chris. He stood transfixed as a blonde woman, her face reproduced 16 times in various shades, earnestly told the host that Mr. Carpenter was doing a lot of good.

"I couldn't disagree more," another panelist interrupted, leaning forward. He was a bland man in a three piece suit and spoke directly into the camera. Pete vaguely recognized him as an important local politician, but couldn't place his name till it flashed across the bottom of the screen. "By appearing to do good, Christopher Carpenter is actually doing tremendous harm. This man genuinely wants us to believe he is God! Simple, ignorant, easily led people will listen to him and believe that he really does hold the cure to their own problems and to society's problems. The man obviously has some serious mental problems of his own, and I'm sure Dr. Westke would back me up on that. . . ."

As the speaker gestured to his left, the camera angle widened to show a balding, bespectacled man. The words "Dr. Ivan Westke, psychologist" appeared on the screen. Dr. Westke nodded, and the camera closed in on the politician again.

". . . but he's not just an ordinary mental patient who can be institutionalized. This guy has tremendous credibility, tremendous charisma, and a tremendous following. He could do untold damage, not just to the religious establishment, but to the whole structure of government in this country. By choosing to focus only the so-called 'good' he does, people like Ms. Martin here"—he nodded toward the blonde woman—"are contributing to a serious upheaval in society." He was gazing straight into the camera again. "This is no trivial matter. This man *must* be stopped."

Pete turned and strode away from the bank of TVs and out of the store. He zipped up his Marselles High jacket and felt in his pocket for his keys. He walked, not back toward the square but in the other direction, toward the parking garage. This would be a good time to take the van out and get it gassed up. He had a pretty good idea they'd be needing it soon.

Chapter Fourteen

Martha plunged her hands into the dishwater and quickly drew them out again. She let the cold-water faucet run for a moment, swished around the water to cool down the rest of the water, and began to wash the dishes.

The doorbell cut across the sound of running water and radio news. Drying her hands on her apron, Martha hurried down the two flights of stairs between the Castillo apartment and the front porch.

When she opened the door, she didn't recognize the dark-haired woman who stood uncertainly on the porch. An awkward moment passed before the stranger half-smiled and said, "Martha . . . ?"

Then she knew, but it seemed too impossible, too absurd, and she found she could not bring herself to say the name. Instead she asked, "Who *are* you?" and it came out harsh.

"Don't you remember me?" The big eyes were half-sad, half-scared. "Maria."

"Maria?" Martha stepped aside and swung the door wider. "Come in . . . Maria. Yes, of course. I only thought . . . you've changed."

"Well, 10 years." Maria shrugged, moving into the hall. She carried a small, cheap-looking tote bag and a large purse. "I guess I have changed. You have, too, a little bit."

Martha put her hand up to her own hair. Maria was still gorgeous, with the same dark hair and eyes and fine features. But her beauty looked cheapened, tired, used up. Her face lacked the sparkling vivacity that had marked her as a teenager. Even so, she was still Maria, the pretty one, and still seven years younger.

"I've got old, I guess," Martha said. "I'm sorry, I . . . it's hard to know what to say."

"Mmm, it's been so long," Maria murmured.

"I shouldn't keep you standing out here like this. Come in, come upstairs." She started up the stairs, and Maria followed.

Inside the apartment, Maria laid down her tote bag, but kept hold of her purse. Martha reached out to take her sister's coat. She examined it quickly as she hung it up; it, too, was tawdry. Wherever Maria had spent the past 10 years, it hadn't been a big step up from Lancer Avenue.

In the kitchen, the two women sat down. Both perched on the edge of their chairs. Maria's eyes flicked around the room, resting for the briefest moment on her old school picture. "Well—this place hasn't changed much," she said at last.

"No . . . well, the fridge is new."

"Oh, really?" Maria asked politely.

"Yes, the old one finally gave out," Martha said, glad to have found something to talk about. Maria seemed to be keeping back a smile. "I could get by with it, but it wasn't so good. I finally got this one after Lazario moved back home."

"Larry's back?" Maria asked. "But I thought . . ." She let the question trail off.

"Oh, they broke up. Sally left him when the baby was only about two. He's been living here ever since."

"And . . . Mom?"

"She died about a year after Lazario came home," Martha said quickly. She stood up and went over to the sink. "Lung cancer."

"Oh, I'm so sorry," said Maria, so low the words could hardly be heard.

Martha reached back into the dishwater and began scrubbing at the frying pan. Maria laid her purse on the table and moved over to the counter, taking a dish towel off the rack.

"That's all right, you don't have to—" Martha began.

"That's all right, I want to."

Martha looked at her sister out of the corner of her eye. Maria was simply dressed, in jeans and a pullover. Her hair was pulled off her face with combs. She was smiling again. Despite her air of world-weariness, she seemed contented, at peace in a way she hadn't been when she was younger.

They washed and dried together silently for a while. In this more natural activity, the conversation, when it began again, flowed more easily.

"I don't suppose you've heard anything about—Simon, have you?" Maria asked, hesitating the barest second before the name.

"It's hard not to hear of him," Martha replied. "He's a real big shot now, on the town council and everything. He's always on the news. Not so much lately, I hear he's been sick."

Maria didn't comment. Martha was nervous. Mentioning Simon brought them dangerously close to the memory of the last time Maria had stood in this kitchen. Martha didn't dare ask what her sister had been doing in her years away from home, but the younger woman raised the subject herself a few minutes later.

"I think I owe it to you to tell you," she began, "that I haven't lived a very—nice—life since I left here."

"Oh?"

"No. I didn't—have the baby. I got an abortion. And then—I had to find some way to survive. I'm sure you don't want to know all the details. But I thought I should tell you because—you may not want me home, knowing what I've done."

Martha slowly rubbed a scouring pad along the bottom of the fry pan, scraping away the burned-on bits. "I'm sure I wouldn't approve of whatever you've done, Maria," she said, "but I turned you out of this house once. I won't do it again."

"As long as you're sure . . ." Maria said.

Martha shrugged. "Anyway, your brother wouldn't let me. Do you know how happy he'll be to see you again?"

Maria's face was alight. "Oh, I hope so! I want to see him again, too. When will he be home?"

"He gets off work at 5:00, so he shouldn't be much longer. At least he has a steady job now, which is more than I can say for most of the past few years," she added. Soon Lazario would come home and that special closeness between him and Maria would kindle again. Again she, Martha, would be left out in the cold, bearing all the responsibility. *All these years,* she thought, *I've wondered why I put up with him. Now it'll be her too. But how could I send her away again?*

"There's one thing I *do* have to tell you," Maria continued. "I need to explain why I came back, after all this."

"Yes—I was wondering."

"Don't worry—I haven't come home to freeload. I'm going to get a job, maybe a waitress or something. I'll even get my own place, if it doesn't work out with me staying here. But I had to see you again, to come home. I wish Mom was still alive—I needed to tell all of you I was sorry for what I did to you, and . . . and forgive you for what you did to me."

"Isn't it a bit late for that?"

"No. I couldn't have come back any sooner. I never would have come back at all but—I've changed. I met someone . . ."

Martha, looking down at the sink, raised her eyebrows. Maria laughed.

"Not like that—not a man. I mean, not *just* a man. His name is Christopher Carpenter, and he—"

"You know Chris Carpenter?"

"Yes, do you know who he is?"

"He's eaten at this table more times than I can count. . . . I worked with him here in Marselles when he first started preaching. . . ."

Maria whirled to face Martha, clasping both her hands. Her face glowed with an excitement greater even than the excitement she'd shown at the thought of seeing her brother.

"Martha, you know him! And Larry too? How wonderful! I was so afraid of explaining to you, so afraid you wouldn't understand what he did for me—but if you know him, then you already understand. Oh, this is so much better than I expected!"

"Well, I don't know him as well as some of the others do—" Martha demurred, drawing her hands away from Maria's. It was, she now realized, the absolute truth. She had cooked and cleaned for Chris and his friends. They had slept on her living room floor, and she had washed and mended their clothes. She had worked as hard for Chris as had any of his followers in Marselles—Erica or Bob Washington or Audrey Johnson—or any of them. She and Lazario had even gone along on one of his trips back last summer. But she didn't know him as many of the others did—as her own brother did, as her sister now seemed to.

Maria wasn't put off. "Oh, but you're so lucky! To have spent so much time with him—I'd love to see him again. I *need* to—there's so much I still have to learn."

"How did you meet him?"

Maria didn't answer for a moment. "It was sort of an awkward situation. I was in trouble, being accused of something, and I suppose you could say he stuck up for me. But that wasn't all. He told me I was forgiven—you know how he says he can forgive sins?

That sounds so crazy, but you know, as soon as he says it, you know it's true. Once he's told you you're forgiven, you don't wonder anymore about this business of him saying he's God because, you know, only God could forgive you that way. But I suppose you know all that, since you've known him so long."

"Yes . . . well." She did know, because Lazario and the others talked like that, too, about sins being forgiven. Hers? She had shied away from conversation with Chris Carpenter partly out of the fear that he might offer to forgive her sins. And the only reply that came to her mind was ludicrous—"I have no sins." Of course you couldn't say that; everyone had sins, but Martha's problems had nothing to do with whatever sins she might have committed. Most of her misfortunes were the fault of other people, or of circumstances, not of her own doings. She knew that something must be wrong with this reasoning, but all she could clearly figure out was that Maria had had her sins—probably really awful ones—forgiven, and now Chris, like all the others, would love Maria best.

But the fact remained; she could not turn her sister away again. Especially if she was a friend of Chris Carpenter's. Martha turned back to her dishwashing. "I'm glad you've come home, Maria." It was not quite the truth, but it was as close as she was likely to get for now.

☆ ☆ ☆

The timer on the stove went off with an insistent buzz. Martha opened the oven door, peered in at her casserole. *Give it another 10 minutes*, she thought. Or would it be overdone? She glanced at the clock. The casserole would have to be left in to warm for at least another half hour, anyway. As usual, she had put it on too early. Lazario wouldn't be home till 6:00, and the others would probably come with him.

Carrots, peeled and scrubbed, waited on the countertop. Deftly she set to work slicing them. No point putting them on to boil yet, or the corn either. She gathered plates from the cupboard and brought them over to the table, unsure how many places to set. With Chris back in Marselles, it had been a busy few days. And when she had asked him, last night, to come for supper tonight she knew today would be especially busy. She knew Chris Carpenter enjoyed the well-set table and comfortable surroundings in her apartment. Perhaps she couldn't bring him sins to forgive or a life to mend, but at least she could cook him a decent meal. She didn't say this to Maria, who would have laughed and then grown serious.

☆ ☆ ☆

Maria's voice mingled with Chris's out in the living room. They never seemed to run out of things to talk about. No awkward silences between Chris Carpenter and Maria—or Chris Carpenter and anyone, for that matter. Except Martha.

She decided to set the table for eight. If more came, she could put in another leaf. She hoped there'd be only eight, though—she hated to give skimpy servings.

She called into the living room. "Do either of you know who else is coming?"

"Most of the guys have gone somewhere else," Chris called back. "The ones who live in Marselles mostly went home to eat, and they've all invited someone home. Matt and Tomas are still down at the Center, though. They'll probably come back with Larry. Is that OK?"

"Oh sure, I can feed eight easy," Martha said. She stood in the doorway of the living room, wiping her hands on her apron.

"Maybe Erica and Bob will come," Maria suggested. She was sitting on the opposite end of the couch from Chris, her feet drawn up under her, the big eyes in her small face turned eagerly toward him. Chris Carpenter was the only man Martha had ever seen who genuinely seemed not to care about Maria's looks—or anyone's. All he noticed in a person was their openness, their willingness to talk with him about—well, about personal things, Martha thought. Unfortunately, Maria had that as well as her looks.

"Come sit down, Martha," Maria urged. "You've been in that kitchen all day. You must have dinner ready."

"Yes, take a break," Chris added, motioning to the other chair. "You always put on such a good meal, Martha, that I'm sure you've got everything under control." He smiled at her, and his warm eyes held appreciation—but was there another message there too? A warning? A challenge? Martha turned away.

"No, no, I've still got a lot to do. Maybe after supper." After supper there would be the dishes, and the others would be here, and the whole group would be wrapped up in some lively discussion. Then it wouldn't be so awkward.

Inside the kitchen she hesitated. What *was* left to do? True, she had been in the kitchen all day. Maria had come home at noon from her shift in the hospital cafeteria and had pitched in for a couple of hours, scrubbing the bathroom and vacuuming, all the while laughing and saying all this fuss wasn't necessary. Martha, who had been rolling pie crust at the time, steadfastly ignored her. In the two months since her arrival home, Maria had been helpful around the house as well as contributing her share financially. But her attitude wasn't serious enough for Martha. Living with Maria and Lazario was in some ways like living with two high school kids again, for they both seemed to have regained the lightheartedness she remembered in them as teenagers.

Anyway, Maria had buzzed off again about 2:30, down to the Center to help take food to some family in a shelter. While she was gone, Martha had launched into a cooking frenzy. Really, nearly everything *was* done now. She'd declined Maria's and Chris's offers of help half an hour ago when they came in, but there were still the last-minute tasks only a hostess could take care of. . . .

She listened now to Maria's clear, lilting voice drifting in from the living room. "With those little children," Maria was saying, "like those little ones today, the Wilson kids, with the big eyes and the shy grins, it's so *easy* to love them. But what about the father, who's lazy and unemployed and drinks up the welfare check so the whole family suffers because of him, am I supposed to love *him* too?"

Martha could picture the earnestness in Maria's eyes as she asked the questions, and her mind's eye could see Chris Carpenter leaning forward intently as His low, gentle voice gave an answer Martha didn't listen to. She had remembered the whipped cream — there was none to go on the pie.

Lucky thing I remembered that, she told herself as she reached for the mixing bowl and poured heavy cream into it. In the middle of whipping the cream, she looked at the clock. Why, it was time to start boiling the water for the vegetables. And she still hadn't put the butter on the butter dish.

As she shut off the mixer, she heard Maria's voice again, ". . . must have thought of another job to do," her sister's amused voice trilled. *Fine for her to laugh*, Martha thought.

"I could use a hand in here, Maria," she called sharply. Martha went to the living room door again. "Christopher, you must see how busy I am. How can you just let her sit out there talking when I need help in the kitchen?"

Maria looked confused. But Chris stretched out his hand and beckoned toward Martha. "Come here, Martha." He gestured for her to take his hand, and hesitantly she put her small hand into his large one. He pulled her down beside him on the couch.

"Martha, Martha." He shook his head at her. "You work so hard and worry about so many things—and you have plenty of good results to show for it." He still held her hand captive. She knotted her apron tightly between the fingers of her free hand. Was he laughing at her? Perhaps. He was smiling, but as he continued he grew serious.

"Don't you see, Martha, that your lovely meal and clean house will all be gone someday? They're good things, but not the essential ones. What Maria has chosen to care about are the more important things—the things that will never be taken away from her."

Martha pulled her hand out of his and pressed both hands together in her lap. Her cheeks flushed. The rebuke stung like a slap in the face—just when she had wanted most to please him.

"Martha—" Both Chris and Maria spoke at once, but their words were interrupted by the sound of footsteps and voices on the stairs, Lazario's voice ringing above the rest.

Martha sprang to her feet and rushed to the top of the stairs. "About time!" she called down. "I almost burned supper because of you. What took you so long?"

Chapter Fifteen

Shivering in the chilly air, Matt pulled his jacket closer around him. Voices and laughter drifted up from the path that led down to the water. Moments later, four or five men emerged through the trees. The Boss strode along at the front of them. He glanced back over his shoulder to toss a joke to Pete, who brought up the rear, then threw his head back in laughter at Pete's reply.

"Catch anything, guys?" Matt called down to them.

Pete held a bucket aloft. "Enough for supper, if nobody eats too much."

"Ah, Martha's doin' the cooking tonight," another of the men spoke up. "She'll make it stretch."

"Yeah, but first she'll make us clean it," Chris reminded them.

But when they clattered up the stairs to the deck where Matt was sitting and then trooped inside with the fish, Chris stayed outside. He swung up onto the railing beside Matt and looked out at the lake. "There's a frost warning again tonight," he said. "Wouldn't be surprised if the cove started to freeze over soon."

Matt nodded. "It snowed last night. Not much . . . it was gone by morning."

"Well, at least this time when winter hits we know we'll all be in a warm, safe place," Christopher said.

"And all together," Matt pointed out.

"Mmm. That too."

Matt was glad to see Chris relaxed and happy as he was now. During the summer and fall, he'd been showing the strain of the growing resistance to his message. None of them felt comfortable staying in large towns for more than a few days anymore. So when one of The Boss's wealthier supporters had offered them the use of this large, out-of-the-way hunting and fishing lodge for the winter, they'd taken the opportunity. About 30 of them stayed there full-time, with visitors constantly coming and going. And every two or three days, Chris would load up the van with whoever wanted to go and drive 30 miles to Elwood, the nearest small town, to talk to people there. It was the most stable life any of them had known since meeting Chris Carpenter. And all of them, even The Boss himself, seemed more content as a result.

Matt wanted to put some of this into words, but it seemed almost presumptuous to say what he wanted to say. He tried anyway. "This is a good place, Boss. I even think it's—good for you, you know?"

Chris smiled. "Yeah, I know. I guess it is good for me. It's nice to have a break before getting back to—to work. Though this is part of my work, too."

"You just seem to be enjoying yourself more."

"I am, Matt."

"But sometimes—like now . . ."

"What?"

"Oh, I don't know, sometimes you look kind of sad . . . underneath it all. And then I wonder what it is you're thinking about."

Chris was silent for a moment, still looking out at the lake. "Yes, it's true, I guess. At the very deepest level, I'm happy no matter what's going on, because I know I'm doing what the Father asked me to do, and He's with me. And when I'm out here with you guys, it's easy to be happy on the surface too, to laugh and have a good time. But in between those two levels somewhere, there's a lot of sadness." He fell silent again for a bit. Geese winged overhead, honking their southward way, and both men turned their faces to the gray sky to watch the disappearing V.

"There are a lot of things," Chris began again, "a lot of things that make me sad, but mostly it's people."

"People?"

"Yes. I mean, sure, we can say we're all here together, but it's not really true, is it? Almost everyone's left someone behind—someone he or she cares about but who doesn't want to be here."

Matt nodded slowly, thinking of his own parents. They thought their MBA-bound son was crazy now. As crazy as any other kid who dropped out and joined a cult. "I guess it'll be like that even in the kingdom, won't it, Boss?" he asked. "Having to leave people you love behind."

Chris looked very sad now. "Yes—it will be. For all eternity I'll be missing people who—" He shook his head as if to clear away the thought, and shoved his hands deeper into his jeans' pockets. "But they're not the only people I feel sad about."

"Who else?"

"The ones who *are* here—all of you. I'm afraid for what may happen to you when . . . when things get rough."

"What do you mean?"

Chris Carpenter wasn't one to talk in generalities. He fixed his clear eyes on Matt. "Well, for example, I worry about you, Matt. You've come so far and learned so much—yet deep down, you still feel like you're not good enough."

"Well, isn't that true of everyone—we're *not* good enough?" Matt challenged.

"Yes, it's true of you exactly as it's true of everyone else. No less, but certainly no more. What I'm afraid of is that someday you'll make some mistake and decide you're not good enough for God's grace, and then you'll give up. I won't always be here to encourage you, and I'm not sure your faith is strong enough to believe in my love, in the Father's love, when I'm not here to show it to you." He reached out and put his hand on Matt's shoulder with a grip almost warm enough to take the chill out of his words about not being here someday. That warmth seemed to flood Matt's heart, making him temporarily short of words.

"It almost scares me, how well you know me," Matt said at last. "How well you know everybody."

Chris swung down off the railing and stood up. "You know, sometimes I think it almost scares me too," he said with a grin. "I'd better go inside and help clean those fish."

"I'll be in in a little while," Matt said. He too, got up, but he walked away from the lodge, down the steps, and toward the water's edge. Down on the dock he sat with his legs crossed under him, listening to the lake's sounds, to the bump-splash of the tied-up motorboat as it nudged against the tires at the end of the dock. The lodge was so full of life, so full of people, that it didn't hurt to get away at times. Probably the others felt that need too, though Matt didn't see why. They all seemed to have a place to fit into, a role to fill, something to add to the conversation. He didn't really have much to contribute.

Out on the edge of the cove, a canoe with a single occupant appeared. Matt watched the canoe cutting through the cold water until he could tell that the tall, upright figure in the stern was John Fisher. He waited, hoping John would come in and they could talk. He liked John—always had, since John had talked to him in the campus square that long-ago day. But although John was a few years younger than he and had never even been to college, Matt felt intimidated by him. He was so smart and so sure of himself.

John must have seen him then, because he raised his paddle in greeting. The canoe drew close to the dock. "What time is it?" John called.

"Four-thirty," Matt replied.

"Want to come out for a while before supper?"

"Sure." As John paddled in parallel to the dock, Matt reached out to draw the canoe closer, climbed in, and picked up the extra paddle lying in the bottom. He waited as John turned the canoe around, then plunged his paddle in and helped push out into the open water. For a while neither of them said anything as they listened to the sound of the paddles dipping and pulling.

"Bit rough today," Matt commented.

"Even rougher outside the cove," said John. "You should've seen it last night, though. The Boss and I were out here around midnight, and it was calm as glass. Moon shining on the water—it was like magic."

"That must've been nice."

"It was."

"You spend a lot of time with The Boss, don't you?" Matt asked wistfully.

"Every chance I get. You know how he doesn't like to single anyone out too much, unless maybe they need a lot of help or something? Well, when I first got to know him, I needed a *lot* of help. I'd lose my temper and blow up almost every day, and I just got in the habit of talking to him about it."

"You don't get mad much anymore."

"Don't I? Thanks." John paused. "I guess it's because I talk to Chris. There's so much love, when I'm with him, that it sort of makes me want to love everyone else. Even the people I'm mad at."

"Yeah."

"What does Chris do for you, Matt?"

"Wow, that's a pretty pointed question."

John laughed. "You should be used to it, living around here.

The Boss's conversation style is starting to rub off on everyone else."

"So I've noticed! OK, I guess I'm avoiding the question."

"Paddle on my side for a second," John instructed as they steered out of the cove and onto the open lake. "Yeah, you're avoiding the question."

"Well, I guess he's just given me a lot more—I don't know, he's made me believe I'm OK, I guess. That I don't have to be any big success to prove myself. Some of the time I believe that, anyway."

"Some of the time seems to be about the best any of us can manage," John agreed. After a few moments he asked, "Ever study much in the way of history or literature, Matt?"

"Only what I had to."

"Typical business student, huh? I would've majored in English and history, if I'd ever made it to college. Well, there's something I was just thinking about. You know how Chris talks about the kingdom of Heaven? I just kind of thought how all through history, back when most countries were ruled by kings or queens, there's been this kind of ideal of what a king should be like. Even though we don't have kings and stuff now, there's still this idea that a king is something different from a president or a prime minister—you know, like there's more dignity, more natural leadership, and yet at the same time a king should be concerned about his people. You know what I mean at all?"

"Sort of. Go on."

"Well, if you read history at all, you know that there haven't really been many kings who've measured up to this ideal—and yet it's still kind of an image people have. And when I got to know Chris, it just hit me—*that's* a king. That's what a king is like. He's a leader, but not a politician like our leaders now. A king. Not so much that he measures up to the ideal as that he's the one the ideal is based on."

"Wow! That's deep stuff."

As John had said, the waves were rougher outside the cove. Matt dug his paddle more deeply into the water with each stroke.

"The Boss says he's heading up to Broderick tomorrow," John continued. Broderick was a town about 50 miles north of the lodge. "You going too?"

"I might. Probably. Chris is never happy unless he's doing something for somebody, is he?"

"Mmm—sometimes I wonder if he's going to be able to stand

it in an isolated place like this all winter," said John. "But things were definitely getting too hot to handle back in the city. Or even in Marselles."

Matt grinned. "Jude's thoroughly disgusted with him for coming up here. He's mad at Chris for getting bad press in the first place, but he says if it had to happen, the worst possible thing he could do was leave his base of support."

"Sounds like Jude," John agreed. "Sometimes I wonder what game that guy's playing. Do *you* know what goes on inside his head? He's your friend, isn't he?"

"Not really," said Matt, meaning to answer both questions. "Well—no, that's wrong. He *was* my friend. It wasn't a very equal friendship . . . he was more like my mentor, I guess. I looked up to him, back—when we were in school."

"And now?"

"Now—like you said, I just don't know what's inside his head. He seems to be looking for something, like all the rest of us. Only, instead of looking for a leader he can follow, he's looking for a property he can manage."

John laughed. "That's pretty good. But you know, maybe that's not really what he wants. Maybe he's just got so used to looking at the world that way that he doesn't know anything else."

"Mmm. Maybe." Matt was silent for a while, thinking of Jude. Always so sure and confident. Here that didn't seem as much of an asset as it had been back in school. "But Chris Carpenter could get through all that, if Jude'd let him. Look what he had to get through with all of us."

"Yeah, we're a pretty rough crowd, aren't we?"

"Lot of variety, though. Losers and snobs and skinheads and rednecks . . ."

"MBA's and mechanics," John chimed in, "—housewives and hookers—"

"Yeah, you and Maria are pretty good friends too, aren't you?" Matt interrupted.

"Sure we are. But nothing else," John shrugged as Matt glanced back at him. "I mean, sure I've noticed she's gorgeous—"

"Has anybody *not* noticed?"

"Well, anyway, she may not look it, but she's like seven or eight years older than me. That's not really the point, though. She makes it pretty clear that she's here to follow Chris and help out all she can, and that's all. Haven't you picked up on that?"

Matt thought of Maria Castillo and her lovely dark eyes that so often shifted away from an admiring gaze. "Yeah, I've noticed that. I guess, with her history, she wants to be really sure that no one's mistaking her intentions."

"Uh-huh. And I think it's a big relief to her to be around people who treat her like a human being, not like an object."

As they turned the canoe around and headed in again, the wind now at their backs, their conversation drifted to other members of the group. John, Matt observed, was picking up Chris's habit of not badmouthing anyone else, always finding something good to say about everyone. It was a habit more of Chris's followers could certainly stand to learn. The atmosphere at the lodge, though usually pleasant, could turn nasty without much warning.

That evening, though, it was pretty free of tensions. Matt and John arrived back at the lodge just as Pete Johnson's station wagon pulled up. Audrey Johnson and Maria Castillo got out of the front seat, and the three Johnson kids tumbled out of the back. As Audrey opened the tailgate, they all started unloading shopping bags.

"How'd the run into town go?" John asked.

"Oh, all right," replied Audrey. "We got the week's groceries and a few things for the kids' schoolwork, and we paid a few visits."

"We found a lot of people who want to meet Chris Carpenter," Maria added. "I think we'll have quite a crowd out here on Sabbath."

"Jenny, let Kevin carry that other bag. It's too heavy for you," Audrey directed. She herded the children into the lodge, and Matt and John followed her. Matt was in awe of Audrey. He couldn't fathom how a loudmouth like Pete had ever acquired such a wife. She was always busy at something, and was unswervingly loyal to her husband, her kids, and Chris. When Chris and the guys had decided to move out to the lodge for the winter, Audrey had pulled her kids out of school and brought them and her elderly mother along. Now she ran a home study school for her own kids and the handful of other children at the lodge. Sometimes Matt thought he had more respect for Audrey than for anyone else except Chris Carpenter himself.

Matt strode across the dining hall to the large open serving window and leaned his elbows on the counter. "Haven't you girls got supper ready *yet*?" he called to the women inside.

"No, and we won't as long as we keep getting interrupted," Mrs. Fisher replied tartly.

"I expected to smell fish frying," Matt persisted.

Martha Castillo, who looked as unlike her sister as you could possibly imagine, swung to face him with her hands on her hips. "There won't be any fish till the boys finish cleaning what they caught today," she assured him.

"Stew tonight," Mrs. Delaney said. She was another older lady, Audrey's mother. "And it's almost ready."

Chris was in the kitchen too, slicing up huge loaves of bread. "You know, you've all been really great about feeding such an army every day," he said.

"Oh, this is nothing," Joanna Hirsch said. Even in an apron, Mrs. Hirsch looked a little classier than the other ladies. Her silver hair never looked ruffled, nor did her smooth face. "When I was still in the city with my husband, we sometimes used to host formal dinner parties for 50 people. Of course," she added with a sigh, "I had kitchen help then."

"And you don't now?" Mrs. Delaney teased, poking her in the ribs as she passed with a bowl of potatoes.

Chris joined in their laughter. "And I bet you always invited people who would then invite you to *their* dinner parties, right?" he said.

"Oh, of course," said Mrs. Hirsch. "It was a big social obligation game."

"It's the same everywhere," Martha put in. "Down on Lancer Avenue, I sure never got invited to any fancy dinner parties, but I knew if Mrs. Rudnicki downstairs had us down for some of her cabbage soup, I'd pretty soon have to ask her up for a meal."

"Want to hear a radical idea?" Chris said.

"From you? What else is new?" The speaker was a fifth woman who had just come in—The Boss's mother, Mary Carpenter. Another lady whom Matt thought was a real class act.

Chris smiled. "How about this? When you give a dinner, invite the people who can't invite you back. The really dirt-poor people, the sick, the handicapped—the people nobody wants. They can't repay you for your hospitality—but God will."

Martha paused in her task of stirring the stew. "I've cooked a lot more meals for people like that since I met you," she said.

"This bread's all sliced," Chris said.

"Then we're ready," Martha decided. "Matt, go yell out in the other room, tell them to come and get it."

When supper was done, the dishes cleaned up, the kids in bed, and the evening chores done, everyone settled in front of the fireplace in the lodge's main room. Most of their days ended here, with some quiet conversation. Sometimes it wasn't so quiet— occasionally a heated debate started. But tempers seldom flared as they did during the day. Here around the fireplace, with The Boss among them, tensions were soothed. Once in a while, Friday nights especially, Tomas would bring out his guitar and they'd sing hymns. Usually there were visitors, but tonight it was just the group who stayed at the lodge, the ones who followed Christopher Carpenter.

Matt looked around the circle at the firelit faces. Audrey Johnson sat with her head against Pete's shoulder. Their younger boy, who'd wanted to stay up late, was stretched out asleep with his feet in his Uncle Andy's lap and his head in his father's. Old Mrs. Fisher sat straight in her chair, her eyes resting eagerly on James and John, the sons she was so fiercely proud of. Larry and Maria Castillo lounged on the floor next to each other, in front of their sister's chair. Martha sat knitting, with her feet tucked neatly under her. Thad was on the floor beside Matt, his head resting against his wife's knee. His wife, Doris, cradled their sleeping baby. Matt thought of his own family and fought back a tightness in his throat. "I wish my folks could be here," he said suddenly. "They don't understand this, but I know they'd like it if they were here."

A murmur of assent ran round the circle. Matt remembered the conversation he and Chris had had earlier. The Boss, too, seemed to recall it, for he said, "Some of us are lucky enough to have some of our loved ones here with us, but almost everyone here has left behind someone they loved—a parent, a child, a wife or husband, a brother or sister, a friend—who they wish could be here." Matt followed Chris's gaze to where Mary Carpenter sat, and he suddenly remembered that Mary had other children. He looked at the room again, seeing what he hadn't seen before: the firelight flickering on the faces of those who were alone. Joanna Hirsch looked down at her hands, folded in her lap. Clyde, the fellow from the AIDS hospice in Pendleton, gazed off into the distance, and Matt wondered about his family. And Simon, with his glittering defiant eyes—he had parents somewhere. Nat Addison, with his teenaged son Mike but without his wife and daughter. So many people were here alone, or with fragments of families.

"You've given up so much," Chris went on, "to come here, to follow me. And that means a lot to me: I know it hasn't been easy." His voice faltered, but after a moment he went on steadily. "I can promise you that it will all be worth it. But you have to know what you're getting into. After all"—a smile lightened his face—"when a country decides to go to war, does the government just say, OK, send in a few planeloads of troops, drop 'em anywhere, and we'll decide what to do when we get there?"

"Sometimes I think that's how they do it," John spoke up, and everyone laughed.

"Well, contrary to appearances," Chris went on, "it's usually carefully planned. They like to know what the odds are, whether they have a chance of winning, before they get into it. And these big companies, when they plan mergers, they don't do it without endless rounds of meetings beforehand. The point is, nobody makes a big, life-changing move without sitting down to figure out what it's going to cost them, right?"

"Right," Matt murmured, along with some of the others.

Chris leaned forward from his seat on the hearth. "It's already cost you a lot to come with me. But this is only the beginning. In the next few months, it's going to cost you even more. You'll lose even more of the people you love. You'll suffer rejection, ridicule, pain. You'll have to give up everything, sacrifice yourselves completely. Are you ready for that?"

The pause was uncomfortable. A few people shifted in their seats, uneasy at Chris's intensity. A few nodded, hesitantly. Only Pete said, "Yes, I'm ready," out loud, and even he said it more quietly than usual.

Under his breath, Matt whispered, to himself, to Chris, to God—"I hope so. Oh, I hope so."

Chapter Sixteen

Y ou might as well not even be in the kitchen if you can't work
any faster than that. Why don't you go out and hang around
the men, like usual?" Martha was more annoyed at herself
than at her sister when she heard the words leave her mouth, but
she couldn't call them back. Frozen in the act of peeling a potato,
Maria stared back at her with wide uncertain eyes.

"Hey, I resent that sexist remark," Andy said in mock
indignation. "Some of 'the men' are on kitchen duty, too, don't
forget."

"And where would we be without you?" Mary Carpenter
patted Andy lightly on the back as she crossed the kitchen. Pulling
up a stool opposite Maria, she added, "We really do need two
people at this. I'm finished with the salads; I'll give you a hand."
She picked up a potato and an extra peeler and set to work,
pretending not to see Maria's grateful smile.

Martha turned back to the counter where she was working on
a roast. Once again everyone had been sweet and kind and helpful
and had made her look just awful. They were all so careful about
Maria's feelings; what about hers?

This was not a good day. Friday was always the busiest day of
the week, with Sabbath preparation and the usual influx of visitors.
Sixty people for supper tonight, probably more for dinner tomorrow. Yes, she resented it. Lazario and Maria quitting their jobs,
uprooting her from her comfortable home, to come out here in the
woods so she could be a kitchen slave for this motley crew. What
a life! She slammed a bowl down on the counter with shattering
force and instantly regretted drawing attention to herself. Better she

should stay quietly and meekly slaving away in the background like the hired help. That was the way they wanted it, wasn't it?

Being on her feet all through supper didn't improve her mood any. When she wasn't carrying some dish or another out to the dining hall, she lurked in the kitchen, busying herself with small tasks. There, at least, she could be distanced from the endless clamor of voices. After the meal was over, she shooed her helpers out of the kitchen. Sunset came early these winter nights, and in theory all work should cease when Sabbath came in. In practice, how would 70 people eat tomorrow if the dishes weren't washed? "No, don't worry, I'll do them myself," she assured the others as she edged them toward the door. "You've been a wonderful help, now go out and relax." She wore her patient smile but avoided looking at Mary, who was the last to leave. The older woman's clear blue eyes were too much like her son's—they saw things that were meant to be kept hidden.

When they were gone, Martha closed the kitchen door firmly. She considered pulling down the screen over the serving counter, but decided she didn't want to shut herself off completely. Let them hear her, far off in the background.

Her feet, her shoulders, the back of her legs, were all sore. It didn't occur to her to sit down; she went over to the sink and began stacking the dirty dishes. She almost liked the feeling of being away from the murmuring conversation out by the fireside. She switched off all the lights except the one over the sink. The kitchen felt even more peaceful that way. Did anyone notice how she was doing the dishes all alone? Probably not; they expected it of her. She turned on the hot water, annoyed again.

"Not coming out, sis?" Lazario was leaning across the counter, flashing her his dimpled grin.

"If I come out, will these dishes wash themselves?" she asked over her shoulder.

"You could leave them till morning," Lazario said. "And then do only the ones you'll need for lunch."

"You know I can't go to bed with a sink full of dirty dishes."

He shrugged and grinned again. "Nobody's asking you to sleep in the sink, sis."

"Oh, you get out of here," she said, snapping her washcloth in his general direction.

"Well, don't stay holed up in here all night," he said as he turned away.

She smiled in spite of herself. It would never cross *his* mind to offer to help in the kitchen — but he could make her laugh, and that counted for something.

By the time she got the cheap plastic plates and glasses loaded into the dishwasher and began scrubbing the pots, they had begun singing out by the fireplace. "Day Is Dying in the West" — she hummed along; she'd always liked that song.

The dishes were actually done before she noticed that the singing had ended and only Chris Carpenter's voice and the crackling fire broke the silence. She finished wiping the counter by the sink, wrung out a cloth, and stepped over to wipe down the serving counter. From there she could see the group by the fireplace at the far end of the room, and through the mass of heads and shoulders she glimpsed Chris's face, lit by firelight, as he talked to them all.

He was telling a story Martha had often heard him tell before — the story of the sheep that was lost so the shepherd had to go and find it. Of all his stories, that was the one people liked best and asked to hear again and again.

When the story was finished, a child's voice spoke up from somewhere in the crowded room, "Tell another story!" Over the slightly embarrassed laughter of the adults, Chris spoke again, and his voice smiled.

"You want another story? All right, here's another one that's a lot like the story about the sheep — but it's different, too. It starts out on a ranch, owned by a rich and prosperous cattle farmer. This man had two sons — the older, a steady, reliable, responsible boy; the younger a bit impulsive and reckless."

Martha had finished wiping the counter, but she stayed leaning there, listening to this new story.

"One day the younger son, tired of the tedious daily chores, went to his father and said, 'Dad, this life isn't for me. I need to go to the city, see new places, and meet new people — broaden my horizons. You understand, don't you, Dad?'

"His father said, 'But how do you plan to support yourself in the city?'

" 'Um, well,' the son replied, 'that's kind of what I wanted to talk to you about. Do you think you could give me my share of the inheritance now — what I'm supposed to get when you die?'

"His father gave him the money, telling him he was sorry to see him go. But the young man hardly heard the sad farewells of his father and mother and older brother. He was off to bright lights and adventure, and with his father's money in his pocket, nothing could hold him back."

The listeners sat attentively as he continued the story by relating the son's escapades in the city. His marvelous storyteller's voice dropped as the boy's fortunes fell, and he spoke sadly of the loss of his money and friends, and how he was forced at last to work as a janitor in a run-down, rat-infested tenement building. His eyes rested first on one, then on another, of the group. Martha could see Maria sitting near him, her face turned eagerly up to his. Did his eyes rest a little longer on her face as he described that lonely boy's sufferings? *Yes,* Martha thought, and then his gaze went tenderly to others in the group who she knew had left behind terribly mixed-up lives to follow him. Each of them, no doubt, identified with that poor lost boy. She found her own thoughts turning to the forgotten older brother, diligently doing his work day after day, probably getting little thanks for it. Wouldn't he have grown bitter as all his parents' thoughts centered on their wayward son, while his own hard work and loyalty were taken for granted?

But all was going well in the story now; the younger son had come to his senses and was returning home. "He had a little speech all prepared," Chris said. "He was going to tell his father, 'Dad, I've done wrong in your eyes and in the eyes of God. I don't deserve to be your son anymore—can you take me on as a hired hand?' But he never got through the speech. His father saw him coming when he was still a long way down the road, and ran to him, enfolded him in his arms, and cried on his shoulder. Then he took the boy into the house and told him to get cleaned up and rested, to take off his ragged clothes and put on the new suit that he had bought for his homecoming.

"The father told everyone in the house to prepare a big celebration dinner for that night. But in the midst of the preparations, his older son came to him and said, 'What's all this? All these years I've stayed home and obeyed your orders and slaved away like a servant, and you've never bought me a new suit or thrown a party for me. Then this irresponsible jerk shows up, after wasting all your money on booze and prostitutes, no doubt, and you act like it's the end of the world!'

"But his father said, 'Son, you are always here with me, and everything I have is yours. But we must celebrate, because your brother was dead and is alive again; he was lost and has been found.' "

Chris Carpenter's eyes swept over the crowd and up to meet Martha's. She stood frozen as he held her with his gaze. She twisted the washcloth in her hands, then abruptly turned away and pulled down the screen between her kitchen and the rest of the lodge.

She moved across the dimly lit kitchen and sat down at the table. Her hands continued to play with the damp dishcloth as her mind raced. So he had seen, and known—he had known her feelings well enough to put into words what she had never said, even to herself. Two brothers, of course, not two sisters—how clever of him to disguise the story. But how *could* he? Tear open her heart and leave it exposed for everyone to see. . . . Her throat constricted; her fingers clenched the dishrag.

Head bowed, eyes closed, mind clamoring with her own pain, she didn't hear anyone come in. Nonetheless she wasn't startled when she felt hands touch her shoulders. Of course he would be there.

Saying nothing, he sat down across the table from her. He took the twisted cloth from her hands and laid those hands flat on the table. Then he covered them with his own hands, bigger and even more calloused and work-worn than her own. She looked down at his hands as long as she could, but she could feel his gaze steady on her, till finally she was forced to lift her own eyes to meet his. The silence lasted a very long time.

"It was a good story," Martha said at last, and was annoyed to find she was blinking back tears.

Chris shrugged. "Like any story, everyone will get something different out of it. What did *you* get from my story, Martha Castillo?"

She found she resented him more than she'd thought possible. *How dare he . . . ?* she thought over and over. But she said, "You're right. I have treated her badly."

"I didn't tell the story so you would realize you've been unfair to your sister, Martha," he said. The steady pressure of his hands on hers did not change. "Your own conscience could tell you that. You've heard enough about Maria. I wanted to tell you something about *you*."

"In that case," she steadied her voice, "you left the story unfinished."

"I suppose I did. But they"—He nodded toward the outer

room—"don't need to hear the rest. They've heard the part about the lost son being welcomed home, and most of them are encouraged to know that God accepts them back after they've wandered away. Only a few people need to be reminded that you don't have to wander far to cut yourself off from the Father's love."

"So—how *does* the story end?" Martha's heart still pounded, but in the intensity of the moment she was forgetting her fear, growing bolder.

"That depends," he replied, "on what the older son says to the Father."

Martha glanced around the kitchen, focusing on irrelevant objects—a spoon, a bowl, a calendar. She swallowed. "What if he tells the Father that he's sick of being good and he wants to go try his luck in the city too?" She darted a bright, hard, challenging look at Chris.

"Then the Father will have no choice but to tell him He loves him and to let him go—and break His own heart again."

"And if—"

"Yes?"

"If the older . . . sister . . . says to the Father, 'I'm sorry I've been so selfish. I was jealous of the love You gave my sister because I never realized all the love You had for me, all along. I've acted like a servant who expects to be paid, instead of like Your child who knows she's loved.' "

She was looking straight at him now, and although his face stayed perfectly solemn, his eyes shone. "Then the Father will say, 'My daughter, don't you see that you could never earn my love by your good deeds, any more than your sister could lose my love by doing wrong? For both of you the answer is the same—my love is there; you only have to accept it.' "

Finally, then, her tears broke loose, running hot down her flushed cheeks. She did not reach up to wipe them away, because Chris Carpenter was still holding her hands.

Chapter Seventeen

The telephone in the lodge shrilled across the subtle early morning sounds. Pete moved to answer it. Across a muffled long-distance line, a woman's voice shakily answered his greeting.

"Hello—Peter, is that you?"

"Yes," he said uncertainly, trying to place the voice.

"Is Chris there?" The woman sounded as if she were speaking through tears.

"No, sorry, he's gone out. He should be back around—"

"Peter, I have to talk to him, this is really urgent—"

"Maria!" he exclaimed.

"What?"

"This is Maria, isn't it? I didn't recognize your voice."

"Yes—Pete, when he comes in, please, please tell him we need him here right away. It's Larry—he's very, very sick. We need Chris here—"

"Maria, I don't think he can come back to Marselles. Have you heard the news? Have you heard what people are saying about—"

"Pete, you don't understand. This is serious. Larry's been sick since—oh, Monday, Tuesday, I can't remember—he's in the hospital, but—"

"What is it, Maria? What's wrong with him?"

The note of alarm in Pete's voice had caught the attention of the half-dozen or so people in the room, and they were quiet, trying to gather the bad news.

". . . meningitis. There've been several cases here in Marselles. Larry is . . ." Her voice broke. A muffled moment later Martha came on the line. She, too, though more controlled, sounded shaken.

"The doctors say his chances may not be very good, Peter. Lazario has been asking for Chris. Maria and I are frantic. We *must* see him—he's so close to Lazario, surely he'll come."

"Of course he will, Martha. If that's how things are, I'm sure The Boss will be there right away."

When Pete hung up and told the news to the others, they all agreed with him. Might as well start loading up the van, because The Chief would want to be on the road right away. With public opinion against Chris Carpenter running so high right now, Marselles, so close to the city, was a dangerous place for him to be. But when had danger ever kept him away from someone who needed him?

It was only a month or so since the Castillos had left the lodge to return to Marselles, after spending nearly the whole winter with Chris. Pete liked Lazario Castillo—he was an easygoing, down-to-earth guy who fitted in well with the crowd and moved in an atmosphere of cheerfulness. Here, where his footsteps and his laughing voice had so recently rung out, it was impossible to imagine him lying in a hospital bed, breathing shallowly, and being watched by worried doctors.

Pete went out onto the front deck, feeling the need of some fresh air. The snow was melting in patches, and the air carried hints of spring. Down in Marselles all the snow would be gone, and perhaps the trees would be starting to bud. In spite of the danger, in spite of the peace the lodge had provided during the past months, it would be good to see Marselles again.

With tension crackling in the air all day, it seemed almost unbearable that Chris and the others who'd gone up to Broderick with him were late getting back. It was already dark when they pulled up. As soon as Chris stepped into the lodge, a clamor of voices tried to tell him the news. Pete raised his voice above the confusion, capturing Chris's attention.

"Maria and Martha called this morning. Larry's in the hospital with meningitis and it's pretty serious. They're not sure he's going to make it, and they want you to come right away."

Pete's only worry was that the sisters' message had taken so long to reach The Boss. Now that he knew, there was really no need to fear. He understood the relief that had flooded Martha's trembling voice at the assurance that The Chief would come. How often had he himself thought that if Audrey or one of the kids were sick, he'd feel completely relaxed knowing Chris Carpenter, who'd healed so many people, was right there! But The Boss didn't even need to be "right there" to work a miracle. They'd all seen him the day he told that businessman his son was cured—and hadn't the man later received a call saying his son's condition had begun to improve at just the time Chris had spoken? No, as long as he knew about Lazario, there was no cause for anxiety.

The Boss's words echoed Peter's thoughts. "There's no need to be afraid. Larry's going to live." Then, as murmurs of relief swept the room, he added, "This is happening for a reason. Larry's illness will bring honor to God and reveal God's Son to the world." For a moment, a look of pain, almost of regret, flickered across his eyes. Then it was gone, and he was assuring the others that all would be well.

His fears about Lazario put to rest, Pete slept soundly. But in the chilly darkness of dawn, the telephone rang again. Pete and Audrey's room was closest to the upstairs phone, so Audrey got up to answer it.

The conversation was short, and when Audrey came back to bed she looked bewildered. "That was Martha," she told Pete. She sat on the edge of the bed, drawing a quilt around her for warmth. "She said Lazario's gotten much worse since last night—the doctors say it's only a matter of hours. When I told her that Chris already knew, she seemed shocked—like she'd been expecting something different. But she said to ask him *please* to come, or something—if he could . . ." Her voice trailed off. Pete was about to scold her for that doubtful little ending—"if he could," indeed!—but he reasoned that she was only echoing Martha's fears.

As that day, a Friday, wore on, Chris Carpenter said nothing about returning to Marselles, and no further word came from the Castillos. That night Pete didn't sleep with the same sense of ease. He lay awake and worried. Going back to Marselles meant trouble—but staying away seemed to mean that Chris Carpenter was not the person they'd thought he was.

The next afternoon, Pete sat on the wharf talking to Jim and John, trying to make sense of the whole thing.

"It's not *like* him," he insisted. "He *cares* about people. He has the power to do something, so why isn't he doing it?"

"He said Lazario wouldn't die," John reminded them. "Aren't we supposed to trust what he says?"

"I *did*," Pete protested, "until Martha called and said Lazario was getting worse. That was yesterday morning, and we haven't heard a thing since. If he were better, she'd have called to tell us. But if he's worse, or—anyway, if he's not better, they probably wouldn't bother calling again. Since The Boss obviously can't or won't do anything."

"He's been acting funny since he heard the news," Jim observed. "All yesterday he was really tense, almost like he wanted to go, but he was being kept here against his will. You know what I mean? And then last night he took the canoe out, and as far as I know he didn't come back till morning."

"That's weird too," Pete said. "You know he had to be gone off praying, that's what he always does when he takes off like that. But how does he usually look when he comes back? All refreshed and peaceful, right? But not this morning. He looked more tired than I'd ever seen him. Almost like he was sick himself."

"I know," agreed John. "He looked awful when I saw him this morning. I tried to talk to him—not about Lazario, I just asked him what was wrong."

"What'd he say?"

"He said 'It's funny how even when you know how something's going to turn out, you still wonder if it's worth all the pain.' Oh, and then he said it was hard enough to suffer yourself, but even harder to watch other people suffer. But that was all he said, and then he went upstairs, and I haven't seen him since."

Pete arched a stone overhead and watched it splash into the water. "You mark my words," he told the other two. "There's something fishy going on here."

☆ ☆ ☆

Sunday afternoon. The miles of road unrolled beneath the heavily loaded blue van. Pete sat in the passenger's seat, next to Chris who was driving. Everyone was silent. Audrey and the kids followed behind in the station wagon, but Pete felt he needed to be in the van with Chris and the other guys. His place in the car was filled by luggage and passengers. For some reason, everyone at the lodge had come along, a caravan of cars following the blue van to Marselles. When The Chief had announced that morning that he was going, everyone had swung into a muted kind of action. They cleaned the lodge and packed their belongings somberly, weighed down not only by Lazario Castillo's illness—of which they'd heard nothing more—but also by the fear that a return to the city would mean trouble for Chris and his followers.

Tomas and a few others had made a halfhearted effort to dissuade The Chief, reminding him of the threats against him, of the attempts on his life that had driven them to the lodge only a few months earlier. Of course they hadn't changed his mind. They hadn't stayed behind, either. Pete suspected they secretly felt the same relief he did that Chris was finally taking action.

Even now, though, they weren't taking the most direct route to Marselles. They were puttering along winding back roads.

"I thought we might stop at Tedley for the night," Chris said casually, into the silence.

"Uh, Boss—" Pete said after a moment, "we could make Marselles tonight if we press on. Don't you want to see Lazario?"

Chris checked the rearview mirror. "Lazario is asleep by now," he said with the calm certainty he always used in telling them things he couldn't possibly know. "I'll wake him up when I get there."

"Oh. Well, I supposed if he's getting a good night's sleep that means he's getting better," Andy put in.

Chris didn't answer for a moment. Something like a sigh escaped his lips, very quietly. "I didn't mean that kind of sleep," he said at last. "Larry's dead."

The relief Pete felt at being on the road melted, revealing dark patches of misgivings underneath.

☆ ☆ ☆

They parked at the Community Center on Lancer Avenue. Martha was already there, waiting for them, her face bleak. In those last weeks before the Castillos had left the lodge, Pete, not normally the most observant when it came to women's moods, had been struck by the change in Martha. The tension that had always seemed a part of her nature had dissolved, leaving her less harsh and defensive. Now the walls that surrounded her seemed to have risen again, and behind them she looked lost—and bereft of more than just a brother.

"Chris." She came forward to meet him, her voice rough-edged from spent tears. He took both her hands. "Why didn't you come? If only you'd been here, I know he wouldn't have died. But even now—" she swallowed and went on, "I still believe God will give you whatever you ask for. That's why I don't understand—" The

111

walls were down again; she clung to him as if he were life itself, though Pete guessed she'd been angry only moments before.

"Your brother will live again, Martha—"

She turned away, and pulled her hands back from his grasp. "I know," she said wearily. "I believe in the resurrection at the end of the world, and I believe Lazario will be raised then. . . ."

The sound of The Boss's voice seemed to pull her toward him. "*I* am resurrection and life. Anyone who believes in me still has life, even in death. And death can never *really* touch someone who is with me. Do you believe this?"

Martha's voice was simple and steady. "Yes, I believe that you are God's chosen one, the one sent to us."

It's true, Pete realized. The Boss *is* life. You couldn't imagine death in his presence. He recalled those two odd incidents—the sick little girl who had died before they got to the house; the young man whose funeral they'd interrupted. In both cases cynics had tried to explain away what seemed impossible, which was easy to do as few people besides Chris Carpenter's close friends had been there, but Pete knew he'd seen The Boss defeat death. Now his words fanned hope wildly alive again.

Maria arrived just then. Less stoic than her sister, she was crying. She broke away from the people around her and ran to Chris, clinging to his arms. "Larry wouldn't have died if you'd been here!" she sobbed.

He reached out and drew her to his side. With the other arm he gathered Martha to him. Both women leaned against him, Maria weeping, Martha still struggling to hold back her tears. Above their heads, The Chief's head, too, was bowed. "Where is he buried?" he asked in an odd voice.

"Come, we'll show you," one of the bystanders said.

Chris Carpenter looked up as the two sisters, arms around each other, moved off. His own eyes gleamed with tears. Pete looked away.

Quite a crowd had gathered. Some must have been friends and relatives who had been at the Castillo house. Others were some of The Boss's followers in Marselles, who had no doubt been awaiting his arrival. Other faces were unfamiliar, and looked curious rather than sympathetic. With a sinking feeling, Pete realized how far word of Lazario Castillo's death had spread. Maria and Martha were not the only ones hoping for a miracle from Christopher

Carpenter today, nor were love and grief the only motives for that hope.

Pete's fears were realized when they reached the shabby little cemetery where the residents of Lancer Avenue buried their dead. More people waited outside the gate; the local TV station's news van was parked on the street and a man shouldering a TV camera stood among the spectators. Chris strode past them all as though he didn't see them.

Larry had died a few hours after the last phone call, Martha told them. Four days—he was already buried. No question this time that he might not be dead—nor, with the TV camera here, could anyone say there were no unbiased witnesses. Pete chilled as he realized what this might mean. He didn't really doubt The Boss *could* do it—though he was no longer so sure of what he *would* do. Was this what had to happen before people would recognize who Christopher Carpenter really was? No wonder he had agonized over the cost.

They gathered at the new grave. "Dig it up," The Chief commanded.

There was no response except a shocked murmur from the crowd. "It's been four days . . ." Martha protested weakly.

"Didn't I tell you that if you believed in God, you would see His glory?" he challenged. It was the voice no one dared resist. Pete didn't ask why there were shovels handy; when someone put one in his hand, he went to work. But he handed it to someone else before the job was done and stepped back to stand beside Audrey. Like everyone else, he was torn between the desire to see what would happen and the urge to shrink back. Most of Chris's friends stood fairly near the grave; the rest of the onlookers kept well back.

Pete heard Maria sobbing—saw Andy firmly steer a reporter away from Chris—heard a shovel striking solid wood—felt his son's hand in his, trembling—saw Chris's lips move again, briefly—heard the slight metallic scraping of latches being turned—heard muffled sounds from the grave itself.

Then a collective gasp, and everyone moved back a bit farther. After the slightest pause, Andy and John leaped down and opened the coffin lid, and the whole crowd surged forward to see Lazario being helped to his feet. Briefly, through the jostle of people in front of him, Pete glimpsed the perfectly healthy, pleasantly bewildered face of the man who had helped him fix the dishwasher at the lodge. Lazario was wearing a suit, but otherwise he looked just like

113

himself. Maria and Martha were hugging him, people were reaching out to touch him, the reporter and cameraman were pushing determinedly toward him.

Pete found himself jostled to the rear of the crowd. A man in front of him turned around. It was The Boss.

Chris still looked tired, but no longer tense. "You were right," Pete said after a minute. "He didn't die. And people *did* see God's glory." He laid a hand on Chris's arm. "So—it *was* worth all the pain, wasn't it?"

Chris smiled. "Yes, it was. But it's not over. This is just the beginning."

"I kind of figured that. But . . . whatever happens, it'll still be worth it, won't it?"

"It will." The Boss's voice was sure now. "Remember that, Rocky. Please remember that."

Chapter Eighteen

I just don't like the idea, that's all." Matt pulled a sweater on over his head and looked in the mirror as he adjusted it. Behind his own reflection he could see Jude's. Jude was still the cool, handsome, debonair young man he had been in law school. Why was it Matt no longer felt intimidated by him? He studied his own reflection in the mirror. He still didn't think he measured up to Jude; he just wasn't sure Jude was the standard anymore.

"It's obvious you don't like the idea," Jude replied. "What you've failed to do is give me a valid reason *why* you don't like it."

Matt, crossing his arms, spoke firmly to Jude's reflection. "OK. I don't like it because you're sneaking around behind his back. This is his life, his mission—or whatever you want to call it—and I believe we should trust him to do it his way. If we're with him, we're with him 100 percent, and to me that doesn't mean manipulating events."

Jude stroked gel into his hair with quick fingers. "The question is, my loyal little friend, if you and I mean the same thing when we say we're 'with him.' To you it seems to mean believing everything he says, blindly and uncritically."

"And what does it mean to you? Riding his coattails as long as it looks like he'll be successful?"

"Don't be nasty, Matt, it doesn't suit you." Jude moved to the mirror to stand beside Matt, adjusting his tie. "Of course I want to be associated with someone successful—so does anyone who has any sense. I think I remember trying to teach you that, back in the days when you were more teachable. But don't accuse me of being shortsighted. Why do you think I spent the whole winter stuck out in that uncivilized lodge with an unpopular leader, when I could have been back in Pendleton finishing my neglected law degree?"

"I have no idea. It obviously didn't have anything to do with loyalty."

"Loyalty means different things to different people. I like and respect Chris Carpenter, and I think his cause is worthwhile. I was confident he'd ride out the bad publicity and make a comeback. And with this Castillo affair, that's exactly what will happen if he plays his cards right." He picked up his wallet from the dresser and put it in his back pocket.

"He brought a dead man back to life, and you make it sound like a publicity stunt—like sitting on a flagpole or something."

Jude shrugged. "If you want to debate metaphysical questions, call a philosopher. If you want marketing, call me. Sitting on a flagpole is just as good a stunt as raising the dead if it gets you the same results."

Matt rolled his eyes. "I give up. I'd laugh if I didn't think you were serious." He flopped down on the bed.

"Very serious, pal. This little shindig tonight—and admit it, you've missed wearing decent clothes and seeing classy people—is a step in the right direction. If The Boss handles this right and doesn't step on any toes, we can forget the critics and ride the publicity wave right to the top. But if he does something outlandish and offends this Noble guy, I'm going to think seriously about provoking some kind of crisis. Force him to take a stand."

"Forget it, I'm not arguing with you. It's time to leave anyway." The two young men galloped down the stairs of the Johnson house, where they had been staying during the most recent trip to Marselles. Down in the kitchen, they could hear Pete spouting off about something, and Andy trying to calm him.

"I'm afraid our host is a little tense about tonight's bash," Jude whispered over his shoulder to Matt. "Pete's hardly used to moving in these circles."

I wish Pete could hear that patronizing tone, Matt thought. *He'd bust your jaw, which right now doesn't seem like such a bad idea.* Ruefully he reflected he must still be a *little* intimidated by Jude, or he would have said that aloud.

Simon Noble, deputy mayor of Marselles, lived in a sprawling house in the Westchester Park subdivision. Jude's snide comments were more true than Matt cared to admit: Pete, Andy, and several of Chris's other companions looked distinctly out of place in the

116

plush surroundings. Lazario Castillo, who along with Chris Carpenter was Noble's guest of honor, looked particularly uncomfortable. Nothing in his life so far had prepared him for the flood of attention that had surrounded him in the weeks since his astonishing resurrection. Normally easygoing, he had handled most of the publicity lightly, but tonight he looked truly ill at ease.

Simon Noble circulated the spacious living room, chatting to various groups. He was a handsome, polished man in his thirties. Matt gathered from the Marselles natives that he had been a well-known public figure for some time, had briefly been rumored to be seriously ill, but seemed now to be at the peak of health. Recently, after the news of Lazario Castillo's resurrection had become well-known, Simon had gone public with the news that he himself had been healed by Chris Carpenter a few months before. Matt instantly disliked the guy—he seemed to share Jude's brand of opportunism—but he had to admit that throwing a party in The Chief's honor was the nicest thing any prominent person had done for them lately.

He edged over to Larry. Talking to him had seemed kind of spooky at first. For one thing, it was hard not to ask him what being dead was like, though he claimed to remember nothing about it at all. After a day or two the strangeness had worn off and Larry was just Larry again.

"You don't seem to be having too good a time," Matt observed.

"I'm not," answered Larry. "I really shouldn't say this—I wish I could be as forgiving as Chris—but I don't like Noble. Even that's pretty mild to what I would have said awhile ago. After what I've been through, hatred seems kind of petty, but I still can't like him."

"Any special reason?"

"He used to go out with my sister, and he treated her pretty bad. I tried to make him pay for it, and he got me in trouble with the cops. All years ago, of course. When we were kids."

Matt raised his eyebrows in surprise. He hadn't imagined Simon Noble would ever have met the Castillos socially, but he couldn't think of a polite way to say this. "Where are your sisters tonight?" he asked instead.

"Martha's in the kitchen helping the caterers," Larry said, nodding in that direction. "Maria's not here. If I don't like being in Simon Noble's house, you can imagine how *she* feels. He ruined her life—at least until The Boss came along and fixed it up for her."

The evening seemed endless. Simon's guests were not a good

117

mix. The media people and politicians Jude was so thrilled to see there had little to say to most of Chris Carpenter's followers. They amused themselves by asking potentially awkward questions of The Boss and Lazario. The meal was delicious, but the after-dinner hour crawled especially slowly as countless conversations were attempted and abandoned. As a city councillor lectured him on the problems of public transit, Matt checked his watch for the fourth time in 10 minutes and hoped he wasn't being rude.

☆ ☆ ☆

She checked her reflection in the large, beautifully lit mirror, then picked up the box that lay on the counter before her. It was time to stop cowering in the bathroom. *Go out there and do it, Maria*, she told herself sternly.

She had had plenty of opportunities to thank Chris for what he had done—transforming her life and Martha's as well, giving Larry back his life. But no words seemed quite enough. A dramatic gesture was required. A public gesture, too. She had tried to avoid much of the attention that had been focused on her family recently, but she couldn't stop rumors about her from flying around. Now, at this very public gathering, she was going to show her gratitude. *I'll make a fool of myself*, she thought as she slipped out into the hall, *but everyone will know where I stand, and everyone will know what I believe about Chris Carpenter. And I must do it while there's still time.* For various reasons, it seemed appropriate that this silent declaration of allegiance would take place in Simon Noble's presence.

She lifted the cover off the elegant box and ran her fingers over the smooth leather surface of the Gucci boots. They were so lavishly expensive that she wondered for a moment if Chris would even accept them. He disapproved of any waste of money; always bought the cheapest and most practical things. He never spent a cent on anything fancy for himself. But she had wanted to give him something beautiful—and when she saw the outrageous price of the boots in a store so elegant she normally wouldn't even go inside, she thought of the worn old sneakers in which Chris walked down so many streets, into so many homes. To place these beautiful boots on the feet she had seen in the town square the day Chris gave her back her life—that would be a true act of worship, a true gift. The ridiculous price had taken every cent of her hoarded savings, but it was well worth it. She prayed she'd made the right decision.

She hoped the modest black dress and the long hair covering her face made her unremarkable in the crowded room. She moved quickly around the edges of the room to where he sat, in lively conversation with a group of people. She dropped quietly to her knees beside him, her heart pounding. Quickly she slipped off his shoes—not the sneakers tonight, but a pair of cheap dress shoes he'd probably bought secondhand. Her fingers trembled as she realized that the little knot of people around Chris had grown quiet, seeing her bizarre action.

Quickly she opened the box and drew out the expensive boots. Her hands caressed the rich leather as she slipped them onto his feet, and she knew from the gasps around that people had seen the gift and recognized its value. Embarrassed, Maria bent her head so that her hair spilled down to cover the scene, then chided herself for her shame. She had wanted to declare openly and dramatically that Chris was her Lord and her God: now she was trying to do it without being noticed.

Then all the present scene was swept away. Once again she was Marie, teenaged and scared, with her sister's angry words driving her out into the night. Marie, alone and trembling in the office of a backstreet abortionist. Marie, tough and unfeeling, on Ellesmere Avenue. Marie, shamed and terrified, in the middle of a derisive crowd. And then came Chris, and the Maria that he saw and loved—the Maria she had begun to be the moment he looked at her. She gave way to tears and leaned her head against the bottom of the chair, her face pressed against the Gucci boots.

Out of the shocked silence, the murmurs began. She heard Jude's voice above others, making some caustic remark about what a pair of boots like that must have cost and what good use the money could have been put to. Chris must be leaning forward, for she felt his hand on her head. He was answering Jude evenly: ". . . an act of love . . . she is preparing for my death. . . ." *His death?* she thought bleakly. Voices continued to murmur, but one from behind her stood out clearly. It called to her aching memory—funny to remember that that voice had once spoken of love for her.

"He obviously doesn't know the girl's reputation," Simon was saying.

"Of course he does," another voice replied. "She's Castillo's sister, everyone knows Mr. Carpenter is a friend of the family."

"Oh, I'm sure she's been careful to cover that up," Simon went on smoothly, giving Chris the benefit of the doubt. "If he knew what kind of girl she is, I'm sure he wouldn't be so quick to defend her or to be seen with her."

More murmurs. Simon's comments had been meant to be overheard. Chris had leaned back in his chair now—Maria lifted her head so she was looking up at him. He seemed so perfectly casual, as if unconcerned by his newly clad feet or the woman kneeling by them.

"I heard an interesting story recently," he was saying. "Simon, with your business skills, you should find this one interesting. Apparently a wealthy man was owed money by two of his employees—one man owed him $50,000 for a major loan he'd needed to see him through a family crisis. Another guy had borrowed five bucks to pay for his lunch in the cafeteria one day. The man who owed the huge debt couldn't begin to raise the money to pay it back, so the boss called him into his office and told him the debt was cancelled—to consider it a gift. The same day, at lunch, his other employee mentioned the $5 he owed, and the boss told him not to bother paying it."

Nobody said anything. They seemed to expect more of a climax to one of Chris's stories.

"The question is," Chris continued, "which of those employees thought more highly of his boss? What do you think, Simon?"

"I suppose the one who owed the bigger debt, obviously."

"Exactly. The one who has been forgiven much, loves much." Chris stood up, then reached down to Maria and helped her to her feet. "It was a lovely dinner, Simon, Mrs. Noble, thank you both. I must be going."

☆ ☆ ☆

"I can't believe it!" Jude stormed. "It was worse than anything I could have imagined!"

Matt sprawled on the bed and looked up wearily at his pacing companion. Jude had been smooth and polite to everyone during their awkward departure from Simon's party. He'd been ominously silent in the car on the way back. Now, the Johnson's guest room seemed about to burst with the effort of containing his rage.

"He had to lower himself—make himself look like a fool. The girl may be Castillo's sister, but she's been trouble from the word go. The newspaper photographer got a picture, you know. It'll be all over town tomorrow. And instead of salvaging what's left of his reputation, he stands up for her! She's hardly so valuable to the cause that he can't afford to hurt her feelings. Can you imagine what they're saying about him? A cheap little sex scandal is all we need!"

"It's hardly that," Matt protested.

"It's hardly that *now*, but you should see what it'll be once the media gets hold of it. Oh, I can see it now. This settles it," he announced, picking up his just-removed jacket.

"What? What are you going to do?"

Jude cleared the anger off his face long enough to look pityingly at him. "I'm hardly likely to confide in you, am I? I'm going to do *something* that will bring things to a head, one way or another. If Christopher Carpenter meets the challenge and you and all the others get lucky along with him, you'll have me to thank for it."

"And if he doesn't meet your challenge?"

Jude, hand on the doorknob, turned back. "Then none of you—including him—will have anyone but himself to blame. Goodnight."

After the door closed, Matt studied the water stains on the stucco ceiling for a long time. Then, thoughtfully, he got up and went downstairs to the kitchen. The five or six people there, deep in conversation, probably hadn't even noticed Jude's departure. Matt realized he has wrong to have stopped being scared of Jude. Jude was scarier than he'd ever been.

Chapter Nineteen

Something's up, and I don't like it." Jim Fisher paced around the dingy hotel room. He paused by the window and looked nervously down at the street below. Pete knew what was down there—the WCTV news van—because it had been parked there all day. In the past few weeks, the WCTV news van had become part of the scenery of daily life. He barely noticed it anymore.

"Relax, Jim. Of course something's up. Something's been up ever since we left the lodge. You're not supposed to like it."

"If there's gonna be trouble, I'm not sure I want to be a part of it."

Pete laughed. "You already *are* a part of it, pal. In up to your neck. We all are. Anyway, since when have you wanted to stay away from trouble?"

Leaving his disgruntled friend fuming in front of the window, Pete strolled out into the hall. He didn't want to be here, in a cheap hotel on the outskirts of the city he hated, on a damp gray morning. He didn't want to be part of a media circus.

He knocked on the door of the room adjacent to the one he had just left. Inside, several of the guys were lounging around, wearing expressions as gloomy as Pete's own. He sat down on the floor next to Nat and picked up the copy of this week's *Time* magazine, which Nat had just tossed aside. Not that he hadn't seen it before. It had hit the newsstands Thursday—today was Sunday—and since then practically every one of Chris's companions had memorized the lead story.

The cover showed the now-famous picture of Christopher Carpenter and Lazario Castillo at the cemetery, gripping each other's hands tightly. "Whoever took that shot must be a million-aire by now," Pete muttered, not for the first time. Across the picture yellow letters blazed: "CHRISTOPHER CARPENTER: FRAUD, FANATIC, OR FAITH HEALER?"

The article itself recapped the main events of Chris Carpenter's public life during the past three years, giving special attention to recent events. It discussed the growing opposition to his work and included comments from some of his supporters as well. Neither The Boss himself nor any of those closest to him would grant interviews, but reporters had no difficulty finding people who were still loyal to him and willing to comment on it. A separate article discussed the "apparent resurrection" of Lazario Castillo and included "explanations" of the "phenomenon" by several scientists—though it ended with the conclusion that no one could say for sure what had happened in the cemetery that day. Though the magazine's coverage appeared to be quite balanced, the overall impression left by the article was that Christopher Carpenter was a potentially dangerous force who needed to be watched carefully and might need to be stopped. The popular view, these days.

Pete closed the magazine and tossed it aside, probably for the same reason Nat had—because he ran across a ghastly unflattering shot of himself, Nat, and Andy, obviously designed to show the kind of low life this Mr. Carpenter attracted. At least they'd balanced it with a shot of Simon and Thad together, hinting at the peace and harmony that reigned among The Chief's followers. Sometimes.

Peace and harmony were not particularly evident this morning. Everyone sat in a kind of discontented silence. Simon, perched on the windowsill and, like Jim Fisher, regarding the news van in the street below, finally broke that silence.

"What are we supposed to be doing here? Does anyone really know?"

"I suppose The Boss does," Matt replied.

Simon wrinkled his brow and rubbed a hand over his close-shaved head. "And does anyone know where he is, or what he's planning?"

Silence settled again.

"It *is* weird," Nat said. "Coming up here on a Saturday night, having to stay in this awful hole—"

"—because there aren't enough people left in the city who like us enough to put us up," Tomas added.

123

"And now The Boss disappears on us, after he's been acting strange for days anyway, and we're stuck here with a bunch of media vultures hanging around down in the lobby. He must have some reason for wanting to be in the city, but I wish he'd tell us what it is." Nat leaned forward and looked around at his companions as though he expected an answer.

He got one. Two short raps sounded before the door burst open. Chris stood there. His face alight with excitement and anticipation. His eyes sparkled, and a smile twitched at the corners of his mouth. This was The Boss as they were used to seeing him. The preoccupied air that had weighed him down since their return to Marselles was gone. He looked ready for action.

"Come on!" he called to them, laughing at their startled expressions. "Did you think I'd left you? Did you think you were going to sit here and brood forever? Not a chance! The time has come! Let's get going!"

They were all on their feet. "What do you want us to do, Boss?" Pete asked. Until this moment he hadn't realized how eager he was to be active, to be out in the streets turning the world upside down again as they had done when Chris Carpenter had first burst into their lives.

Chris met Pete's eyes with a grin that said he recognized and shared that eagerness. He handed him a slip of paper with a few words written on it. "Go look up this address. The man there has a car I need to borrow. Tell him The Boss needs it." Noticing Tomas' dubious glance, he assured them, "He'll understand."

"This is crazy!" Tomas informed the others in the van as they drove to the address Chris had given them. "We *still* don't have a clue what we're doing."

"But at least we're doing it!" Pete countered, slapping the steering wheel.

"I wonder what he meant?" John mused. "About this being the time?"

"Well, you know how many times someone's tried to get him to make some kind of political move—try to get hold of some real power—and he always says 'My time hasn't come yet'?" Pete glanced at the others for affirmation. "Well, now I guess it's time. He's making his move."

"I think you're right," John agreed. "But I've got a feeling that whatever kind of move he's going to make, it's not going to be anything people are expecting."

"Whatever it is, I'd like to know what borrowing a car has to do with it," said Tomas.

The car turned out to be a vintage convertible—a blue-and-white '57 Chev—in good condition. As Chris had assured them, the owner was quite willing to lend it, although he seemed to have no more idea what it would be used for than they did. The top was down, and Pete drove it back to the hotel in style. The day was warm for early spring, and though the skies were still gray, the dampness of early morning had ended. It was going to be a good day—for whatever they were doing.

Back at the hotel, Pete was surprised to see the lobby crowded with familiar faces. The night before, Chris had invited only the 12 men to go to the city with him. But this morning the Castillos were there, and Audrey, and the Washingtons—in fact, most of Chris Carpenter's supporters from back in Marselles, and from other nearby towns as well. Pete ambled over to Audrey and gave her a hug. "What're you doing here?" he asked.

"Chris called and asked us to come up, just for the day. I left the kids with Mom. I told them we might come up Friday, for the long weekend, if you guys are still here. What's going on?" she asked, glancing at the crowded lobby.

"I don't know," Pete admitted. "That's what we're all wondering."

"It *feels* like a celebration."

"Mmm." Pete stood there, his arms still loosely around his wife, her head nestled under his chin. After a moment's hesitation, he said, "You know, I love you, Audrey."

She laughed. "I love you too. But what did I do to deserve this right now?"

Pete shrugged. "Just a weird feeling . . . something's happening that I don't understand, and I just wanted to make sure you knew."

"That's very sweet. I really do love you—and I'm proud of you."

"Proud of me?"

"Sure." Audrey lifted her face to his. "You always were a good man, but since you've met *him*—well, I'm really proud of what you've become and the way you've thrown yourself into his cause."

"I couldn't have done it without you." He gave her an extra squeeze, then turned to Chris, who was moving in their direction. He smiled at Pete and Audrey.

"I'm glad you two got a few minutes to spend by yourselves,"

125

he said. "We're about ready to leave, Pete. Can you drive the convertible? And Audrey, can you take a few people in the station wagon?"

Within 15 minutes Pete found himself behind the wheel of the open car, with The Chief in the passenger's seat and Jim and John in the back seat, still with no clear idea where they were going. Behind them, the blue van and a long line of dusty cars and trucks stretched out like a working-class motorcade. Which might very well be what this was.

"Head up to Grandview, Pete," Chris instructed him, "and take it nice and slow." He was wearing a shirt and slacks Pete hadn't seen on him before—still casual, but dressier than the familiar jeans and T-shirt. He was clearly prepared for some kind of an event.

The long line of cars slowly made its way up to Grandview. As they turned onto the broad shopping avenue, the clouds overhead shifted and a beam of sunshine forced its way through. The sunlight glinted on the smooth white hood of the old convertible, and Pete's spirits lifted again.

Grandview was a busy street any Sunday afternoon. Today, at the beginning of the holiday week, it was crowded with shoppers. Pete forced himself to drive slowly, but it was hardly necessary. Within minutes the unusual procession had attracted attention, and people were clustering on the sidewalks to see the man whose face had become so familiar. He could hear the shouts of "It's Chris Carpenter!" and out of the corner of his eye he saw Chris waving to the crowd as regally as any world leader on a state visit.

The news van, which had dogged their steps since they left the hotel, must have cut down a side street, because now it was up ahead, filming this strange ride. Normally the drive up Grandview to the city center took Pete perhaps 20 minutes. Today that much time had passed, and he was barely a quarter of the way up the long avenue. As they inched along, the crowd grew. No longer was it merely curious; it was openly supportive. Cheers rose up from the spectators. Chris Carpenter's name rang out again and again in the air.

As they reached the intersection of Grandview and Wellington, Pete saw that crowds of people had lined up on Wellington east of Grandview. "They're expecting us to turn down there!" John yelled, leaning forward from the backseat.

"Well, do we?" Pete turned to Chris.

"Sure!" was the reply, and Pete turned right onto Wellington.

There was no other traffic, though double-parked vehicles on both sides narrowed the street. People sat in cars or on top of them, or stood along the street, cheering as the white convertible inched its way along. Driving so slowly, Pete was free to look more closely at Chris, who was still waving at people, acknowledging their praise with a leader's confidence, but Pete thought he saw a difference between The Boss and the sort of man who usually traveled at the head of a motorcade. Instead of smiling and waving into a faceless crowd, as a president might, Chris Carpenter seemed to seek out individual faces and smile at *them*. It was the same as it had always been—for him, there were no crowds, only individuals.

Perhaps that warm personal glance was what caused people to begin rushing forward into the street. First one, then another, then a flood of them rushed the car, reaching in to touch Chris. He clasped hands with as many as he could, and the crowds in front of the car parted to let them move on.

Up ahead a crowd of teenagers perched in the bed of a pickup looked vaguely familiar. Pete thought he recognized them from a church youth rally they all had visited last year. The kids were waving jackets and sweatshirts over their heads and chanting in unison, "Christopher Carpenter comes from God!"

The chant caught on. As the open car crawled down the long street, Pete could see more and more people waving jackets as the shouts of "Christopher Carpenter is the one who comes from God! CHRIS! CHRISTOPHER! CHRISTOPHER CARPENTER!" shook the air.

They cruised past the town hall and turned left up the hill toward the city park. Again, the crowd seemed to have anticipated their route, for the spring sunlight glinted off the hoods of innumerable cars in the parking lot. As Pete slowed the convertible to a stop just inside the park's entrance gates, throngs of people surged around the car.

Of course the police had shown up by now. Three or four officers vainly struggled to keep the yelling crowd under control, while another pushed his way through to the convertible.

"Mr. Carpenter, sir, this is disturbing the peace, you know. Can't you keep your people under control? Calm them down!"

Chris just shook his head at the officer, half-laughing. "I can't do it, officer. Not now. If I were to make these people be quiet, then the rocks themselves would start shouting. It's time to celebrate!"

The officer retreated, swallowed by the crowd. Pete sat behind the wheel of the convertible. There was a tightness in his chest, as if his heart really were about to burst with pride and joy. How foolish they had been to worry about the disapproval of politicians, preachers, and reporters! This was what really mattered—the people. And the people knew Chris Carpenter—they had heard him speak, had been healed and fed by him. They loved him and worshiped him as did everyone who knew him. Their love would support him as he began—now, today!—to really change the world. And Pete Johnson was here, part of it all, behind the wheel of this impromptu victory parade.

He looked back over his shoulder to share a grin with Jim—who was no doubt feeling just as happy, only he wasn't sitting in the driver's seat. Out of the corner of his eye he noticed that John's expression was thoughtful and troubled. "Lighten up, kid," Pete said. "Like The Chief said, it's a celebration." He didn't catch John's reply.

Chris climbed out of the car. Pete wasn't sure what he—or the crowd—expected. Perhaps for Chris to stand up in the car and start talking to them, as he had been known to do before. Instead he moved among the people, touching, talking, healing the sick who were thrust toward him. For a while Pete lost sight of Chris or any of his friends as strangers milled around. Many of them recognized him as the driver of the car, and plied him with questions. Most of them wanted to know what Chris Carpenter planned to do next. Make an announcement? Give a speech? Organize a movement? Pete thought it would look bad to admit he didn't know, so he mostly said, "Wait and see."

Quite a while passed before people began asking where Chris Carpenter was and discovering that no one knew. John sidled up to Pete and asked, "Have you seen him lately?"

"No, not since he got out of the car. Why?"

"He was around for a while after that, but now no one can find him."

"He does have this way of disappearing in crowds," Pete muttered.

"Come with me. I've got a hunch. . . ." John grabbed Pete's elbow and led him through the crowd.

Beyond the throng clustered around the cars, people sat in small groups on the grass and on picnic tables. The place had a holiday atmosphere—and something that went beyond the regular holiday season, a mood of expectation, of hope and change.

They found Chris well apart from the crowd, in a quiet clearing on the hill that overlooked the city. He was standing quietly, and as they drew near they saw that he was crying. It shocked Pete, as it had on the day Lazario Castillo came back from the dead. Chris Carpenter was their strength, and to see him in a moment of weakness shook all the foundations of their world. If, indeed, it was weakness.

Pete and John stopped just behind Chris, not wanting to interrupt his privacy. Looking out at the city, he repeated, "If only . . . if only . . . I wanted to take care of you all, to gather you together like a mother gathers her children—but you rejected me. I wanted to protect you . . . but now it's too late."

Unable to stop himself, Pete sprang forward and grabbed Chris's arm. "No, Boss! You can't say that!"

He turned to look at Pete, an unreadable expression in his now-clear brown eyes. John said, "Pete—" in a warning tone, but Pete hurried on. "I mean, how can you say they've rejected you? Look at the response you got out there! This isn't the end, this is just the beginning!" All of a sudden he felt foolish, standing there giving The Chief a pep talk. Chris's face grew stern, and Pete recalled the sharp rebuke he'd gotten on another occasion when he tried to get The Boss to stop talking so pessimistically. He faltered and stepped back, but Chris only said, "Yes, Pete, it is the beginning. But it's not the beginning they're expecting." He nodded toward the park, where the holiday crowd was still gathered.

"What are you going to do?" John asked.

"Today? Not a great deal; not make the speech they're all waiting for. Can you guys bring the van around to the back entrance of the park? I know a place outside town where we can spend the night without being interrupted. If you like, you can spread the word that we'll be back in town tomorrow." He turned in the opposite direction. "I'll walk down to the other entrance and meet you there."

Pete and John stood together, watching him walk away, confident and determined. "I don't understand," John said unnecessarily. "First he's happy, like we're off to conquer the world, and then we get all this response from the people and he seems depressed. I can't read him at all. What *is* he going to do?"

Pete hadn't said anything since The Boss had turned and looked at him. Now he shrugged and said what he thought Audrey or Andy—or Chris himself—would have said: "Let's not worry about it. We know what we're supposed to do. Let's worry about that for now."

Together they walked back down the hill.

Chapter Twenty

Matt woke up not knowing where he was. The ceiling seemed unusually low and narrow, and the windows were too small. Also, he was sleeping on the floor.

As the pre-dawn dimness gave shape to the objects around him—most of which turned out to be sleeping bodies—his memory reassembled itself. Chris had brought them here yesterday evening, after the drive through the city with all the accompanying excitement. A friend of his had offered the loan of her mobile home in this trailer park on the edge of town. Chris's supporters had returned to their homes at the end of the day—all but the 12 of them, who went with him in the blue van (the Chevy convertible having been returned to its owner) to this now-cramped retreat.

Matt sat up, then stood. Carefully maneuvering his way around bodies and furniture, he groped his way to the door. He slid his feet into what he thought might be his shoes; slipped into a denim jacket that felt like his, and stepped outside.

It was cool. Zipping up the jacket—which meant it wasn't his, since his didn't have a zipper—he walked between the rows of trailers. Across the road next to the trailer park lay an open field and beyond that a small patch of woods. Matt sat down on a rock in the field, looking to where the eastern hills were edged with rose-gold.

Matthew Levy, MBA student, had not been a watcher of sunrises. If you had to get up this early, you should either be jogging or be on your way to a power breakfast. Though in real life he'd most often risen early to cram for a test—if he hadn't managed to get the answers beforehand. He smiled at the memory. No, in university he'd never gotten up just to watch a sunrise. But before that, much further back, he remembered rising early on summer mornings. During his high school years, he'd worked at summer camp, and there he often used to sit and watch the sun come up. He had known something then that he had lost in the process of getting educated, something that Chris Carpenter had found in him again. He'd changed so much over these past couple of years, but he felt he was finally becoming someone whom that teenaged Matt would have admired. He felt, oddly, that his younger self might at last be proud of him.

As the sun shot its first fire over the ridges, Matt heard a noise from the woods. Turning around he saw that he was not alone with the dawn. A man walked out of the woods and paused, shading his eyes, to look at the sunrise. Though Matt couldn't make out the features, that confident pose was impossible to mistake. The Boss, intent on the sunrise, did not see Matt, and after a moment he turned and walked away, back toward the trailer.

For a moment Matt wondered if he should follow. He wanted to talk to Chris. Like all of them, he wanted to know what yesterday's parade had meant and what was going to happen in the days ahead. They were used to having things explained to them; but now, when there was so much to be explained, The Chief seemed reluctant to talk.

Just then Matt noticed that a third member of their group had risen early this morning. From between the trailers another man stepped onto the road and headed in the opposite direction, away from Matt. He walked with hands thrust in his pockets and head down.

Matt rose to follow Jude instead. Funny, how parallel Chris Carpenter and Jude were in his life. For two years in school he'd followed Jude loyally, learning from him how to be a success, trying to copy him. Then he'd spent the past couple of years following Chris loyally, learning his ideas of success and trying to be like him. Though both his heroes were obviously out to change him, Chris's influence made Matt sure of himself in a way he'd never been before. Still, he couldn't discard his old friend entirely. Sometimes he even felt a recurrent desire to be Jude's satellite again, one of the Bright Young Men on the way to the top. That feeling hadn't come for a long time now—and when it did, he usually dealt with it by putting as much distance between Jude and himself as possible.

Lately he'd had the feeling that Jude was dangerous, that someone should keep an eye on him. But it was more than that which sent him hurrying down that early morning road after Jude. Loyalty or friendship or whatever you called it. It simply was there.

"Oh, hi," Jude said. "Want to walk with a very confused person?"

"Unusual for you to admit to being confused," Matt commented, falling into step beside him.

"Well, enjoy it while it lasts." Jude walked in silence for a moment, then burst out, "I just *wish* I knew what he meant by yesterday's performance. Just when I'm convinced he hasn't got a clue what he's doing, he does something that makes it perfectly clear that he's got goals and intends to reach them. But what *are* his goals? How am I supposed to know what to do? Should I just trust him?" He turned to Matt, his eyes filled with genuine questioning. "Should I?"

Hope surged eagerly inside Matt. "Yes," he said, trying to keep his voice level. "Yes, I think you should."

Jude laughed his short, cynical laugh. "You can relish this little irony, too. My asking you for advice."

Matt shrugged. "I owe you one, after all the advice you've given me."

"All of which you've now rejected as completely shallow and twisted."

"No," said Matt, shaking his head. "Not all of it. You've given me some good advice."

They stopped walking, and both stood looking at the horizon as the sun burst above the hills and poured its full glory onto the ground, casting long shadows behind them. Then, abruptly, Jude turned and began walking back the way they had come, leaving Matt to catch up to him.

A few hours later, after everyone else had arisen and eaten breakfast, they piled into the van and headed into town.

"Where are we going today?" Matt asked as they pulled out of the trailer park.

"The Randall Hotel and Convention Center," Chris answered.

"To the conference?" Tomas asked incredulously.

During this holiday week, the city was host for a nationwide conference on "Religion and Society." Every major denomination was represented, as well as several minor ones. Along with the usual seminars and workshops, there were public events—concerts, panel

discussions, worship services—planned throughout the week, cul-
minating in a huge ecumenical church service at the end of the
week.

"You've got to admit, his timing is perfect," John commented
to Matt as they strolled through the Convention Center lobby,
looking at the displays various religious groups had set up. "He
brings Larry Castillo back to life and captures everyone's attention,
and then just at the time of year when everyone's likely to be
thinking about religion anyway he makes this big mysterious drive
through the city and disappears again, and now this conference
tops it all off. He's got people crazy with anticipation. I bet if one
of us just mentioned his name now, 50 people would hear it."

"Some people have recognized us," said Matt, glancing around.
"I've been getting a few stares. Where is he, anyway?"

"Beats me. He said he was going to park the van."

Matt surveyed the display in front of them. The banner draped
across it proclaimed the name of a popular TV evangelist. Women
with hair-spray-stiff curls and wearing shiny polyester dresses were
offering "free" prayer medallions in return for donations. A few
booths down, a slightly larger crowd milled around a man dressed
in flowing robes who was demonstrating meditation exercises. At
the next table, people were browsing through tapes and CDs by a
well-known religious singer, and across the lobby a group of
earnest biblical scholars selling hardcover books had collected no
crowd at all.

"From the sublime to the ridiculous," John remarked, raising
an eyebrow.

"Tell you the truth, I don't see a whole lot of sublime around
here," Matt replied.

Then they heard the crash.

It could have been the sound of a door crashing open, except
that the Randall Hotel and Convention Center had only revolving
doors. Actually it was the large notice board welcoming visitors to
the conference, which stood at the front of the huge lobby. When
everyone else in the room turned around, Matt and John turned
too. Matt had a sinking feeling he knew what he'd see.

Christopher Carpenter stood there, one man alone in a
crowded room, not unusually large or tall, completely commanding
the attention of every person there. *This is it,* Matt thought. *He's
flipped, He's gone completely crazy. Jude was right.* The toppled
notice board lay sprawled at The Boss's feet, and in his right hand

he carried what seemed to be a stick or something.

A corridor had suddenly opened through the middle of the lobby, and down this Chris Carpenter strode. His ringing voice silenced the murmurs and echoed to every corner.

"Get this foolishness out of here!" he commanded. He barely glanced at a display of books topped by a large blow-up picture of the author; he simply reached out and pushed it over. "You have taken the vital truth God has given you, His Word and His message and His mission, and turned it into a money-making machine!" Reaching the table with the prayer medallions, he flipped it over with his left hand, spilling the tawdry merchandise on the floor. His right hand still clutched the stick, though he did not raise it.

The hair-sprayed proprietors of the booth stumbled over spectators in their eagerness to back away from Chris. He cut a wide swath through the room, taking in the books, pamphlets, and religious paraphernalia with unconcealed disgust. A couple of flashbulbs popped. When Chris Carpenter's voice rose again, the murmur of the crowd ceased instantly.

"You think you can put God into boxes, into books, into seminar rooms! You think you can analyze and dissect and explain what you call 'religion and society.' What would you do with a religion that turned your society completely upside down?"

He stood still in the center of the room, a powerful and vaguely menacing figure. He said nothing more. Silence gathered around him like something tangible. Quite suddenly he turned and walked away, off to the side of the room. People murmured, stirred, shifted position. Matt, glancing around the room, noticed that very few of the people who remained wore the red-and-white convention badges on their lapels.

At the edge of the lobby clustered a group of people in wheelchairs, probably waiting for the faith healer who was supposed to speak at 10:00. Toward these people The Chief walked, and they were the first to call his name and reach out to him, breaching the barrier of silence.

Half an hour later, the people connected with the convention still had not returned, but more and more people thronged into the lobby of the Randall Hotel to see Chris Carpenter. He healed sick people, talked to them, told the stories they loved to hear. He perched on top of a bench at the far end of the lobby, and the people sat, knelt, and stood 10 deep around him.

"I absolutely cannot believe this," Matt said to John, shaking his head.

"I know, isn't it incredible?" John's smile flickered from his mouth to his eyes. He was elated, hardly able to stand still. "Oh, here comes the ubiquitous WCTV crew. And a few guys who look pretty official—"

"Does this mean trouble?"

"Who knows? It doesn't matter; they can't touch him now. Look, he's got people in the palm of his hand. I knew it; he had it planned all along." John moved away, eager to get closer to the scene of the action.

Whatever the official-looking men said to The Boss, he must have had a good answer. From Matt's vantage point on the edge of the crowd, he only saw the pinstriped suits edge away, annoyed. There were cops in the lobby, and it had occurred to Matt that Chris could certainly be arrested for disturbing the peace, but no one moved toward him as he continued to sit among the crowd, talking to them.

The morning stretched on: people came and people left. Noontime passed, and the convention reassembled itself after a fashion. The afternoon seminars and speakers went ahead on schedule, and some people even attended, though far more stayed in the lobby with Chris. The booths that had previously occupied the lobby remained conspicuously absent.

All afternoon, Matt hung around the lobby, listening to Chris, talking to friends and curious spectators who drifted by. At about 6:30, Andy sauntered over to the steps where Matt was sitting and dropped down beside him. He handed him a bag of greasy french fries and a can of root beer.

"Thanks," Matt said, surprised.

"Not the fanciest food around, or the healthiest, but the cheapest," Andy said. "I bet The Chief is getting hungry."

"Aw, you know how he is once he gets talking to people. He never thinks about eating."

"Well, he won't have to do any miracles to provide food here, anyway," Andy said with a smile. "The fast-food joints out there will take care of that."

They ate mostly in silence, listening to Chris's voice alone in the unusually quiet crowd. "I hear they offered him one of the seminar rooms, but he said no," Matt told Andy after a while.

"Probably wants to make it clear he's not part of the convention."

Matt popped the tab on his root beer can and tilted his head back to drink. As he finished, he glanced over at Andy's pleasant face—one of the most open and straightforward faces he'd ever seen. He felt comfortable with Andy, although he wasn't with most people. In fact, the young mechanic was probably the closest friend Matt had made during their journeyings.

"When I went down to get this stuff," Andy said, gesturing with the bag of fries, "some guys were asking me about him, so I brought them up here to see him."

Matt nodded. Bringing people to meet The Boss was nothing new for any of them, especially for Andy.

"One of them asked me if I didn't get tired of hearing him talk, you know, because I'd be hearing the same things all the time."

Both men shared a laugh at that. Though Chris Carpenter often did tell the same stories to different audiences, no two of his talks were ever quite alike. "I can't get enough of listening to him," Matt admitted, then added, "Especially now."

Andy nodded. The feeling was unspoken but shared; right now it was especially important to listen to what Chris had to say.

He was beginning a new story, though his voice sounded hoarse. "Once there was a multi-millionaire, head of several big corporations. This man had only one child, a son, a brilliant and handsome young man who was the apple of his father's eye. The time came for the son to marry, and he chose a beautiful, talented young woman—the ideal match.

"Their wedding was to be the social event of the season, and the boy's proud father invited everyone he knew—business connections, old family friends, and all the local celebrities.

"But when the RSVPs started coming back, a strange thing happened. Though this was clearly going to be the wedding of the year and people talked in the streets about how great it would be to be asked to attend, the invited guests all seemed to have excuses why they couldn't come. One was on vacation, another planned to be away on business, and a few simply said it wasn't convenient."

Matt had heard this story, with variations, many times before. But still he leaned forward to hear. It was one of his favorites, as it was with many of Chris's followers. Matt saw in it an explanation for his own presence in the circle of Chris's friends. He watched the crowd's reactions as the story continued, as the rich man's social secretaries were insulted and abused when they called on some of the guests, and the millionaire finally grew angry at his friends and told his secretary to extend invitations to all sorts of ordinary people who had not been originally invited.

"Even then it looked like the crowd wouldn't be large enough to fill the church or the vast hall they had rented for the wedding. So on the very morning of the wedding, the father sent out several of his employees and told them to find whomever they could—the poor, the sick, the hungry, even the homeless and the criminals and the mental patients—anyone at all, and bring them to the reception dinner.

"And for every guest, however ragged and dirty, he provided a suit of good clothes to wear to the wedding. So all the homeless and unwanted people came to the wedding of the year, and the great hall was filled with an unlikely assortment of characters.

"How the bride and groom—not to mention the bride's family—felt about this, we're not sure. But the groom's father himself seemed strangely pleased and went around to each table welcoming his odd guests."

The expressions on the faces of the hearers—the ones who understood the story, for, as always, some missed the point—reflected emotions Matt knew well. It was hard to believe, the amazing truth that God wanted the unlovely and the unwanted, that He invited them in. But some faces looked uncomfortable. Who were the wealthy friends who had been invited, but refused? Matt had given that some thought, too.

Tonight, the story had an epilogue. The Boss wasn't finished.

"Then at one table the host saw a man dressed in jeans and a tattered sweatshirt. 'Who are you?' the millionaire asked, 'and why are you not wearing a suit?'

"The stranger stared up at him blankly, but made no reply. The host beckoned to two of the waiters. 'Take this man,' he said, 'and throw him back out on the street where he came from!' "

The listeners were quieter still. Chris Carpenter surveyed them with an unreadable expression.

"Because, you see," he concluded, "not everyone who is invited to the party is going to get in."

Chris jumped down from his elevated seat and moved into the crowd, talking to people in small groups. He had taken breaks like this throughout the day, though they hardly seemed restful, with people clamoring for his attention. Matt sat still, his thoughts locked on the end of the story. Chris was always that way—offering the ultimate acceptance, demanding the ultimate sacrifice. He both gave and asked no less than everything. Matt shivered involuntarily. Was there meant to be a note of warning along with the invitation?

Chapter Twenty-one

The day was warm. Maria considered slipping off her jacket, but, thinking of the people standing around, decided she didn't want to. Instead she pulled it closer, though the spring sunshine poured down on her shoulders.

"What time is it, Maria?" John asked.

"Almost 2:30." Two-thirty on Wednesday afternoon, and since Monday morning Chris Carpenter had been the center of attention at the Randall Hotel and Convention Center. When Tuesday morning had dawned sunny and warm, Chris had moved out to the courtyard, and all day yesterday and today people had come to listen to him there. For much of the day he preached to the crowd. In between, he talked to smaller groups of people, and healed the ever-present sick.

"Were you around this morning, when that bunch of ministers came out?" Pete asked.

"No, I wasn't here then," answered Maria.

"That was worth seeing!"

"They weren't just ministers," said John. "They were theology professors from some university—"

"Whatever. Anyhow, they were asking The Boss questions again, trying to back him into a corner—but he's just got an answer for everything. They couldn't get nothing over on him!"

John joined in Pete's laughter, but Maria couldn't smile. Sure, it was great to see people flocking to Chris, but where was all this leading? It was great to see him rebuff his opponents, but why did he suddenly seem to have so many?

Not for the first time in the past few days, Maria wished she could push through the crowd of people surrounding Chris and sit near him, listen to his voice without straining to hear. Surely just being close to him would make things all right again. All right, the way they hadn't been since—well, since Simon's party, anyway.

"What time did you guys leave here last night?" she asked John and Pete.

"Oh, must've been around midnight—no, later," Pete said.

"Chris preached till almost 10:00 and then stayed around talking to people for a couple of hours. Even then, he pretty much had to tear himself away," added John.

"Did you go back to the same place you stayed last night?"

"No, another place."

"We haven't slept two nights in the same place since we came up from Marselles," Pete grumbled. "The Boss seems to want to keep moving around."

Maria nodded. Most of Chris's followers, except the 12, were still back in Marselles. She had come up along with Chris's mother and a few other women, and they were staying with a friend of Mary's. They hadn't seen much of Chris Carpenter or the other guys, for that matter, except in the courtyard of the hotel.

"It's funny," said Matt, who had been standing by quietly. "The way he keeps moving around, it's almost like he doesn't want people to know where he's staying."

"That's no surprise, is it?" The question came from a stranger standing near Matt, a short man wearing a tweed cap. "Your man must know that there's an awful lot of people who'd like him out of the way."

"But he's here, every day at the hotel," Maria said. "If they want to find him—"

"Sure, but they're not going to take him here in front of everyone, are they? Can you see the publicity?"

"But what can they get him for anyway?" Matt wondered aloud. "Disturbing the peace, maybe, that'd be about it."

The man in the tweed cap snorted. "That doesn't matter. Nobody wants to see Christopher Carpenter go to trial and get a fine or a short jail sentence. They've been digging around for months, trying to find some dirt that could land him in a real scandal like all those other preacher-types. But they can't get anything solid."

"Shouldn't that tell you something?" asked Maria.

The stranger shrugged. "I don't know about that. I don't take

141

sides. I'm not a religious man anyway. I just know that it doesn't really matter what kind of charge they get him on. What's important is that they'll arrange to have some 'accident' happen to him while he's being held in jail. Or they'll release him into the hands of the right people . . . and make sure justice never gets done."

"Are you saying . . ." Matt began slowly.

"I'm not sayin' anything," the man countered, crossing his arms in front of him. "I just know the way these things work. There are folks in high places who want Carpenter out of the way for good—and they've got ways of doing these things." He stared straight ahead impassively, refusing to meet their eyes.

The world swayed around Maria. "It's impossible," she breathed. "They can't . . ."

Pete Johnson reached out to put a steadying arm around her shoulders. "Don't worry, nothing like that's going to happen. Look at all these people . . . would they let anyone hurt Chris Carpenter? Would *we* let anyone hurt him?"

Maria shook her head, but the words did not untie the knot of fear inside her.

Matt spoke softly. "Nothing will happen to Chris that he doesn't want to happen. You know that."

Those words, of all words, should have reassured her. But as she looked across the crowded square at Chris, for some reason her fears remained.

Chapter Twenty-two

Candles flickered on the table in honor of the occasion. The holiday dinner, the meal they should all be eating at home with their families. Only, "home" didn't mean what it used to. And as for family . . . well, Pete partly regretted that Audrey and the kids were celebrating without him back in Marselles, but he also recognized that there were ties binding him to the other 12 men in this darkened room, ties in some ways stronger than those he shared with his wife and children, if that were possible.

Blocking out the faces of those around him, Pete let his eyes focus on the candle flames. The voices receded to a pleasant murmur, which was unusual. If a conversation was going on, usually Pete was at the center of it. But tonight he was more tired than he'd ever admit, and it was good to just relax. He wasn't naive enough to think this quiet evening marked an end to the current turmoil, but he was grateful just for a break.

The past week had been weird, to put it mildly. He found it hard to believe that the drive through the city had taken place only Sunday. Monday had begun with that bizarre scene in the hotel lobby, where The Boss had asserted his authority in some way everyone respected, even if they didn't understand.

The rest of the week had been a blur of comings and goings, all centered around the crowds at the hotel who were bent on seeing and hearing Chris Carpenter. Every day more people had flocked to him, confirming what Pete kept telling his dubious friends: that people were more supportive of Christopher Carpenter than ever before. Things were moving toward the climax of The Chief's ultimate victory. Or so he tried to reassure the rest of them. Yet he couldn't deny that Chris was attracting a lot of negative attention too. Pete had spent a large part of this afternoon arguing with Tomas' skepticism and trying to allay Andy's worries, but in the privacy of his own thoughts he had to admit that an uneasy feeling permeated the air. That man in the courtyard whose words had so frightened Maria had been the most blunt, but the feeling was not hard to pick up: The Boss was putting himself in a dangerous situation.

Yet Pete still felt confident. He pulled his eyes away from the dancing candle flames to scan the familiar faces all around him. A few of these men he still didn't like much, more of them he'd never trust, but they had seen and done some amazing things together. *I'm not the same guy I was,* Pete thought. *And neither is Andy or Jim or John—any of us. You can't go through what we've been through together and not be loyal.* For himself, he knew he'd be willing to kill or die for Chris Carpenter without a second thought. If the others felt that way too, then surely only good could come out of the past week's events.

Chris's words rose out of the murmur of conversation, jarring harshly with Pete's thoughts. "To tell you the truth," he said, seeming almost matter-of-fact, "I know already that one of you at this table is going to betray me."

Pete didn't know what conversation had led up to that remark, but that statement effectively silenced all further talk. There were a few gasps of "What?" Then, after a moment, Pete saw that Chris's eyes were fixed on his own, and in them he read pain and disappointment so deep he hardly knew how to respond.

"You can't mean me, Boss!" The words were torn out of him.

Chris made no reply, but almost at the same moment John cried out, "Not me!" Chris was looking around the table, meeting each pair of eyes. And each man there, Pete knew, was uttering his shocked disavowal to cover the sudden nakedness of soul that Chris Carpenter could so easily reveal. What each of them really wanted was for this man, who knew them better than they knew themselves, to say, "No, of course it's not you. I know *you* could never do that."

Pete picked up his fork and fingered it nervously. He, too, looked at the other men around the table. Only moments before, he had felt a surge of comradeship and affection for them. Now he assessed each face, trying to detect which one hid treachery. Simon . . . he'd never trusted that skinhead. Anyone who wore that much black just *looked* sinister. And Tomas—Pete met his eyes and quickly glanced away. He thought of the simple, powerful story Chris had told them that afternoon in the park when they'd finally managed to escape the crowds. He'd been talking about the end of the world, the day of judgment, when people would be separated into two groups according to the simple acts of kindness they'd done or left undone. Pete thought of Tomas' cool, passionless intellect—probably he would consider such ordinary goodness beneath him. Yes, Tomas was capable of betrayal.

It could even be Jim Fisher, who sometimes seemed even now to smolder with stifled anger. Or Matt, who was still so often unsure of himself and where he stood. Or Nat, who had never really gotten over losing his wife. Why . . . it could be any of them!

After Chris's strange statement and the shocked denials that followed it, conversation around the candlelit table was reduced almost to whispers. Chris himself broke the silence, gathering everyone's attention with a tone of voice that was oddly ceremonial.

He held in his strong hands the loaf of bread that had lain on the table before him, and he tore off a piece of that loaf and held it up before them.

"Do you see this bread?" Again his eyes moved from one to another. "This bread is my body, which I am giving for you. Take it and eat it." He handed the loaf of bread to John, seated beside him, who held it as if he were dazed. Finally John broke off a piece and passed the loaf to Pete.

So the loaf of bread made the circle of the table, each man taking a piece. No one ate until The Boss did, and then they all followed his lead. Chewing, Pete thought that it tasted exactly like every other piece of bread he'd ever eaten. But the difference was there. He remembered a sermon Chris Carpenter had preached a long time ago, in which he'd compared his body and blood to food and drink, and told people they'd have to eat and drink him to know God's eternal life. Some people then had been repelled by the imagery, but Pete felt he understood it at a gut level. Now, much later, he understood those words even more strongly, knew how much closeness to Christopher Carpenter had to do with closeness to God. Tonight's ritual seemed like a more concrete way of carving that picture into their minds.

But back then Chris hadn't spoken of his body being offered.

He had talked of his own death on other occasions, but Pete had never wanted to listen.

Now he was lifting the pitcher and pouring the dark liquid into his glass. "This is my blood, which will be spilled as a promise for you." He passed the pitcher to John. "Drink this, and remember me."

Remember me. Could any words point to a darker future than those? As Pete took the pitcher to fill his own glass, his hands shook. But Chris's hands had been steady.

Looking at those hands, so familiar, that face and those incredible eyes, Pete felt a rush of love for Chris Carpenter. This man was, quite simply, everything. *He knows me inside out,* Pete thought, *and I hardly know him at all. I haven't got a clue what's going through his mind now. He's more than any of us, and he's the closest friend I'll ever have.* He thought back to Marselles, to the comfortable days when he was the proprietor of Pete's Garage—before The Boss came along. The impossible adventure that had started when Christopher Carpenter came to Marselles had been worth it, every minute. The past three years had contained more shining moments than Pete Johnson had ever dreamed of knowing.

Chris held his now-empty glass up to the light. "I want to remember this evening too," he said. "I won't drink this again until we're all together again . . . in my Father's kingdom."

The tension in the room seemed to break at last, and they were all questioning him, wanting to know what his strange predictions meant. Above the anxious babble of their voices his broke in. "Don't worry! Don't be afraid! Put your minds at rest. You believe in God, don't you? You believe in me?"

Pete nodded, as the others did.

"Then believe this. My Father has a home—a house with many rooms, and I'm going there to get it ready for you. But I'll be back to get you, to take you all with me." A note of gladness tinged his voice now; they all caught it and held to it. *He's still talking in pictures,* Pete thought, *even now.* The image of the house with many rooms appeared in his mind as a picture of the Elwood lodge up north, where they had spent those happy untroubled months.

"You all know where I'm going," Chris went on, "and how to get there."

"What?" Tomas spoke abruptly. "With all due respect, Boss, that doesn't make much sense. We *don't* know where you're going—and if we don't know even that, how can we possibly know the way to get there?"

Chris's eyes burned a bright challenge at his skeptical friend. "*I am the way there*—and *I* am truth and life. Without me no one can find the way to the Father."

"The Father." Phil's voice was flat. "If we could see God, then maybe we'd understand."

Now The Boss shook his head. "All this time we've spent together, Phil, and still you don't know me? Look, if you've seen me, you've seen God. He is in me and I'm in Him. All that the Father is, I am—that's what I came to show you, what God is like."

It must be frustrating for him, Pete thought suddenly, though Chris's tone hinted at nothing but patience. *All this time, and we're so slow to catch on to what he's really all about.*

Chris Carpenter went on talking, answering their questions, trying to explain, though not as clearly as they'd have liked. Through it all, Pete heard only one thing: The Chief was going to leave them. For the second time in his life, he saw a yawning chasm open at his feet.

Quite abruptly, Chris said, "Come on, it's time to get out of here." Then, as the men shifted in their seats, he added, "First, let's sing a hymn to close our meal."

The song he led them in was one of praise, a favorite of his, and his voice was so strong and clear above the rest that Pete, ever the optimist, dared to hope everything would work out. No matter what, he knew he would stay by Chris Carpenter as long as he could.

He felt it was important, after all that had been said tonight, to let Chris know how he felt. The Boss was the last to leave the room, straightening the chairs and table as the others put on their jackets. Pete stopped him at the top of the stairs and laid a hand on his arm.

"Boss—I just want you to know, whatever happens, I'm with you. All the way."

Chris's eyes were terribly tender. "Oh, Rocky," he said softly. The name he'd first called him. Then, "Pete, the enemy wants your soul—he wants to tear you to shreds. But I've prayed for you; prayed God will give you strength to remain faithful."

"What?" Despite the tenderness, the words were a slap in the face after his assurance. Did Chris Carpenter doubt his loyalty? Why did He think Pete needed special help? "Don't you know I'd follow you anywhere? To prison, to death—anywhere!" The words burst from him, loud above the shuffle of his friends who were descending the stairs, going out into the night.

"Will you?" Chris's voice did not accuse, but its edge was sharper. "Peter, before the sun rises tomorrow morning you'll swear—three times—that you never knew me." He turned away from Pete's shocked glance, from Pete's hand on his arm, and suddenly looking terribly weary headed down the stairs.

☆ ☆ ☆

The grass was dew-damp under Pete's back as he lay, listening to Chris. He wasn't really hearing much of what The Boss was saying. The hurt inside him hadn't diminished any during the past hour. They had all journeyed together from their borrowed dining room to the city park, but Pete had for once been on the fringes of the group, wrapped in his private pain. Did Chris Carpenter really trust him so little? After everything?

He's just testing me, Pete thought. *He wants me to prove that I really will be loyal to him. He'll see—I won't let him down. Even if the others do.* Determination lifted his spirits for a moment, but sheer exhaustion dragged them back down. The crowded events of the week had meant little sleep for the past three nights, and the emotional turmoil had taken its toll, too. Now, even on a damp hillside on a cool spring night, sleep was calling. Several times Pete brought his mind sharply back to what Chris Carpenter was saying, realizing that he'd been drifting in some dim world beyond thought.

Now Chris was saying earnestly, "I'm telling you these things because I want you to have my joy living in you—so that joy will fill your lives!" The repeated "joy" sounded out of place on a night so full of strangeness and sadness. But, looking up the hill at Chris's face, Pete had to admit there was something to it. No matter how bad things got, The Boss still seemed to love life, and that joy sustained him. The words, and the thoughts that went with them, teased the edges of Pete's brain, but he was too tired to pursue them. He looked over at John, leaning forward on his elbows, listening eagerly, wide awake. *Great to be young . . .* Pete thought.

When he drifted back to reality again, his eyes opened to stars overhead, and Chris was still talking. Only, Pete realized, now he was praying. Praying, it seemed, for his friends gathered around him on the hillside. "Keep them from getting drawn in to the evil of the world around them, Father. . . . Bring them together as one, the way that You and I are one—give them that unity. Then You will be living in them, as You live in me. . . ." The words made Pete ashamed of his own concerns and his own weariness. He tried to shape a message to the Father in his own mind, but couldn't quite do it.

He realized that the prayer was over and that Chris had been silent for a while. Looking up, he saw that most of his companions on the moonlit hillside were as tired as he. All around him they were sprawled or huddled into sleepy shapes. Propping himself up on his elbows, Pete surveyed the faces around him. Only John had his eyes open—flat on his back, he stared up at the sky. Vaguely, Pete thought that someone seemed to be missing, but he wasn't sure who.

Chris was still sitting up, gazing off beyond them all into the night sky. As Pete looked up at him, their eyes met. Chris didn't look angry, but his eyes held some clear sad knowledge that excluded Pete, just as the words he'd spoken earlier did. So it was a surprise when The Boss stood up and said, "I'm going to walk on a bit farther. Want to come with me?"

"Sure." Pete got to his feet. John darted a quick look at Chris, who nodded to him, and he too rose. His brother Jim, next to him, opened drowsy eyes and sat up also.

The three of them followed him up the hill, onto the hiking trail between the trees. Pete was vividly reminded of that other time when he, Jim, and John had followed The Boss up a hill and seen that strange vision of glory. He had often been glad, since, that he'd been there that day. Like Chris Carpenter's miracles—more, even, than the miracles—that memory gave him a reason to believe during those times when the whole thing seemed ridiculous.

On that far-off day, The Boss had walked up that hill with an eager buoyancy—a heightened version of his usual stride. Tonight all that was gone. Despite his earlier words about joy, it seemed that the sadness which had hovered over him all evening—or had it been all week? or longer?—had finally descended. He moved with slow heavy steps, his hands thrust deep in his pockets, his eyes on the ground. The others slowed their pace to match his. John moved a step or two ahead to walk beside him on the narrow path; he seemed to be searching for something to say but finding no words powerful enough to pierce that deep silence. After a moment he reached out and put his hand on Chris's shoulder.

At the top of the hill, the hiking trail leveled off and opened into a small clearing. A few benches faced out over the vast expanse of the city lights, and on the other three sides lay the deep quiet of the trees.

Here Chris turned to the three of them. His tired, moonlit face startled Pete. In all the troubles of the past three years, he'd never seen The Boss look discouraged or afraid as he did now. Afraid? Could he be? The calm certainty in his eyes had reassured Pete countless times. To find it gone tied his stomach into a cold knot.

"I need to be alone," Chris said, "but I'd like it if—if you'd wait here for me, and pray with me . . . for me."

He turned away from them and walked to the edge of the clearing, where he knelt on the ground in front of the farthest benches, resting his elbows on the bench and burying his head in his hands.

John, James, and Pete looked at each other uncertainly. Then Pete sat down heavily on one corner of the bench and leaned against the back. He shook his head. "Weird night," he said. Jim just nodded and sat down on the opposite end. John moved a little away from them and sat down on the ground, watching Chris Carpenter intently.

The Boss's voice was audible, barely, and Pete heard the pain, the pleading in his tone. He tried a prayer of his own. "Dear God, I don't understand anything anymore; everything's so messed up. I don't know what's wrong with Chris, but I know You won't let anything bad happen to him, or to us. . . ." Images from the past weeks flooded his mind, drowning the optimistic words. He let his mind drift, sliding in and out of the pictures of memory. Finally, all the pictures faded into darkness.

Something nudged the edge of his sleep—a voice or a movement—and he opened his eyes to see James asleep on the bench beside him. Farther away, John lay on the ground, his head cushioned on his arms. And Chris stood a few feet away, wearing that same sad expression and saying something—but Pete slipped quickly back into sleep, and afterward was never sure whether that moonlit tableau was memory or dream. He drifted in and out of a fitful sleep filled with short, disjointed snatches of dreams, and he didn't wake up fully till he heard John shout, "What's that?"

Blinking, Pete turned to look back down the hill. He saw lights flickering through the trees and heard excited voices rising above the sound of car engines and slamming doors. Obviously one or more cars had driven to the area where the rest of the group was sleeping, and from the sound of the commotion below, it wasn't a friendly visit.

Pete was on his feet immediately, as were James and John. "Let's see what's going on down there," James said, heading toward the path.

"No, Jim," John said. "Let's wait—"

James was already out of earshot, crashing through the underbrush, but Pete stayed where he was. The Boss walked up behind them almost silently and placed a hand on each of their shoulders. "It's time," he said simply. His face, though still sad, looked perfectly calm. Pete, with his legs trembling and his stomach churning, wondered how The Boss could look that way.

Then there were loud voices and crashing footsteps and bright lights on the path, moving up the hill toward them, and suddenly the little clearing was full of men. Pete froze when he saw the one carrying the flashlight: he wore a police uniform.

Several of the others were also policemen, but he saw many who just looked like thugs. *Of course,* he thought, *they brought a crowd along because they knew Chris always had a crowd with him. Well, we'll give them the fight they came for.* He didn't see many of his friends in the crowd, but he did spot his brother Andy, struggling with a huge man who was trying to hold him back. And wasn't that Phil over there . . . ?

"Which one is he? Where's Christopher Carpenter?" The officer held up his flashlight, sweeping its beam across Pete, Chris, and John.

"There he is! That's him!" a chorus of voices called. One man stepped forward from behind the flashlight's glare, and Pete realized with a jolt that there was another familiar face in this crowd. Jude, the college boy, looking a little dishevelled and uneasy, walked over to Chris. Chris too took a step forward, ahead of John and Pete. Jude placed a hand on Chris's arm and said to the policeman, "Here he is. Here's your man."

The Boss didn't shake off Jude's touch, only turned to look at him. *Of course,* Pete thought. *He's the one who was missing, ever since suppertime. He knew where we'd be; he led them here. I knew all along he was—* Here his thoughts broke off for lack of words, but his fists itched to connect with Jude's smug face. Instead he took a swing at a big, burly stranger who was moving toward Chris.

A firm hand caught his wrist, stopped his arm before the blow could land. It wasn't the tough, who had only just now noticed

Pete's attack; it was The Boss, who had moved swiftly to Pete's side. "Not that way, Rocky," he said quietly.

Pete's arm dropped. Anger and frustration surged through him. They were trying to hurt Chris Carpenter, and he wasn't allowed to do anything. How could he prove that he meant what he'd said? Why was The Boss letting all this happen?

The mob moved forward, but both police and thugs seemed curiously reluctant to touch Chris Carpenter. Chris looked at them, almost amused, and spoke to the policeman behind the flashlight.

"All week I've been speaking in public, out in the open. If you had any cause to arrest me, why didn't you do it then? What were you so afraid of that you had to come at night, bringing a gang?"

An angry murmur of voices drowned out the cop's words, and men moved in to surround Chris. Pete was pushed away; his arms were forced behind his back and held there. As he twisted to free himself, he heard Chris's voice, still full of calm authority, in the middle of this bizarre scene. "I'm the one you've come for; let the others go." And even as they forced him down the hill between them, they couldn't disobey him. Pete felt the grip on his arms break away. Ahead of him, he saw the man Andy was struggling with deliver a brisk blow to Andy's face; again Pete was overwhelmed by the desire to lash out, but before he could move toward his brother the man had shoved Andy into the bushes.

John's voice spoke close to Pete's ear. "Don't run and don't try to fight. Let's just hang around and see what happens, then we'll know what we can do."

So Pete and John followed the crowd at a slight distance and watched in horror as they forced Chris into the police car. Jude moved to get in beside him, but the cops pushed him away. "They don't need him anymore," John commented. Jude was squeezed into a rusted old car with some of the thugs; it was the one small moment of satisfaction Pete had all night.

Panic overtook him again as the cars pulled away. "What do we do now?" he asked John.

"I don't know. Maybe Chris has a plan and we should just wait for him."

They had always trusted him to have a way out of any situation, and he always had. But seeing him manhandled by that mob had broken something in Pete. Glancing into John's eyes, he saw the reflection of his own uncertainty and fear.

152

☆ ☆ ☆

"Look at the crowd," John said, stopping the van at the corner.

The city was still shrouded in predawn darkness, but a crowd had gathered outside the police station as Chris Carpenter was brought in. Illuminated by the floodlights in the city hall square, they huddled on and around the steps, waiting. At first Pete had dared to hope that they were there to protest Chris's arrest, but their reaction as Chris was led up the steps told him clearly which side they were on.

"Right across the street from the hotel," John muttered, furious. "Just yesterday they couldn't get close enough to him. Now look at them. Scum!" He turned off the van's engine and looked at Pete. "Want to go over and see?"

Pete shrugged, but he got out. He hadn't said anything since they had found the van and discovered that none of their friends were around. First Chris had let himself be taken, then everyone else seemed to have run away, now the people had turned on him. Nothing was left; nothing at all.

He trudged down the street behind John. As they neared the edge of the crowd, John glanced down the side street that ran beside the police station.

"I've got a buddy who's a janitor in there," he told Pete. "Night shift. I bet he could let us in. You coming?"

Pete shook his head. He didn't want to go inside, near Chris; he didn't want to be a part of whatever horrible things were going to happen. He was Pete Johnson, an ordinary guy. Part of the crowd. If everything else was gone, that was what was left, and that was what he would be.

He moved through the crowd, not listening to their babble. When some woman elbowed him and said, "Hey! Do you know what's going on? Do you know Christopher Carpenter?" he kept his head down and ignored her till she turned her question elsewhere.

At the bottom of the steps he stopped, not wanting to push in any closer. To his dismay he saw a reporter and cameraman elbowing through the crowd just in front of him. He looked away, hoping not to be recognized. But the reporter's sharp voice was aimed straight at him. "Excuse me, you're a follower of Mr. Carpenter's, aren't you? Can you tell me how you—"

Pete recoiled from the microphone thrust in front of him. He shook his head and raised his hand in front of his face to cut out the glare of the camera's light. "No, sorry, I can't help you," he mumbled. "I don't know anything about it."

"But you *are* a friend of his, aren't you?" the young man persisted. Still shaking his head, Pete turned his back on the camera and edged away from the reporter, up the steps.

The crowd's movement jostled him, pushed him farther and farther up the steps till he was leaning against the railing near the door. The people were impatient, huddled together in the chilly, gray half-light. What were they waiting for?

A hand grasped his shoulder and pushed him forward; a flashbulb popped in his face. "Here's one!" someone shouted. Pete looked up to see a young woman with a press badge and a clipboard. The people next to him were pointing her in his direction.

"Yes, that's right! You *were* with him! I saw you there when I covered the Castillo story!"

Pete hated her, hated the noisy people around him, hated his friends who had deserted him, hated The Boss who had abandoned them, hated himself. This pushy girl with the fluffy red hair was the easiest person to hate, though, and Pete lashed out at her with the first words that came to his mind. She looked back at him, startled—it wasn't the kind of language anyone expected to hear from a friend of Chris Carpenter.

Then another voice cut in. "Sure he's one of that crowd. Can't you hear the Marselles accent?" Everyone laughed, and Pete swore again, then said, "Look, I'm telling you, I don't know the man. I don't know anything about this, now leave me alone!"

His very vehemence betrayed him, but she must have been an inexperienced reporter, because she didn't press her advantage. Instead she turned away. Pete thrust his hands deep into his pockets and stared at his feet. One man, nearby, persisted in saying, "I know he was—" but a glower and a muttered warning from Pete made him subside.

Then the crowd stirred, craning their necks to see. The side door of the police station opened, and a pair of cops leading someone between them bustled out. The crowd surged away from the steps and across the square, past the city hall, toward the courthouse, where the policemen were heading.

From his vantage point on the steps, Pete could look down at the man between the two cops. Handcuffed and guarded, he still walked with dignity. Then he turned to look up, behind him, as if knowing Pete was there, and their eyes met.

Misery cut like a knife-edge through Pete's dulled emotions. This was *Christopher Carpenter*—his Chief, his best friend—looking at him with such pain and disappointment. Pete gripped the railing fiercely, wishing he could send Chris some sign, some signal of his loyalty. He couldn't even nod his head, for the look on Chris's face told him he would know it was a lie. That look was the same as it had been when Chris had said, "You'll swear—three times—that you never knew me."

The Boss turned away.

Pete tore his hands from the railing and bolted down the steps, tripping, running into people. He raced away from the crowd, from the square, from Chris, down side streets and alleys. At last he stopped at the end of a deserted lane. He stumbled there, fell to his hands and knees, and stretched full length on the ground, his face pressed against the cold gravel. He had no thoughts—only memories. Chris's face, troubled and knowing, all evening. His own brave promises of loyalty. The Boss at the Community Center in Marselles, when he'd first said, "Rocky Johnson." Chris, happy and singing, at the wheel of the van. Chris, gentle and strong, by a hospital bedside. Chris—blazing in glory on the hilltop. Pete ducking to avoid the camera. Chris in the square tonight, pain on his face.

Between the buildings, behind the hills that ringed the city, the first sunlight of day shot out, touching streets and cars and people, utterly missing the dark alley where an ordinary man lay sobbing bitterly on the ground.

155

Chapter Twenty-three

The air had turned suddenly cooler, and Matt Levy, aimlessly pacing the tree-lined walks of the university campus, wished he had brought a warmer sweater. In fact, he had brought nothing except his wallet and keys to the rented car. He'd made a fast getaway on Thursday night, hating himself for leaving but rationalizing that he couldn't do anything to help, so it would be better to get out of the city until things were resolved. He had arrived in Pendleton about 3:00 Friday morning and had slept in the car, then spent all Friday wandering around town, avoiding people he might know, loathing himself, and waiting for news. Then on Friday night, news arrived. Things were resolved—but it was not a resolution he'd ever dreamed of.

Friday night—that was last night—he didn't remember at all. He must have rented that room at the Y, because that was where he woke up this afternoon, dulled and disoriented. Probably he'd gotten drunk. And now, walking through a campus steeped in a Saturday stillness, he thought it might be a good idea to get drunk again. As soon as possible.

He looked up to realize he was standing in the square where he had first met Christopher Carpenter. His fists clenched in anger—at what? At Chris, for cheating and fooling him? For giving him a new life that had promised so much, and then shattered into emptiness? With himself, for running away as soon as he saw The Boss forced into the car by those men, running away to save his own skin and to avoid watching his world come apart? Or with the people who had killed Chris Carpenter, neatly and horribly, just as that man in the hotel square had predicted they would?

That was the impossible thought—that Chris, so full of life that it spilled over onto everyone he touched, could be dead. The pain that ripped through Matt's body—betrayal, despair, emptiness— was the most intense he'd ever known. *No, Matt thought, I was wrong to believe, wrong to care. Jude, the smooth-talking cynic, had it right all along.*

Jude. Where was he? He had been there in the park Thursday night—not part of The Boss's group, but part of the crowd who'd come to take Chris away. Seeing Jude with those people had hit Matt harder than he had realized it would. Of course he'd known that Jude didn't trust Chris, that Jude had something planned. But that he could be responsible for this? Standing there in the shadows behind Chris, Matt for a moment had met the eyes of his old roommate. Then Jude had looked away. Maybe it was Jude, as much as anything, that had sent him running away from the park, away from the others, away from Chris. Back to a past that had long since ceased to be real.

His feet were moving, involuntarily it seemed, toward the apartment high rise where he had lived with Jude. He knew that Jude had kept the apartment there, subletting it to students. Unlike Matt himself, Jude hadn't recklessly left everything behind to follow Chris Carpenter. He also knew that Jude had left the apartment vacant this semester—one of the things that had warned him that Jude's dissatisfaction was reaching a crisis.

Could Jude be there now? As he stood at the door of the building, Matt tried to imagine a confrontation between himself and Jude. He couldn't. But perhaps it had to happen—they had to meet one more time, so that Jude could gloat over having made all the right moves once again. Be cautious. Don't get in too deep. Keep your head. He could hear Jude's voice now.

The lobby, the hall, looked unreal. He studied his reflection in the mirrored wall—unshaven, hollow-eyed, clothes rumpled. Look what the Bright Young Man has come to. He'd thrown all his trust behind another young man, and now that man was dead. And the Bright Young Man was dying inside.

The whole group of them had crashed at this apartment while passing through Pendleton a few times, and the key was still on Matt's chain. He stood in front of number 804 for a long time, fingering the key. Finally he knocked—it was Jude's place, after all—but no one answered. So, Jude wasn't here. No confrontation.

Still, curiosity had dragged him this far. He turned the key in the lock.

The room was dim, blinds pulled down. It looked barer than it once had. He went down the narrow hall and glanced into his old room, then into the bathroom, then into Jude's room.

That room was dim too, so dim that at first he didn't notice what was in the middle of the room, hanging stiff and lifeless from the sturdy ceiling fan. When he did see it, he couldn't understand at first . . . until he looked down and saw the chair lying on the floor, and looked up again to see what had been Jude's face.

He bolted down the hall and ran wildly out into the living room, but didn't make it to the door. He barely made it to the kitchen sink. Retching and shivering, he leaned there against the counter. He was almost too weak to move afterward, but the crawling horror all over his cold, sweaty skin made it impossible to stay in the apartment with . . . that. Even with the door closed behind him, he could still feel it beyond the walls, and again he ran blindly, this time toward the elevator. He didn't feel free of it until he was down in the lobby, and there he crouched on a bench for a long time, his body shaking and his mind numb.

Finally he called the police from the lobby pay phone. He sat in the lobby, waiting for them to arrive. When they came, he followed them back up to the apartment, trying to deaden his feelings. It must have worked, because he felt no shock of horror when he looked for a second time at Jude's lifeless body. In the living room, he told the police everything he knew about Jude and how he had found the body. When they were done taking his statement, he was free to go. He followed them out of the building and stood uncertainly in the parking lot. Darkness had fallen. He wasn't sure where to go, but he began walking away from the building that had once been his home.

I did care about you, was the first coherent thought Matt formed. *I resented you and I was scared of you, but I did care. If I'd known . . . I would have done something, I swear to God I would have. You had me fooled, Jude. I thought the image was the real thing—that you really didn't care. But I guess you did.*

He thought of his own awkward attempts to pierce Jude's armor, to get him to see what Chris Carpenter was really about. If he'd tried harder, perhaps they would both be alive. He couldn't handle that thought.

Again, he'd been walking without purpose or direction. He saw that he was walking past Troubadour's, a bar popular with university students. At least, it had been popular two years ago. He went inside, sat down at the farthest back table he could find, and ordered a beer.

He tried to lose his thoughts in the music and the surroundings, but it was far too early in the evening for a distracting crowd. He hadn't even finished his first drink when the next wave of pain crashed through his numbness.

It wasn't just the horror of seeing Jude's body, or the knowledge that two of the best friends he'd ever had were dead. He had looked up to them both, and both were gone. One had given him a life of false glitter and promise, a life that not only Matt but ultimately Jude himself had failed at. The other had given him a hope that seemed utterly real—then failed to deliver on His promise. *I've always been a follower,* Matt thought dismally, *and now there's no one left to follow.*

How could Chris Carpenter be dead? How could all that they'd believed be untrue? He drained his glass and set it on the table in front of him, looking down at its murky bottom.

Jude's death was, in its own way, just as inexplicable. If Chris's murder had disproved everything Matt believed about him, Jude's suicide had done the same. It was so ironic. Jude hadn't cared about Christopher Carpenter, it seemed, yet when his plan brought about Chris's death, he felt so tortured by guilt that he took his own life. Chris Carpenter, who had never found a way to reach Jude, had touched him at last by dying. Matt's hands tightened around the glass. It was as if by hanging himself, Jude had testified that he had been wrong, that Chris Carpenter *was* worth believing in. Only now it was too late, because there was nothing left to believe.

Matt drank his second beer more slowly. A few people drifted into the bar. He tried to remember himself sitting here, almost three years ago now, being handsome and witty and charming to some girl, desperately hoping he could keep the facade in place long enough to get her into bed with the man she thought was Matt Levy. He knew how much he'd changed since then. Now there was something real inside there, something he could afford to reveal. The raw aching core of emptiness had been filled by Chris. That was another thing which made it impossible to believe that Chris had cheated them all—he had made a new man out of Matt.

The events of the past few weeks played relentlessly in Matt's mind, as steady as the thudding soundtrack of music from the speakers above his head. Why hadn't they all seen where it was leading? Jude wasn't the only one with a plan. They had all noticed how The Boss had carefully timed things so that he would attract as much attention as possible. They had all known something was about to happen—why hadn't they guessed it might be something tragic?

A new thought struck Matt, making his slumped shoulders lift for a moment. What if this tragedy *was* what Chris had planned? What if he had chosen this? *He knew how some people hated him,* Matt remembered, *and he did talk about his own death, though I tried not to listen. Was this what he meant when he'd said that his time had come? Is this what he'd chosen for himself?*

It wasn't possible. Matt leaned his head into his hands and knotted his fingers into his thick hair. He gazed into his empty glass, but shook his head at the waitress when she stopped by his table again. It wasn't possible, because his trust had been founded on the belief that Christopher Carpenter was God not-so-incognito. But if he was God, he wouldn't have died, and that huge fact crushed all the little hints of evidence that had been building up in his mind.

Yet the hints persisted. Chris Carpenter had been able to change Matt inside, in a way Jude couldn't, because Chris Carpenter wasn't just another man. He was God, and it was the power of God that had rearranged the inside of Matt Levy's head. That power hadn't been able to rearrange Jude, because he'd refused to allow it. Yet it had affected him, had finally convicted him with a certainty so great and so awful he could escape only by escaping life itself.

If Chris was dead, he couldn't be God—perhaps there couldn't even be a God. But if Chris Carpenter was God, he couldn't be dead—or else his death had some meaning. Matt looked up, up from his empty glass, up from the table, up beyond the potted plants to the walls hung with neon signs and fake collectibles.

"God," he said, half aloud, "I've never had such a good reason not to believe in You, and mostly I don't. You've taken away everything, and nothing makes sense, and if You do exist I'm not sure I like You, because all I knew about You was through Chris and he's not here anymore. . . . But the tiny, tiny bit of me that still thinks You're there says please, I need you . . . show me what to do. . . ."

The song playing was insistently familiar, a number one hit from a few years back. In fact it had come out the spring he graduated from college, and he had danced to it here, in this bar, on graduation night. He saw himself on the dance floor just a few feet away, smiling and flushed with success, impeccably dressed, dancing with a pretty redhead whose name now escaped him. The song synchronized with his heartbeat as he stood up, leaving the money for two beers and a tip on the table. Was there anything left of that Bright Young Man to salvage? He'd never know, now.

Rain had begun to fall. Through the dark wet streets, neon-lit, he strode. In the street outside the Y he found his rented car, with a parking ticket on its windshield. Pocketing the ticket, he started the car and drove through the familiar streets, out to the highway exit and away from Pendleton.

He was driving back toward the city, and he didn't know what was there to pull him back. Maybe by going back he could undo running away. He was still bewildered with pain, but he felt a curious excitement, too—the excitement he used to feel when The Boss had led them all off into the unknown on some adventure. Only when the realization hit that Chris was not around to lead this journey, did the ache inside begin again in earnest. He turned the wipers up to fast to clear the windshield. But it was not rain that blurred his vision of the road; it was his own tears.

Chapter Twenty-four

Rain drummed against the window. Pete didn't see it. Though his forehead was pressed against the pane, his eyes were closed. There would have been little to see at any rate. The dull glow of a streetlight illuminated a narrow back street in the city he hated. Behind him lay a dingy room—a cheerless little parish meeting hall, filled with shabby furniture, off of which branched numerous storage rooms and offices and conference rooms and even a kitchenette. All the rooms, whatever their original purpose, had now become bedrooms for people who belonged nowhere except together. And the dimly lit main hall was a waiting room in the truest sense—all the men and women in it were waiting for someone to come and tell them this was only a bad dream.

He knew the expressions on those faces—the unbelieving despair, the unfathomable hurt. Since yesterday afternoon's news had swept the city, those same feelings had been lodged in his own heart—but they were mostly dwarfed by the other feeling, the enormous self-hatred that had been with him since yesterday's dawn.

He couldn't look any of the others in the eye. Sure, it was probably stupid of him to think their glances were accusing. None of them knew what he had done. But he imagined the accusing looks anyway. What he didn't imagine was the pleading in every face. They all looked to each other in bewilderment, hoping to find an answer, but Pete had come to realize during the past 24 hours that, with The Boss gone, they were looking to him, Pete Johnson, for some kind of guidance or leadership. Nobody actually said,

"What do we do now, Pete?" but it hung in the air behind everything that was said.

He hadn't realized he'd become such a dominant member of the group. He grinned to himself, humorlessly. Amazing what a fast tongue and a confident appearance could do. He'd always wanted to be what Chris had called him—a leader of men. Now here he was with a roomful of men and women who wanted to be led, and he had no explanations, no assurances, no guidance, nothing to offer. Less than nothing—he was a fraud. The irony was priceless.

For a room with more than 30 people in it, the space around him was oddly quiet. People spoke in murmurs. Partly it was fear that had herded them all into this drab hall—the same room where they'd eaten supper with The Boss Thursday night. Pete was amazed they hadn't been kicked out, given how people were feeling about Chris Carpenter and anyone who'd known him.

He himself had stumbled back here Friday morning, looking only for a familiar spot in the crowded city. He was surprised to find Andy, Nat, and Phil already here. Others of The Boss's followers trickled in throughout Friday morning, talking about the strange events of the past night and wondering what Christopher Carpenter was going to do. Though shaken, they were still hopeful. Only Pete sat apart from them, silent. He had already lost everything. He didn't even have a right to be there—but where else could he go?

Then, as Friday afternoon slipped into evening, Maria Castillo had arrived, weeping and incoherent. Behind her came John, leading Chris's mother, who for once looked utterly lost. A few more of the women accompanied them, and together they poured out the story of what they had seen on one of the city's back streets that day.

John—just a boy—and the women. Those had been the only ones of The Boss's followers to see him die. He died at the hands of the people he had lived for, died horribly and in pain, while most of his friends were hiding. Pete looked around at the other men in the room and for a moment felt almost as much disgust as he felt for himself.

Later that night, as the news of Chris Carpenter's death flashed across TV screens, the others came. From around the city, from Marselles, and from other towns, they gravitated to this spot. Now, Saturday night, the room was full of stricken people, afraid of what might happen to them.

They didn't talk much. Oh, they had at first, but everyone quickly realized there was little point in voicing agonizing questions to which no one had any answers. So they huddled there all day, as if waiting. *But God alone knows what we're waiting for,* Pete thought.

Footsteps sounded on the stairs. Pete could feel everyone else look up, though he didn't turn around. They had no password, no secret knock: every arriving friend might as well have been an enemy. But the voice at the door was that of Matt Levy, and Pete realized that now all of the original 12 were here in the room—except, of course, Jude, the traitor, the double agent. Pete found that for the first time he couldn't hate Jude. At least the college boy had been clear about where his loyalties lay.

Then he noticed that Matt was talking about Jude, in a slow voice that seemed to be still in shock.

"I found him back in our old apartment. . . . He was—he killed himself. I guess he couldn't live with what he did, after all."

Murmurs ran round the room. *So,* Pete thought, *even Jude had divided loyalties. Surprise, surprise.*

"It's weird," Matt was saying. "I felt like everything was over when I heard that The Boss was dead. But when I realized that even Jude hated himself for hurting Chris—well, it just seemed like I couldn't stop believing. I know it doesn't make any sense . . . but I had to come back here, to try to figure it out."

Other voices rose to meet Matt's, to express their own fears and shattered dreams. *What about me?* Pete thought. *Why am I here?* He was as guilty as Jude—more so, because Jude had made no rash promises. Pete looked down at the street below. This was only a second-story window. He could hurt himself from here, but not kill himself.

Well, he had to stay alive—and around—anyway for Audrey and the kids. Though a fat lot of good he was doing them now. They'd arrived early this morning, and Pete had been unable to reach out to them in any way. He remembered Audrey saying, so often, that she believed in him, knew he was doing the right thing. How could he face the woman who'd had such faith in him? She'd always been his strength, but now she was pale, silent, shattered, and she needed him. And he couldn't say anything or even touch her.

Someone was standing behind him, leaning on the window frame. He looked up to see his younger brother. Andy sat down on

164

the bench beside Pete and joined him in looking out the window.

"I don't understand all this mess," Andy began. "Why did he—no, there's no point, is there? I've asked myself a million times, and I'm not getting anywhere."

Pete only shook his head.

"I keep blaming myself," Andy went on. "I ran away. There in the park—I ran for my life. Maybe if I'd stuck around—well, even if I couldn't do anything, at least I'd have been there when he died."

Pete turned to look at Andy, savage anger ripping through him. "*You* feel guilty? *You* blame yourself! Do you know what *I* did? *I* went to the courthouse! *I* was there! People kept asking me if I knew him—and I said no! Over and over, I told them: I—never—knew—Chris Carpenter." On each of the last four words he pounded the glass with his fist. "How do you think *I* feel?"

He felt as if he were on fire inside. It hurt like crazy. But Andy still kept his amazing calm. "So that's it," was all he said. "I knew something was bothering you." He paused. "Who knows, Pete? Probably I'd have done the same thing if I hadn't run away."

"You wouldn't."

"You don't know. Any of us could've."

"John didn't."

"No. John didn't." Andy looked down at his hands. "Look, you feel awful, and what you did was wrong. We all feel awful, and the worst part is The Boss isn't here to make it right. And me, I don't understand anything. But look—you're still here, with us all. Not like Jude. That's got to count for something."

A car drove through the street below, tires swishing on wet pavement. "Yeah. Maybe," Pete said.

They sat in silence for a long time before Larry Castillo called Andy away. Pete continued to watch the rain. His mind was blank. It had to be—he had to erase everything, if he was going to survive. Christopher Carpenter was dead. Nothing meant anything now anyway, so why try to understand?

A small form crept up on the bench beside him. "Daddy? I can't get to sleep."

He looked down at his golden-haired daughter, but found no words. Out of habit, he put an arm around her, and she leaned against him. He tightened his hold on her.

"Everybody's very sad, aren't they?"

"Yes, babe, I guess they are."

"It's because Mr. Carpenter is gone away, right?"

He picked up a strand of her hair in his fingers and played with it. "Yes," he said at last.

"Is Mr. Carpenter coming back?"

"No." His throat tightened. He felt he was going to choke.

"Oh." She was quiet for a minute. "I asked Uncle Andy that, and he said he didn't know."

"Oh."

"And I asked Mommy, and she said that we did the right thing to believe in him and that God will take care of us no matter what, because we loved Mr. Carpenter." She repeated her mother's words solemnly, like a lesson, and could not know how deeply they wounded her father.

Pete laid his cheek against her silky hair. "You believe that, sweetheart. You hang on to whatever Mommy tells you. Mommy's a very smart lady."

And a very strong one. He'd been wrong. Audrey was not shattered. Bruised, yes, but with her woman's strength she was rebuilding what she could out of their collapsed dreams — rebuilding a faith that could give hope to her children. And to herself, too, for she was too honest to tell them what she herself didn't believe. That faith couldn't help her husband, because he was really shattered. But that was his fault, not Audrey's.

Chapter Twenty-five

Tall golden flowers—the flowers of spring—bloomed all around in the grass at Maria's feet. She picked a few of them and added them to her bundle of daisies. The other women were going off later in Audrey's car to a greenhouse owned by someone they knew, but Maria had come here, to this field on the edge of town, to pick wildflowers. She hoped that when she placed them on Chris's grave, no one else would be there yet. That was why she had come out so early, long before dawn. All Saturday night she'd lain awake, as she had Friday night. Finally she had decided that any action was better than lying there, waiting to go crazy, so she got up and went walking.

The problem—or rather the worst of her many problems—was that she couldn't stop remembering Friday afternoon. She sank to her knees in the dew-damp field, overcome by the pictures in her mind. Just as she had been unable to close her eyes throughout that horrific scene, so she was unable to close the eyes of memory when the images began to play themselves back to her.

Everything about it was horrible. The almost savage hatred on the faces of that small but vicious mob. The smug complacency of the plainclothes police who hovered in the background. They were there only to make sure that not too much attention was drawn to the affair. They had done nothing to stop the murder and would do nothing to punish it; they'd been in on the whole plan. She saw their bland faces again, and the sick eagerness of the couple of reporters there. They wouldn't tell the real story either, because the media hated and feared Christopher Carpenter too. Any reporter who hadn't been invited to be there and who might somehow find out the truth and want to publish it would, no doubt, be paid off or silenced.

She saw their faces, and she saw his face. They had done horrible things to his body—they wouldn't even kill him quickly, but what she remembered most was his face. It showed the simple agony of physical pain, and it showed the hurt of someone betrayed and rejected. She knew both those feelings, in a smaller way, and she recognized their marks on his face. But there was something else there too—an anguish so intense that no physical or psychological torture on earth could account for it. It was so huge that it made her feel as if all her worst sorrows had been trivial. And it had echoed in his voice when he twisted his bruised and bleeding face to the sky and shouted the tortured words, "God! GOD! You've abandoned me! *Why?*"

No. Not that. She could feel that God had abandoned her, anyone on earth could feel that, but not him. The presence of God had been in and around Chris so clearly that it was impossible not to believe in God when he was there, impossible not to believe that he was God. If the Father whom The Boss had spoken of had abandoned *him*, then either that God didn't exist, or else He hated the world.

That was what Maria had thought then, jostled on all sides by a screaming crowd, watching the man who had saved her life dying. She would still have thought it now, as she knelt weeping for him in a dark field, except for the one good picture to come out of that horrible Friday. Just before he finally died, Chris's features had cleared, and she saw again the traces of his perfect calm confidence. He looked up again and said, "Father, I give myself into Your hands." He said it as if everything was all right. But then he died, and everything was all wrong.

Maria stood up, brushed bits of damp grass from the knees of her jeans. The sun was rising. Back in their borrowed room, no one would be sleeping much. Audrey, Martha, Erica, Mrs. Fisher, and the others would leave early, and if she wanted to get to the cemetery before they did, she'd better start walking.

As she walked along, clutching her wildflowers, she saw a city bus in the distance. Automatically she checked her pocket for change. If it went anywhere near the graveyard—and it did, she could see now it was Route 17—she could save a lot of time by taking it.

At this early hour, she was the only passenger. She sat halfway back to avoid conversation with the driver. How strange she must look, a woman with a bouquet of wilting flowers, alone at dawn on a Sunday morning.

She wondered if she'd have any trouble getting past the police guard they were supposed to have posted at the cemetery. What sort of trouble were they expecting? Didn't they know that Chris Carpenter's followers were no threat without him? Perhaps they thought a new leader would emerge within the group. *Which shows how much they know about Christopher Carpenter*, Maria thought.

They were lucky, she supposed, to have a grave for him at all—lucky he had a rich friend brave enough to offer a plot of land and arrange for the burial. No funeral service, of course—it had all been hastily arranged on Friday afternoon. She supposed that they might have some kind of service there this morning, when the other women came, if the police didn't interfere. But it would be so pointless. What kind of prayers could they pray?

Somewhere in the back of her mind Maria recognized a deeper grief in all this. She had lost more than just a friend and leader. She had believed in God because of Chris Carpenter, and what did his death do to that faith? She shook her head as if to clear it. That question couldn't be tackled yet. The personal pain of losing him was still too sharp. Later, she'd have to think about what it all meant. Now she could only think how awful it was that her only contact with Chris would be putting flowers on his grave. Those gentle eyes would not look at her again; that humorous smile would no longer coax laughter from her tears; that purely loving voice would never again say her name, the first thing he'd ever said to her.

She hadn't even had a chance to say goodbye, she thought, digging a tissue out of her pocket. The last time she had spoken to him had been in the hotel courtyard, in the middle of a crowd, and she couldn't remember what either of them had said. She thought of her impulsive display of gratitude at Simon's party, of the gift she'd given him then, and despite the embarrassment was glad she had done it. Hadn't he said then that she was preparing for his death? So he'd known. . . . But at least he'd died knowing how much she loved him. She wondered if he'd been wearing those boots when he died—if, perhaps, he'd been buried in them. It would have been nice.

She wiped away tears, fiercely and uselessly, and remembered the days when she had stood, tough and untouchable, on the street corner. She had learned, once, how to build a wall against emotion. Could she do it again? Chris Carpenter had torn down all those defenses, and she hadn't minded being defenseless as long as he was there to protect her. But now. . . . Despite the tears, she felt a tiny relief at the discovery that she couldn't go back to being that old Marie.

Vale and Eastmount—the stop nearest the graveyard. She reached up to ring the bell and stood up as the bus lurched to a halt. The driver raised his hand in acknowledgment as she got off, and she waved back. When the bus pulled away, she headed up Vale Street to Mount Pleasant Cemetery.

There was no police car parked by the gate—no sign of anyone around at all, in fact. The just-risen sun threw grotesquely long shadows of the gate, the tombstones, and Maria over the green, dewy grass. Picking her way through shadows and sunlight, she found the unmarked plot where Joe Armstrong had told her he'd buried The Boss.

It couldn't be the right spot. This grave was open, freshly dug up. She looked to the right—there was the Whiting family monument with the enormous granite angel she had been told to use as a landmark. This had to be it, but—as she walked through the loose dirt to the edge of the grave, she recoiled in shock. This was not an empty grave waiting for a burial. There was something in there. A coffin, with its lid flung open. An empty coffin.

She stumbled away from the gaping hole and leaned against the Whitings' angel for support. Her flowers dropped, unheeded, to the ground; her hand went to her mouth. What had happened here? Something unthinkable—someone had taken his body! But why had they left the coffin? Couldn't the malicious, filthy creatures leave him alone even in death? What worse could they do to him now?

Or else, perhaps, they wanted it to look as though Chris Carpenter's friends had stolen the body—to frame them. She would have to warn the others—anyway, they would have to know.

She ran from the graveyard, uncertain feet tripping in her haste. She was as anxious to get away from that strange place as she was to find her friends and tell them. Blindly she pushed the gate open and raced down the street.

After a block she slowed to a ragged walk. It was a long way; she couldn't hope to run the whole distance. This time no bus appeared—in fact there was no other traffic at all on the streets. She half-expected to get lost, so blindly was she walking. When she looked up and saw that she was at the far end of the street where the church hall was, she again broke into a run. She wanted desperately to be among friends now.

Finally she was there, pulling frantically at the door handle. It was locked. She pounded on the door and heard footsteps clopping down the stairs toward her.

When John opened the door, she half fell into the entryway and clutched at his arm. She gasped for a moment, trying to catch her breath, and then tried to tell him.

"What? Slow down, Maria. I don't understand."

She shook her head. "It's—the grave, his grave. It's empty. They've taken him away. He's gone—"

"What?" John repeated. "Are you sure?"

It was a stupid question, but she didn't blame him. He had to say something while the news sank in. "Come and see," she urged.

"OK. Just a second." He ran up the stairs and looked into the room. "Maria's here—she's just been to the cemetery and she says the grave's been dug up or something. The body's gone. I'm going to go see. Does anyone—Pete, you want to come with me?"

There was a second of silence, then Maria heard someone stand up. "I guess so," said Pete.

Outside, John said, "It's a long walk. Should we take the van?"

Pete seemed unusually short of words this morning. He just shrugged, then dug into his pocket and handed John the keys.

As they drove along, John asked, "Did you see Audrey and the other women there?"

"No, they weren't there yet. Maybe they'll be there now. Or maybe they came after I left."

John drove tensely, leaning forward over the steering wheel as if he were eager to prod the van along. Pete, who usually drove, sat slumped in the passenger's seat and stared out the window. Maria looked straight ahead, trying not to think.

John stopped the van in a no-parking zone outside the cemetery gates. He was racing up the path before Pete and Maria were even out of the van. They followed more slowly. Pete seemed reluctant to get there; he didn't say anything to Maria.

When they got to the grave site, they found John at the edge of the open grave, looking down and frowning. His hands were stuffed in his pockets. He didn't look shocked, the way Maria had felt, but puzzled and almost intrigued. "This is weird," he told them. "Look at that dirt. It's not like it was dug up—it's scattered all over the place. And who would take the body and leave the coffin?"

Pete sat down on the low concrete wall. John looked at Maria.

"I know, I wondered about that too," she said. "But then I thought . . . maybe they wanted to—to do something with it. I don't know—maybe they don't like him being buried here. You know, it's one of the biggest cemeteries in town, they probably don't think . . ."

John shook his head as her words trailed off. He ran a hand through his hair. "You know what this reminds me of?" he asked, still looking down. Pete looked up at him blankly, but Maria knew. They had stood like this before at an abandoned grave.

"Larry's grave," she said, though she hadn't meant to speak. "My brother. When Chris brought him to life!"

John nodded, a half smile on his long, slender young face. "Remember what everyone said on Friday, when Chris was arrested? 'He's supposed to have raised the dead, but he can't save himself.'" His eyes met Maria's, and she saw that they were radiant with hope. "Kind of makes you think, doesn't it?"

"No!" Pete jumped to his feet and grabbed John's arm. "No, John, don't try to fool yourself into believing that. Whatever else happens, The Boss is dead. You've got to accept that."

"You're forgetting all the things he said—"

"I have to forget!" declared Pete fiercely. "And so do you. You've always been a dreamer, kid, but you've got to stop somewhere. This is one dream that ain't coming true."

"Don't forget," John said quietly, "that everything I believed in turned out to be true."

"Not this. Not this. How can you ever get on with your life if you keep believing he isn't really dead?"

"Who said anything about my whole life? If The Boss did come back, don't you think he'd let us know?"

"I don't know." Pete let go of John's arm. "I don't understand a lot of the stuff he did."

John shrugged. "Well," he said, "let's go back and see what the others think." As he turned to go, Maria could see that already he looked stronger, more hopeful, than when he had come. Pete, just a few steps away, seemed to be standing in shadow.

"Coming, Maria?" John asked.

She shook her head. "No, I want to stay here for a while. I'll walk back later."

"Sure? You don't want us to wait?"

"No, that's OK."

She heard the gates creak shut again, heard the van drive away. She knelt in the grass and dirt, picking up the scattered flowers. Her heart wanted to fly at the thought of what John believed—what John wanted to believe—but she knew Pete was right. It wasn't safe to hope. She was already living through the worst disappointment of her life—she couldn't survive a second one.

Her tears began again—tears for Chris, for the hope he had given her and for the loss of that hope, for herself, and for her brother and sister and friends. They had all been so lost and empty before Chris Carpenter had entered their lives. What would they be without him? And now she would not have even his grave to come to, to be near him.

A sound made her look up. She was shocked to see through her tears two people sitting on the ground just ahead of her. Both were strange men, and she thought immediately of the police. Her old hatred and fear of cops flooded back. These men were not in uniform—both wore brilliant white—but she backed away from them anyway.

"Why are you crying, ma'am?" one asked, not unkindly. He sat at one end of the open grave, his companion sat at the other end.

She was too surprised, and too miserable, to say anything but the truth, "They've taken away my Lord's body, and I don't know where . . . " Something about the steady gaze of the two strangers unnerved her, and she dropped her eyes. Neither of them made any movement, and when after a moment she looked back at them, she saw no one there.

Her mind must be playing tricks on her. Of course. Why shouldn't she lose her mind? It was all she had left to lose. Her old sarcasm, which she'd thought she'd lost forever, was almost a comfort now.

Now she thought someone was standing behind her. This was too much. She didn't turn around, even when a voice said, "Are you all right, Miss? Who are you looking for?"

The voice was kind, so it couldn't be a cop—the caretaker, perhaps? She didn't even notice at first that his second question was a rather strange one. She answered it, though she still didn't turn around. Whoever this man was, he must know whose grave had been here. "Sir, if you know where he is . . . if you've taken him, please tell me. I'll take his body myself, I'll—"

"Maria."

Her name! His voice! The first word that voice had ever said to her! She half rose, turning quickly, and fell back on her knees again. As she had also done the first time, for here again was God, whom she must worship.

"Oh, my Lord!" The words sprang from her in a burst of joy, and she reached up to take his hands. To her surprise, he pulled away, but he was smiling down at her.

"Not yet," he said. How could she, even thinking him dead, have mistaken that voice for any other? "Let me go—I still have to go and see my Father."

She thought, dimly, that this visit must be something special— that he would come to see all of them later. And she thought how kind it was for him to meet her here, knowing how wretched she was. But her mind wasn't on those thoughts: it was on him. He stood with his back to the morning sun, but instead of looking silhouetted against that light he seemed to shine in it. It was the same familiar form, the same confident pose, though he was dressed not in the familiar jeans and T-shirt but in a suit of some light-catching material, far finer than anything she had seen him wear before. And, of course, his face was the same—those eyes and that smile could belong to no one else. Yet, too, there was something different. His face was as strong and clear as if it were a sculpture; the lines of weariness that she had remembered had been polished from it. And he, who had always been so full of life, glowed with new vitality. Everything about him seemed more vivid—it was as if she were looking at a living human being for the first time.

She knelt at his feet, gazing up in worship, taking in all the details. He was back. He was the God of all the universe, and he was looking at her as though seeing her again was his greatest joy.

"Go to the others," he said at last. "To my brothers," and as he called them that, the same pleasure flashed again in his eyes, and she knew how eager he must be to end their suffering. "Tell them I'm going to see my Father, who is their Father, too, and to my God, who is their God." Then, with a last smile, he turned to walk away. She looked back down at the ground, and up again, and, as she had expected, he was not there.

But he had been real. Her mind, no matter how tired, could

never have created him as he had stood here a moment ago. He was so real that the joy of his presence lingered after he had gone.

She stayed by the grave that was not his for a long time, wanting to be alone with her glorious discovery. She ought to go back and tell the others, she finally realized. But as she left the cemetery, a familiar brown station wagon pulled up beside her.

"We came to look for you," Audrey said, rolling down the window. "We went back to tell the others what we saw, and John told us you were here."

"Have you seen anything?" Audrey's mother asked, leaning over eagerly. "We saw—"

"Get in, first," Audrey suggested. "You'll have to ride in the back, though."

Maria went over to the back of the wagon, opened the tailgate, and climbed in beside her sister Martha, who was crouched there. Martha looked radiant. "We get to sit in the back 'cause we're the smallest," Martha said. The car was jam-packed. Maria really didn't want to be around other people just now, but she knew she had to share the news. Though it was obvious that the women had news of their own.

"We saw an angel," Erica Washington bubbled. She tried to check her own enthusiasm. "Course, we don't know for sure it was an angel, but he sure looked like one, dressed all in white, standing there by The Boss's grave."

Maria remembered that she, too, had seen two white-clothed figures, before she had seen Chris. Maybe they were angels—but they hardly seemed worth remembering, now that she'd seen him.

"And he spoke to us," old Mrs. Fisher added. "He asked us, 'Why are you looking among the dead people for someone who's alive?'"

"And we just stood there," Audrey continued. "So he said, 'You're looking for Christopher Carpenter, aren't you? He's not here! He has risen.' I couldn't think what to do, so I just stared at him."

All the women were talking at once now, tongues tripping over themselves in excitement. Erica's voice rose above the others. "Don't you remember that he told you he'd have to die and rise again on the third day? That's what the angel said to us, and I was thinking, *Of course! Of course I remember The Boss saying that!* Then he told us we'd have to go back and tell the rest of you that Chris Carpenter was alive and that we were supposed to meet him back up at Elwood Lake—at the lodge!"

"Wow," Maria said. So far she hadn't gotten a chance to tell her news.

Audrey interrupted the conversation to ask, "Does anyone feel like stopping for some breakfast?"

Everyone did—there hadn't been much in the way of food around over the weekend. They pulled into a fast-food restaurant. Most of the men were afraid even to leave their borrowed room for fear of being recognized and attacked, but the women were less recognizable, not having had their pictures splashed throughout the media quite so much. And now, buoyed up by the morning's news, they felt no one could ever hurt them again.

"So we went back to the hall and told the guys and everyone," Audrey continued the story over breakfast. "And they didn't believe us!"

"Really?" Maria asked.

"No kidding! They thought we were going crazy."

"Well, I think maybe John believed us," Audrey's mother amended. "And Chris's mother—she looked like she wanted to believe it, anyway. She was so badly hurt, poor woman, I don't blame her for not knowing what to think."

"But the others just wouldn't listen," said Audrey. "Not even Lazario!" added Martha indignantly. "And if anyone should know, he should!"

"Not even Pete," Audrey added sadly. "He was worse than anyone else."

Maria nodded, remembering his outburst by the grave. "Maybe they'll believe when I tell them what I saw," she said, half-shyly.

"What did you see?" her sister asked.

So Maria told them her incredible story, all the time looking down at her tray. After she finished, there was silence around the table. She looked up to see several of the women close to tears, "You really saw him," Erica said softly, at last. In every pair of eyes she saw that hunger to see him and hear his voice again.

It wasn't enough just to know he was alive. They spent the rest of breakfast retelling their stories, speculating on what would happen next, chuckling over how Chris would get their stubborn menfolk to believe he was back. When they left the restaurant, still deep in conversation, Audrey was the first to notice the figure of a man leaning against the back of her car, but Maria was the first to recognize him.

She ran toward him, and this time he reached out in welcome to all of them. Taking his hand—so real and solid—Maria fell again to her knees, as did the other women all around her. *We must look crazy,* she thought, *a bunch of grown women on their knees in a parking lot in front of a man who—* No, she realized, *they couldn't look crazy, because anyone who saw this risen man would know it was impossible not to kneel before him.*

Joy lit up his new yet familiar features as he grasped each of their eager hands. "Don't be afraid!" he told them. "It really is I. Go and tell the rest of my friends"—his eyes paused on Audrey's for a moment—"and tell Peter, and the rest, that I'm going to meet them at the lake. They'll see me there."

Suddenly he was gone—he had simply disappeared. None of the women seemed to question whether he'd really been there. Martha's eyes met Maria's, full of awed delight. "I see what you meant, Maria," she half whispered. "He really is—I see what you meant."

Maria took her sister's hands and met her eyes. She had no words to share this joy, but that was all right. Now that Martha had seen him, too, no words were needed.

Chapter Twenty-six

About the only thing Matt was sure about was that he was glad he'd come back. This Sunday had been the strangest and most eventful day of his life. He'd have hated to miss it by wandering around Pendleton in a drunken haze. But so far, it was 7:30 p.m., and not a thing that had happened today had made sense.

He had arrived back in the city around 2:00 in the morning and had found The Boss's friends hiding out in the first place he'd looked—the hall they'd used for supper on Thursday night. Even at that late hour, many of them were still awake. He could sense the tension, confusion, and fear that had built up during two days of being caged in that room without hope. He felt he'd had to tell them about Jude, but he didn't stick around to hear them hash it out. Exhausted by the drive, and much more, he found a corner to curl up in and fell asleep.

His sleep had been interrupted not long after dawn, when a bunch of the women had come in all breathless and excited, babbling about having seen someone at Chris's grave. Well, "babbling" was an unfair word—they'd told their story pretty rationally, despite all the excitement. But when everyone had finally figured out what the women were saying, it seemed obvious that the anxiety and tension of the past few days had made them vulnerable to some kind of group hysteria. Either that or they'd been tricked. As the men scorned the news that Chris Carpenter was alive, Matt tried to ignore the certainty that women such as Audrey Johnson, Erica Washington, and Joanna Hirsch were not likely to be susceptible to either hysteria or hoaxes.

After the offended women left again, Maria had shown up, weeping and half hysterical, and John and Pete had left with her. They had come back without her a little later, both strangely quiet. Then, at around 10:00, just as Matt was trying again to catch another wink or two, the strangest event of the morning occurred. Maria and the other women came back. They were quieter this time, and calmer, but they had an even stranger story to tell. They all claimed to have seen The Boss and spoken to him. They even brought back messages from him.

Matt sat at the edge of the room, away from the center of action, watching the untroubled certainty on Audrey's sensible face. Most of the men were still reluctant to believe them, but the women didn't seem annoyed or eager to convince them. Audrey smiled almost smugly and told the men arguing with her, "Just wait and see. You'll change your minds."

Mary Carpenter had not gone to her son's grave with the other women. She sat listening quietly to this news. Her face showed the pain she had been through, and she looked years older than she had a week ago. But she nodded as the women told their story. Matt, who was sitting near her, heard her say softly, "Of course. I hoped, but I should have known." When Matt questioningly looked up at her, she gave him a faint smile. "I knew who he was," she said. "I should have known he couldn't die, but it hurt so much—I suppose it always does, when a knife stabs you through the heart." Her last words brought another ironic smile, as though she were remembering something.

The only other person who was ready to believe was John. His face grew brighter as he listened to the women, and finally he exclaimed, "I knew it!"

"Knew what?" Andy asked.

"I knew he was alive. He had to be! Didn't he say he'd rise on the third day? Don't you remember him saying that? And this morning at the grave—it didn't look like it was dug up or anything. There was something eerie about the whole place—it looked—it felt—" he gestured helplessly.

Pete, who had been there too, cut in harshly, "It looked like a grave. Look, don't believe it, you hear me? It's a trick. He's dead! John, you saw him die!"

Strangely, Pete seemed to be the one most firmly opposed to believing that The Boss was alive. *Almost*, Matt thought, *as though he doesn't want him back—or as though he's terrified of being hurt*

179

a second time. . . . Well, we're all scared of that.

The rest of the day had been spent in endless conversation, with occasional outbreaks of argument. Most of them wanted to believe that Chris Carpenter could be alive, but were afraid to hope for anything so wonderful. Lazario Castillo quickly took the side of the believers, but most were not as quick to accept the news. No one, however, was as dead set against it as Pete. Looking at the resolutely despairing face of the man they so naturally looked to as a spokesperson, Matt realized he wouldn't be surprised to come in and find Pete's body swaying from the ceiling, too. Though perhaps he just had a morbid imagination, since finding Jude.

Nobody else went to the cemetery that afternoon. Indeed, nobody left the crowded, stuffy rooms at all, except Bob Washington and his buddy Chuck Barnes, who were planning to catch the bus back to Marselles. They both had jobs to go to on Monday morning, and Matt could see in their faces a determination to get on with their normal lives and try to make as much sense as they could out of things. Matt almost envied them—but he had no life to go back to.

"I want to believe it," he told Andy as they sat talking in the late afternoon. "In fact, I think in a way I have believed it, ever since last night. But it's like I'm afraid to—to really take hold of it. I don't know why."

"Scared it might not be real," Andy suggested. "I want to see him again, but I'm almost afraid to hope."

Matt nodded. "And in a weird kind of way, I'm half scared of what will happen if he does come back. I mean, it'll be great, but it won't be the same."

After supper, Pete and John had another argument. This one ended with Pete stomping down the stairs and slamming the door. Matt exchanged a glance with Andy, who stepped forward as if to follow his brother. Audrey placed a restraining hand on his shoulder. "Let him go," she said softly.

Matt looked up to find he had been joined by Tomas, who, as usual, seemed the calmest of them all. "What do you think of it all?" Matt asked him.

Tomas leaned against the wall, folded his arms in front of him in his typical posture, and allowed his usual cynical smile to twitch the corners of his mouth. "I think it's much ado about nothing," he said. "Chris Carpenter was very special, but people just don't rise from the dead. And if, by some chance, he did, we'd know about it.

I suppose anything's possible, but I'm not going to hang all my hopes on some fairy tale."

"You never did, did you? You never believed in him the way the rest of us did—you always reserved your judgment, so you'd have nothing to lose. And now you haven't lost anything, right?"

Anger flickered for the briefest of moments in Tomas' dark eyes. Then all was calm again. "I suppose you could look at it that way," he said.

Moments later, the door burst open. Apparently Pete hadn't bothered to lock it as he went out. Everyone's nerves jumped at the sound. Before anyone could move to see who had come in, footsteps thundered—the sound of someone taking the stairs three at a time. Then Pete was at the top of the stairs, his hair windblown and his eyes very bright.

"I saw him!" he announced to his captive audience.

Silence for a split second, then—"Where? When? What did he say? Is he coming up here? Are you sure it was him?"

Pete's story emerged through a tangle of questions. "I just walked down as far as the corner and—there he was. Like he was waiting for me. He looked kinda different, but it was him all right. I touched him—oh yeah, he was real. But then he just disappeared. I don't know where he went."

"What did he say?"

Pete looked guarded for a moment. "I can't say what he said to me, but I knew it was him from what he said. And he told me to tell you all that he'd meet you soon."

Pete's announcement—and perhaps, even more, the change in his appearance—electrified the room. And it tipped the scales for the undecided. Now they were not talking about whether or not Chris Carpenter was alive, but when they might all see him alive again. Matt, listening to it all but saying little, had forgotten that Tomas was beside him until he heard a quiet voice say, "I'm going to slip away, I think. I don't want to be part of the mass hysteria."

No one seemed to notice Tomas' leaving—they were all too caught up in the conversation. Matt caught Audrey's eye. Her face glowed.

"Pretty typical, isn't it?" she said when she saw him. "None of you would believe it when we told you, but now that one of the men sees him, suddenly—" she broke off with a laugh.

It did seem pretty low-down. "Maybe, it's not just because it was men . . ." Matt tried feebly. "Maybe it's that it was Pete—you know, because he . . ."

Audrey nodded. "Because he was so dead set against it. And he needed it so much." Her eyes rested on her husband with unmistakable relief. Matt wondered if even she knew what it was that had tortured her husband so all weekend, but he knew better than to ask.

Later in the evening, after dark, another knock came at the door. Everyone in the room exchanged glances; no one said, "Is it him?" but the question was in every eye. But it was only Bob and Charlie, who had left for Marselles earlier that day.

"Bob!" exclaimed his wife Erica as he came upstairs. "It's really true—Chris is alive—Pete's seen him, too, now."

Bob stood at the top of the stairs, with Charlie behind him, scratching his head. "Talk about having your thunder stolen," he said above the clamor of voices that rose to confirm Erica's news. "We know he's alive. That's what we came to tell you."

Chairs were pushed forward and the two men sat down to tell their story.

"We got off the bus at Marselles," Bob began, "and we started walkin' for home, and this guy starts walkin' along beside us. We didn't look at him real close, I guess, but he started askin' us what was up and why all the excitement up in the city, and we got to tellin' him about The Boss."

"And he started settin' us straight," Charlie continued, "and tellin' us stuff from the Bible, like how if Chris really was sent from God then he'd have to die, because it said so. He went on and on, just the way The Boss used to—don't know why we never recognized him."

"Probably because once you know someone's dead, you don't expect to run into him," said Bob. "And, like I said, we didn't look real close—still, I think it was like there was something keepin' us from seein' him."

"He even told us where it says the Son of God is supposed to rise again."

"Anyway, we started gettin' up around the old neighborhood, and we thought we'd stop in at McDonalds for a bite to eat, so we asked this guy to join us. And when the food came, he bowed his head to pray over it like Chris used to, and it was like I could see all of a sudden, and it was him!"

"He did look a little different," added Charlie. "But once we recognized him, there was no doubt about it. It was him. And then—he was gone. Just disappeared."

"What time was this?" John asked.

"Oh, I don't know, about 5:00 by the time he left us," Bob said.

"But, Pete, you saw him here around 6:00. How could he—" John's words trailed off as he realized no one was listening to him. He turned around. Matt, who like John was sitting with his back to the little kitchenette, turned too in the direction everyone else was staring.

"Hi! Don't be afraid."

Chris Carpenter was standing in the doorway of the kitchenette. Absolute silence greeted him, and after a moment he smiled at their shock. Those who had seen him before seemed to relax, but Matt, like the others who were seeing him for the first time, remained frozen, awestruck at actually seeing him again.

The first person to move was a tiny golden blur—Pete's little girl Jenny, her blonde hair flying, who launched herself at him, crying "Mr. Carpenter!"

He caught the child and lifted her in his arms, then looked around at the grown-ups. "What, are you still afraid to believe? Look, it's really me! Do you think I'm a ghost?" he teased. "See . . . I'm real—touch me and see! Real flesh and blood!" He held out his free hand toward them, and Matt's eyes fell on the horrible scars of the torture John had too vividly described.

John broke at the sight of that scarred hand. He reached forward and clasped it, then fell on his knees. "It really is you," he said, forcing back sobs.

Then the others, too, crowded around, hungry for his touch, his smile, the sound of his voice. Matt, not wanting to push through the others, waited off to one side. But Chris saw him and met his eyes. Matt took a step forward. The Boss held out his arms, and Matt stumbled into his best friend's embrace.

"Matt," Chris whispered as they hugged, "I'm sorry—about Jude, but there was nothing you could have done." Matt just shook his head, unable to find words. "The important thing," Chris added, "is that you came back. That makes it all worthwhile."

Then The Boss was asking for something to eat, and Martha was scurrying around in the kitchenette, opening a tin of tuna and a jar of mayonnaise. Chris slipped away from the others to where his mother sat and knelt beside her, putting an arm around her shoulder. The others left them alone for a few minutes, but when

Martha returned with a sandwich and a glass of orange juice, apologizing that there was nothing else in there, Chris sat down on the dilapidated couch and everyone gathered around him.

Matt settled into a comfortable spot on the floor. He knew they were in for a long evening of talk. Already The Boss had a Bible open in front of him and was gesturing with his sandwich. Matt couldn't take his eyes off Chris—that face which was so loved and familiar, and yet so wonderfully changed. The Boss was explaining, with the help of his Bible and through a thicket of questions, what they were all so eager to know. What had the events of the weekend meant—his death and now his return to life? Matt knew that Chris had suffered something far more terrible than just the physical torture and death. And as he tried to tell them what that sacrifice had meant, the words he had spoken earlier tumbled through Matt's mind.

"The important thing is that you came back. That makes it all worthwhile."

Does he mean, Matt wondered, *that he went through all that just to make sure I'm safe? That if only I stayed true to God, it would be worth it to him? Does he care that much about me?* And as Chris's bright eyes met his across the room, the glowing spark in his heart leaped into flame, because he knew it was true.

Chapter Twenty-seven

The lake was completely flat with an eerie predawn calm. Pete leaned on the rail, staring out at it.

"It's good to be up here again," Andy said.

"Yeah. Not the same without The Boss, though."

"Oh, he'll be up here. He told us he'd meet us up here."

Pete just nodded. "Guess he won't be needing the van to get around anymore."

Andy laughed. "It *is* different, isn't it—the way he comes and goes? Takes a bit of getting used to."

"I know. It's funny, though, he hasn't really been around much since—since it all happened, but in a way it's like he has. Like even when he's not here, it still feels like he's here?"

The Fisher boys had come out of the lodge and joined them on the deck while Pete was speaking. Now Jim added his voice in agreement. "It's true, you know. Before, I always used to feel different when he was around—like everything was gonna be OK and I didn't need to get upset. Now I feel that way pretty much all the time. Like he's here with me."

"I keep looking around and expecting to see him standing here," Andy agreed.

The four men walked down to the boathouse. "What really amazes me," John said as they pulled the largest of the fishing boats out into the water, "is that now that Chris has come back to life, we know he really *is* God. And that means—God is someone we hung around with. Someone who helped us fix the van and cook a meal and buy the groceries. He understands us. That blows my mind."

Three more shadowy figures emerged through the trees and out onto the dock. "We woke up early and thought we'd join you guys," Nat said. Phil was behind him and, somewhat to Pete's surprise, so was Tomas. Tomas had been very quiet these past few days. About a week after The Boss's return, while his friends were still hanging around the city not quite sure what to do with themselves, Chris Carpenter had appeared again. No one asked where he'd been for a week. He had seemed especially eager to talk to Tomas, who hadn't been there when he first appeared and who maintained his usual cynical stance. Since that encounter, they'd heard no more skeptical remarks from Tomas. He didn't even seem to want to argue about things.

The boat, with seven men in it, was soon loaded and sped away from shore. When they were well out on the lake, Pete cut the motor and got busy preparing bait and tackle like everyone else. This early morning fishing trip had been his idea—a release of tension, but also a necessity, since so many people were staying in the lodge and there was no surplus of either food or money. They'd been up here all week, waiting for Chris to come or something to happen. Pete and Andy had taken on a job fixing a truck for someone in town—Pete couldn't stand being idle, and someone had to bring in a little cash. That job was finished now, and a few big bass wouldn't go astray at the crowded breakfast table.

Luck, though, seemed to be against them. They fished in silence, and the water remained as calm as glass, but no fish were biting. More than an hour slipped by. Dawn streaked the sky rose and gold, and the sun slipped through the trees on the eastern ridge.

The boat had drifted closer to shore. Looking up, Pete noticed a man standing on the shore. He thought he saw a movement—was the man waving at them? Then, clear across the water, a voice called out, "Catching anything, boys?"

"Not a thing," Pete called back to the friendly stranger.

"Try casting off on the other side!"

Pete rolled his eyes and looked at the others—then he caught John's glance. John lifted his eyebrows. "Does something here seem familiar?" he asked.

Wordlessly, Pete reeled in his empty line and cast off on the other side—not that he hadn't tried over there before. The others began to do likewise, but even before John had his line in the water Pete felt a tug. He looked at John and they both nodded.

"It's *him*, all right," said John, grinning.

Pete dropped his fishing rod without even bothering to reel in the line—there were plenty more fish out there, no doubt. In a single movement, he leaped from the boat into the chilly water. "Hey, watch out!" yelled Jim as the boat rocked dangerously.

As his head broke the surface, Pete couldn't help remembering that other night on this lake when he'd left the boat to go to Chris Carpenter. This time he was in the water, not on top of it, swimming for all he was worth. No eerie miracles on the lake this spring morning—except the miracle of Chris being here at all.

His feet scraped bottom, and he splashed into the shore. He was close enough now to see that it was really Chris on the beach— though as always since his resurrection, you couldn't be sure just by looking. The face and form were familiar, but also changed—fired by the same glory Pete had seen once on a hilltop. But that smile, and the handclasp that helped him out of the water, could not belong to anyone else.

From the boat came the shouts of the other men as they reeled in one big fish after another. Pete noticed a fire burning on the beach and some fish that were already cleaned and frying on it. He decided not to ask where the fish had come from—or for that matter what Chris was doing on the far side of the lake without a boat.

Soon the others were pulling the boat up on shore, laden with their catch—a truly amazing amount of fish for such a short time.

"Bring a few of those over and I'll clean them," Chris said. He led the way over to the fire and took the already-done fish off with his knife.

"Man, that smells good," John said.

"Sit down and have some breakfast." He had bread there, too, warming on the edge of the fire, and he passed it around as the men helped themselves to the fish.

Pete neither talked nor thought much as they sat around the fire, sharing their simple meal. He listened to the voices of Chris and the others, and the early morning cry of loons far out on the lake, and the snapping of sparks on the fire. He had traveled a long way from Pete's Garage to this fireside, and he had a feeling there was a long way yet to go, but he knew in this moment he'd found whatever it was he'd set out looking for.

After the food was gone, Andy and Phil set to work putting out the fire, and the others drifted back toward the boat. Pete found himself walking up the beach with Chris. He was still almost scared to be alone with The Boss. They hadn't talked since that one brief encounter on the day Chris had come back to life. Then Chris had said all Pete needed to know to be sure that he was forgiven. Still, it felt funny to be alone with him. Maybe he'd changed even more than The Boss had.

"Rocky?" That name called back so many memories.

"Yes?"

"Do you love me—more than everything else?" The Boss's gesture took in the beach and the boat and Pete's friends and the lodge where Audrey and the kids were waking to a new day. All the same, it was an easy question.

"Yes, Boss. I do love you."

"Do you *really*, Pete?"

He thought then of their last conversation before Chris's death, of the pain and concern in The Boss's eyes. He heard his own voice saying, "Look, I'm telling you, I don't know the man!" He felt again the cold gravel of a deserted alley against his face and saw the tortured death he had not been brave enough to watch. *No*, he decided, *I don't really know a thing about love. But whatever I do have to give, I can't hold anything back from him.*

"You know I love you, Boss."

"Then care for my children, Pete—my little ones."

They walked along the sand in silence, as Pete wondered what that command might mean. Chris's voice broke into his thoughts again, and this time he stopped walking and looked into Pete's face. "Do you *truly* love me, Pete Johnson?"

This time it cut to the core. Didn't The Boss believe him? But what could words prove that Chris Carpenter didn't already know—especially now? The answer was torn from him. "You know everything! You know how I love you!"

The Boss's smile was quiet, but it said everything. "Then take care of my people for me." He was placing a responsibility on Pete's shoulders. Pretty ironic now that Pete had finally proven himself unworthy of the kind of leadership he'd always wanted. But knowing Chris, this was what he was waiting for all along—for Pete Johnson to fall off his pedestal. He gave Chris a grin, wondering if The Boss could read his thoughts.

"Right," said Chris, placing a hand on his shoulder. "You're ready for it now."

Only then did Pete think of the other implication of those words. "You're going away again, aren't you?" he asked reluctantly.

Chris Carpenter nodded. They walked on. "I do have to go away—I told you that, but I told you I'd come back, too. Remember?"

"I remember." Pete thought of the house with many rooms—a room in it for everyone. "But I can't imagine life without you. Can we get by without you?"

"You won't have to. I promised I'd sent my Spirit—haven't you found that out by now?"

Pete remembered the feeling they'd all talked about—that The Boss was there even when he wasn't. "You mean—"

Again, Chris nodded. "After I've gone back to my Father, you'll be even more aware of that Spirit."

"It still won't be quite the same," Pete said. "But that'll give me something to look forward to."

They turned back to walk toward the boat and the others. "You know, Pete," The Boss said, "when you're a young man, you get up, you dress yourself, and you go where you want to go. But someday you'll be old, you'll have to depend on someone else to dress you and take care of you—and he'll lead you where you wouldn't choose to go."

Pete frowned at the picture of himself, old and feeble. *So,* he thought, *Chris Carpenter won't be back in a couple of weeks or months. I'll have to live my whole life, get old, maybe even die before I see him again. Not that death means anything now.* He looked into Chris's face.

"When that time comes—just keep following me," and then Pete knew he didn't care about what the years ahead might bring. He'd be following Christopher Carpenter, which meant that everything would be OK.

John was walking up the beach toward them. His hair tied back and his shirt off for the morning's activity, the sun glinting off his sweaty forehead and chest, John looked like the kid he still was. Pete could imagine himself growing old and dying, but he could never imagine John's youthful fire and idealism fading in middle age. "What's going to happen to John?"

The Boss smiled. "If I choose to let him live till I come back again, that shouldn't matter to you."

It shouldn't, Pete thought, *and I don't need to envy John.*

"The important thing," Chris repeated, "is for you to follow me." He turned to John, who had just reached them, and included them both in his smile. "I'll always be with you, right till the end, whatever happens."

Pete grinned and slapped John on the shoulder. He strode off to join the others in the boat and was happy to see The Boss, a moment later, climb in with them.

"So he's not going to disappear this time?" Andy asked quietly, below the roar of the motor.

"Not right yet," Pete replied. "He's got to go away, but I think he's going to spend a little time with us first. There's probably a lot of stuff he needs to say to everybody—telling us what he wants us to do."

"Good," said Andy, keeping his eyes on the water.

Pete, too, watched the lake as the boat sped across to the other shore. The sun glinted off every blue ripple in the water, the morning wind cut fresh and clean across his face, and gulls cried overhead. He wished there were some way to make the boat go faster. He couldn't wait to get back and tell Audrey about—well, everything.

"Jesus did many other things as well.

If every one of them were written down,

I suppose that even the whole world

would not have room for the books

that would be written."

John 21:25, NIV